INVITATION TO A KILLER

Also by G.M. Malliet

The St. Just mysteries

DEATH OF A COZY WRITER
DEATH AND THE LIT CHICK
DEATH AT THE ALMA MATER
DEATH IN CORNWALL *

The Max Tudor mysteries

WICKED AUTUMN
A FATAL WINTER
PAGAN SPRING
DEMON SUMMER
THE HAUNTED SEASON
DEVIL'S BREATH
IN PRIOR'S WOOD

Novels

WEYCOMBE

Augusta Hawke mysteries

AUGUSTA HAWKE *

* *available from Severn House*

INVITATION TO A KILLER

G.M. Malliet

SEVERN
HOUSE

First world edition published in Great Britain and the USA in 2023
by Severn House, an imprint of Canongate Books Ltd,
14 High Street, Edinburgh EH1 1TE.

Trade paperback edition first published in Great Britain and the USA in 2023
by Severn House, an imprint of Canongate Books Ltd.

severnhouse.com

British Library Cataloguing-in-Publication Data
A CIP catalogue record for this title is available from the British Library.

ISBN-13: 978-1-4483-0664-0 (cased)
ISBN-13: 978-1-4483-0825-5 (trade paper)
ISBN-13: 978-1-4483-0824-8 (e-book)

All Severn House titles are printed on acid-free paper.

Typeset by Palimpsest Book Production Ltd.,
Falkirk, Stirlingshire, Scotland.
Printed and bound in Great Britain by
TJ Books, Padstow, Cornwall.

For the people of Ukraine

ACKNOWLEDGMENTS

Once again, heartfelt thanks to my agent, Mark Gottlieb of Trident Media Group, and to Joanne Grant, Carl Smith, Natasha Bell, Martin Brown, Sara Porter, Piers Tilbury, and more – all the publishers, editors, copyeditors, marketeers, publicists, and designers who help make this writing journey so pleasant and worthwhile.

And as always, to Bob.

'Anyone who tries to write a memoir needs to keep in mind that what's interesting to you isn't necessarily interesting to a reader.'

—Mitch Albom

PART I

ONE

I hoped more people would show up for my funeral than showed up for my book signing that cold October night in Old Town.

Mind you, it *was* cold and threatening icy rain, besides. But that was the forecast for midnight. My signing was timed for eight p.m. when the dinner crowd should have been starting to leave the nearby restaurants, on the hunt for entertainment. There being no live shows in Old Town, I was it for entertainment. And apparently, I wasn't enough.

My name is Augusta Hawke and I am a writer. I have killed approximately forty-four people over the course of nineteen books. That's one person for each year I've been alive. It seems less disturbing when I do the math that way. When I spread out the deaths over time.

These are of course fictional deaths. An occupational hazard for a mystery writer.

I've been at this murder game about twenty years, and apart from an early flirtation with the idea of becoming an artist, writing was the only thing I ever wanted to do. My first effort was a mystery book, as they're called in the US – a crime book elsewhere – and I've been writing them ever since, turning out novels at the rate of one per year. I don't write books that are gory; I shy away from those books even in my personal reading. Ditto books that feature cases solved by cats, goldfish, or zoo animals.

I would probably sell more books if I were more interested in plasma and pain but I'm not. I am an admirer of Agatha Christie and I like to think my appreciation for her is reflected in what I write. Agatha surprises me every time, even on rereading her stories.

I'd never met a villain I didn't like, at least in theory, but then again, I hadn't until that cold night met Calypso Moore – Callie, to her friends. She was married to a well-known lobbyist who in any other part of the world could walk about unrecognized but who was in these parts what passed for a celebrity – one of those people known to operate the levers behind the curtain of everything to do with commerce and politics, a Wizard of Oz hired to get things done, a gun for hire working for whatever side would pay the highest price.

On short acquaintance with Callie I would come to wonder that she seemed to have so many friends, but a powerful lobbyist's wife is of course as sought after as the lobbyist. She is assumed to be the power behind the throne, and an easier target to get to.

I also wondered how many people had been coerced into friendship with her, despite her good looks and surface charm. By coerced I mean threatened or blackmailed. But I'm getting ahead of my story.

At my book signing, Callie helped by being one-third again the size of most of the women in the audience, giving the room the illusion of being fuller than it was. She was strikingly beautiful, shaped like a work of religious art from a long-forgotten tribe of hunter-gatherers, and wonderfully dressed in clothes worth stealing to a burglar with good taste. I was in my usual jeans, sweater, and jacket, with a plaid black-and-purple scarf looped rakishly (I hoped) around my neck for a spot of color and to disguise my emerging wattle. The design clashed with the pattern of my sweater, but I hoped people would write it off to artistic choice. Some days it's a delicate balance between looking like a cracked bag lady or a creative writer, but generally I aim for somewhere in the middle.

The other occupants of the room were the usual blend of young aspiring authors and old aspiring authors with the occasional genuine bibliophiliac thrown in – those who read purely for pleasure despite the increasing cost, without a thought of trying to write a book themselves. I am intrigued by this kind of person. To me it's like studying to be a doctor and getting the degree but never wanting to practice medicine.

Still, it was getting harder and harder to persuade an intelligent reading public to part with thirty-some dollars plus tax for a hardback book, even one signed by yours truly, paperbacks and eBooks having come to dominate the market. That books – good and bad, enlightening and scandalous – should be tax-free is a truth self-evident to all.

Despite the crowd – hardly a throng as I've made clear – Callie stood out. There was something about the guarded way she surveyed the room before choosing a place to sit that reminded me of an FBI agent I had briefly dated. Phil's paranoia had been the end of 'us,' among other of his faults I won't go into except to say they included installing spyware on my computer. That's a big minus in the trust-building department, but this was the type of white-collar guy one met in the DC area, and it helps explain why I'm single and mostly looking to stay that way. At restaurants Phil would feel compelled to clear the men's room of Russian mobsters or whatever he thought was lurking in there before we could take our seats.

I did see a familiar face or two in the crowd, and one of those faces took me by surprise: Old Town Police Detective Steve Narduzzi, whom I had met during a criminal investigation into my neighbors' whereabouts – a case I had been instrumental in solving, if I do say so myself. Inspired by this successful foray into real-life crime solving, I'd signed up for Virginia's sixty-hour private investigator course, passing all the tests and learning more than I'd ever wanted to know about unlawful search and seizure. What I planned to do with the license was anyone's guess, but I'd had the certificate framed and it now hung on my office wall. It was a case of, 'If you build it, they will come.'

His vitals, as I'm sure Narduzzi would call them: 6 ft, 180 lb., dark brown hair, and green eyes. He was basically a younger version of Chris Meloni, the actor, which is not a terrible condition to be saddled with. His sidekick from when I had first met him was not there, so it didn't look like official business. I doubted if Sergeant Bernolak was a big reader anyway.

I wondered fleetingly if he was there because he had come to believe I was after all guilty of something or other (I may have tested a few boundaries in solving his crime for him), but in answer to my little wave he gave a reassuring nod before settling back in his chair, crossing his arms, and waiting expectantly as if for the Christians to be dragged into the Roman Colosseum. Honestly, it was hard to guess what he was doing there. I knew he had a wife somewhere in Del Ray, a few miles as the crow flies from the bookstore. Eight at night struck me as the kind of time for him to be off duty; tucking children into bed, if applicable; and starting to wonder which horrible aspect of World War II was playing out on the History Channel.

The bookshop owner waited until the latecomers were settled before launching into a brief introduction. Chester Lewis was a true friend who had supported me from the early days. Even if there had been just three people in the audience, all of them blood relatives, I would have done my bit as though millions were watching. Short, spare, bespectacled, and balding, Chester looked the kind of man who had been born in the aisles of a bookstore. His mother had owned the shop before him.

'I feel after so many years, local mystery author Augusta Hawke needs no introduction. She lives mere blocks from this store and has graced us many times with her presence when her yearly book is published. This latest is number nineteen' – here he turned to me for confirmation, and I nodded, although I wasn't sure myself – 'and continues the saga of a team of intrepid crime hunters in the Dordogne. With no further ado I give you your neighbor and friend and mine, Augusta Hawke.'

Smattering of polite applause, with Narduzzi smiling broadly and clapping louder than anyone. *Clap clappity clap*! He looked like a proud parent at a child's ballet recital, inordinately glad that all that special tutoring and investment in embroidered tutus had paid off. I stood (rather embarrassed now by the attention and hyper-aware of his eyes on me) and launched into a description of the plot of my newest book, a plot which even to my own ears sounded wholly contrived and absurd. I was always stunned people didn't seem to notice this. Of course, detectives spent half their time trapped in basements or attics or huddled in trees in the French countryside surveilling the bad guys! The main protagonist of these stories was the ever-resourceful Caroline, and although I had not intended it to happen, she had turned out to be the brains of the team of police investigators. Sadly, the member of the team with whom she had most to do was her boss, a Gallic chauvinist who was essentially a buffoon.

Anyway, my heroine Caroline has chosen to get through life by pretending she doesn't notice buffoonery and not-so-subtle harassment and putdowns and by going behind Claude's back to solve the crimes by herself. Needless to say at the end of every story, he grabs the credit for solving the case, leaving me,

Caroline's creator, to wonder if she wouldn't one day just haul off and clock him.

This latest caper I'd based on the true story of a man living only ten miles away from Old Town proper who had buried his father in his backyard and thought no one would notice the solitary old man was missing. The son took up residence in the house, which was paid for, and was living quite high on the hog with only utility bills to worry about, getting his food from the vegetable garden (fortunately for him, he was a vegetarian) and doing odd jobs or bartering for incidentals. But the old man was eventually reported missing by a woman to whom he owed money; the son's behavior was suspicious enough for her to call the authorities. It all unraveled from there, the son never having quite made up his mind if he should pretend his father had gone off on a road trip and never returned or had told him he was leaving to commit suicide or something. It was a sad story and the only thing remarkable about it was it took two years for anyone to notice the fresh new grave site in the garden out of which the vegetables were growing.

I summarized all this as best I could for the audience, playing up the true elements of the story and how they had woven their way into a novel about a detective in a land far, far away. Then I read aloud a random, brief passage from the stiff white pages of my newly published book. The audience always seemed to enjoy this. It must be a vestige of our childhoods when some kind-hearted adult would read us to sleep at the end of a long working day. I was generally comfortable reading and talking in front of a group like this, partly because for several years I'd been involved in amateur dramatics at a small theatre near my house.

I was so caught up in my recital I didn't at first notice Narduzzi looking at his phone, a concerned look creasing his handsome brow. He paused just briefly at the exit to wave an apologetic goodbye in my direction, and he was gone. There, thought I, goes another sale. But in truth, of course, I was hoping he'd been there to run another case by me, stumped for clues himself. This was an unlikely fantasy, but it was mine and I owned it.

I signed a few dozen books for the audience that night – many people would order a copy from Amazon from their phones right there in the store – and then I signed seven boxes of books for the store to sell online or to passers-by in the coming weeks. That was where the real sales would kick in, but Chester was always taking a risk with this practice. Once I signed a book it could not be returned to the warehouse, and he was stuck with it until he sold it or wrote it off as a business loss. In a pinch he could have brought books to my townhouse for signing but he always said he didn't want to bother me. This was why Chester had my undying loyalty. He had no idea how I longed to be interrupted some days, but then again, no one including me could predict those days.

I was collecting my things to leave, wondering what might be on *Masterpiece Mystery!,* when I noticed the beautifully dressed woman hanging back, making sure everyone else had left before approaching the signing table. She looked vaguely familiar, like someone I might have seen in the news. Not in a big movie star way but in a supporting cast way. She'd been browsing the stacks, pretending interest in a book about how to catch giant fish, which made me guess she was waiting to talk to me privately.

Inwardly I sighed. This could only be one of those persons wanting an introduction to my agent or my editor or my publisher or the entire team up there in New York because they had a terrific idea they knew would make a bestselling book and perhaps I could help them write it.

'Hi,' she said. She was not holding a copy of my book for me to sign so we were not off to a great start.

'Hi,' I said warily.

'I was confused about the dates and I thought tonight was when Bridget Carlisle would be here.' Bridget, for the few of you reading this who have not heard of her, which means you have been shipwrecked for twenty years on a remote island, is the bestselling author of what used to be called bodice rippers and are now called women's romance fiction, with clinch covers suggesting a very bad date getting worse by the minute. You've seen the kind of thing: a man who has spent far too much time in the gym crushing a scantily clad woman to his chest. This generally happens, for reasons best known to publishers and their marketing teams, in an historical setting which varies with the current trends. At the moment Vikings were all the rage. Next year it would be pilgrims, which might present a challenge to the cover artists, since scantily clad pilgrims are generally thin on the ground.

It's difficult for me to talk about this because Bridget Carlisle outsells me by zillions of copies on her worst day and has become a legend in the publishing industry – as well as in her own mind. We nod and smile cordially at one another with what I assume is mutual loathing when we happen to cross paths at writers' events, but she tends to stick to the romance reader events and I to the mystery reader ones so there's little crossover except for the panels covering romantic suspense. Think *Rebecca* but with fewer clothes.

Anyway, this fan of Bridget's whom I would come to know as Callie Moore continued speaking as I recalled my most recent frosty encounter with the 'authoress' – Bridget's term for herself, not mine. The woman was clutching a copy of what was undoubtedly Bridget's latest effing book, which had a thicky glossy cover in shades of pink and red, the title and authoress's name in embossed print. Embossing costs money and publishers don't waste any on high-end print jobs unless they know they've got a sure hit on their hands. I looked at my own unembossed but colorful and appealing book cover and reminded myself comparisons are odious. Didn't embossed paper, apart from possibly harming the environment, look like you were simply trying too hard? There was a school of thought, founded by me, which held that to be true.

'That was a wonderful presentation,' Callie said, after introducing herself. 'I feel it's serendipitous I came here tonight. But also, somehow fated.'

That sounded ominous. 'Yes, and I'm delighted you were here. I think the owner wants to close the store though – it's past the usual time for him. I ran later than I realized.'

She looked over one shoulder and indeed Chester was making the motions of a man ready to set the burglar alarm and head off to his own television set for the night.

'I'll tell you what,' she said. 'Let me buy you a drink at the Port. It seems like the least I can do.'

Actually, the least she could do would be to buy my book, which would help both Chester and me. But I'd been curious about the new restaurant – the latest talk of the town targeting the wallets of the thirty- to thirty-nine-year-old crowd – and I was reluctant to wander in there by myself even with a book to hide behind. I felt I had been stuck to my desk for months and I was just gearing up for the plotting phase of the next book – the most interesting but challenging part of writing.

So going out for an hour just sounded like harmless and well-deserved fun. I told myself I could talk Callie out of whatever it was she wanted without too much trouble. I'd had lots of practice.

'Sure,' I said. 'Sounds lovely.'

'Let me just pay for this book,' she said, indicating Bridget's latest masterpiece which she held against her heart. 'I can't wait to read it. I've heard it's a *tour de force*. She is *such* a genius.'

'Isn't she just? I'll tell you what, I'll wait outside for you. Catch a bit of fresh air.'

She only kept me waiting a few moments. The shop was at the corner of Royal and Queen Streets and just two blocks from the fleshpots of King Street – row upon row of boutiques and bars and restaurants of every type. Callie was shorter than I but as I've mentioned she had that presence which was even more noticeable when she walked – in fact, I noticed men's eyes following her hip movements as we passed.

She had red hair – deep auburn with lots of expensive streaks in it, so her natural shade was hard to guess. I put her age at a well-preserved fifty. Her eyebrows were sort of stenciled on – one of these new trends I couldn't understand the need for. Microblading was the word for it, I thought. Her hands as they clutched her purse were beautifully manicured, a deep purple color on quite short but unbitten nails. Generally, it was people who worked with their hands who kept their nails short like that. Maybe after all that's what she was, perhaps a writer or painter or sculptor. I vowed to hear her out and be patient about it, reminding myself she hadn't actually asked me for any favors but had simply offered to buy me a drink. However, this was Old Town, a few miles as the crow flies from Washington DC. And absolutely no one does anything around here without expectation of recompense in one form or another. No one.

It had been so long since I left Maine I couldn't remember a time when people helped each other out simply because it was the decent thing to do, with little expectation of reward in this world or the next. I often asked myself why I didn't move back there, buy a cabin in the woods to write undisturbed by anything other than the occasional moose wandering by and the sound of a shotgun going off in the distance. But the fact was for all its annoying inhabitants, for all its pretensions, despite its hideous traffic and sometimes broiling weather, I loved Old Town. I had made a stand here too many years ago to think seriously of uprooting myself for anything more than a brief summer vacation back home.

Even my future experience of Callie Moore didn't change my mind, but it was a close thing.

TWO

We were in luck at the restaurant. Either the place wasn't as popular as I'd read – the *Gazette*, like most small papers, liked to prop up businesses, not tear them down – or the first shift of diners had left and the second had yet to arrive. Callie asked for a seat near the fireplace in a way that suggested she was of course entitled to the best seat in the place and didn't the hostess know who she was? I was really beginning to think I could learn something from this woman in terms of entitled behavior that got results. Once we were seated, I ordered a brandy and water from the waiter and Callie ordered one of those complicated sugary drinks with stuff sticking out the top that I avoid as guaranteed to keep me up all night.

We settled into captain's chairs in the flattering, subdued lighting of the place and I looked about me at the upwardly mobiles. All around was a show of privilege, everyone looking spit-polished and trendy.

I sighed in contentment. There is a certain strain attached to book readings and signings. Whatever size crowd turns up, it is a performance and when your default position is introspective introvert it takes a lot out of you to try to live up to other people's expectations. After all, they're paying good money to read the fruits of your labor, God bless them. At least on the stage you have a script to follow.

Just as I was wondering what Callie really wanted from me, she went straight to the point.

'I have a confession to make,' she said.

Never a good conversation starter, I'm sure you'll agree. Any number of confessional possibilities ran through my mind, ranging from 'I'm originally from a Mafia family' to 'I once slept with your husband' – the second option being a definite possibility, knowing Marcus.

'I'm all ears,' I said.

'I knew Bridget Carlisle wasn't signing tonight. I just wanted to swing by the shop and pick up a copy of her book.'

'Oh.'

This was sounding worse and worse, although I told myself I didn't care. If Callie wanted to throw good money at the already fabulously wealthy Bridget, I couldn't stop her. My real competition in the mystery field was bestselling author James Rugger, up with whose sales I would never catch. Nowadays he was collaborating with a former prime minister of England writing spy thrillers, so I had abandoned the race some time ago. She seemed to read my expression and added hastily, 'It was you I wanted to meet.'

'Oh. OK. Well, that's fine and very flattering, but why not just say so?'

'It's awkward,' she said. 'It's really a small favor to ask but small is relative, isn't it?' She did little air quotes around the word 'small' accompanied by a shrug and a little moue of fake embarrassment. I was beginning to guess it would take a lot to real-embarrass this lady.

'It certainly is. Let me say up front my agent isn't taking any new clients the last I knew. I think she finds me enough trouble without my dragging other people into our relationship.' This was a joke I often used to diffuse the awkwardness of situations like this. The chances I would stumble upon the next Hemingway at a writer's conference and arrange an introduction to Ali Wilkes were slim.

'I don't need an agent,' she said, smiling. 'I have an agent.'

'Oh! Well, great. Who is it?' I knew most of the world's agents by name and reputation, having been rejected by nearly all of them at the start of my career.

'Rem Larsson.'

As I was in mid-sip of my very excellent brandy, I nearly choked at the name. Rem Larsson was a DC literary agent with a *Who's Who* list of clients, so renowned even people who didn't give a toss about publishing knew who he was. Saying Rem Larsson is your literary agent is like saying the Pope is your religious confessor. Rem handled all the big deals coming out of Washington DC – all the memoirs of politicos, current and past; all the spy novels; all the character assassinations disguised as memoirs; all the salacious tell-all books by former spouses and interns; all the weighty historical tomes destined one day to grace the shelves of a future presidential library. Callie had my interest now.

I still didn't understand why she didn't just come out and say she wanted to meet me and – for God's sake – buy a copy of my book if only to make it look good; I mean, would it have killed her to soft-soap me a bit? And if she had an agent, what did she need me for?

'The thing is – if I can be perfectly honest?'

I made a *sure, why not?* gesture with my free hand. The other hand continued to clutch the stem of my brandy glass. I had a feeling I would need ready access to it.

'To be *perfectly* honest, what I really want is an ambassadorship.'

I looked around the room almost as if I might find official ambassadorship application papers lying about on the floor or on top of the bar.

'I really cannot help you with that,' I said. 'Truly, I cannot.' I said this as plain as day. It was impossible to miss my meaning. Just so you know; I was firm with her. I am a person who has trouble being firm with anyone, but I was firm that night with Callie Moore.

'I am so unconnected it's a joke, really,' I continued. 'I don't go to fancy embassy events – because I'm not invited and I don't have the clothes for it, anyway. I don't hobnob at Martha's Vineyard or in the Hamptons with the good and the great. I don't contribute large sums of money to people wanting to get elected. Both the Democrats and the Republicans have learned not to bother me with their fundraising appeals, although I've probably given twenty dollars to an Independent candidate here or there. I repeat: I really cannot help you.'

'Oh yes, you can!' she said.

'Oh no, I can't!' I said. I made a half-hearted move to go, but I had two-thirds of my drink left and it was delicious and I didn't want to chug it down.

'You misunderstand me, Augusta, it's not your connections I'm interested in.' She leaned in closer, lowering her voice so as not to be overheard. 'My husband is a lobbyist and so well connected that, well, how do you think I got Larsson as an agent?'

'OK, I'm going to guess you didn't send him a query letter written in iambic pentameter, but I'm really not following you. How can I help you? What exactly is it you've written, anyway?'

What fatal questions those would turn out to be but there was no point in beating about the bush. I was sure she'd say she was writing her memoirs, a field of literature about which I knew nothing. Luckily, she didn't need an agent because my own would run screaming at the very mention of a memoir written by a lobbyist's wife, however well connected. Ali hated politics and all politicians.

'My memoirs,' Callie said.

'OK, then, well, we are completely out of my field now, and again I don't see how I fit into this if you are all lined up with an agent.'

'The thing is I haven't actually written my memoirs yet. For that I need a talented writer. What they call a ghost writer. Someone like you.'

Oh, my. I imagined she had no idea how to write a book, much less a memoir. She probably thought writing a book looked like a lot of work, which it was.

But, why me? Perhaps Bridget Carlisle had already turned her down. The only advantage I could see was that I was local, making collaboration easier.

'No.' Once again, you will notice, I was clear and firm. 'There's no way—'

'When I mentioned you to Larsson, he was hugely excited. That's what got his attention, to be honest. That and – well, a few other things. A few other things I plan to write about. You could call them scandals, I guess. Yes, definitely, you would call them scandals that will rip this city – and the world! – wide open. I've lived around here for a very long time, you see. And there's nothing I don't know about what goes on behind the scenes.'

'Larsson really said that? About me?' OK, I was flattered, I'll admit. I wasn't looking for another agent, I really liked the one I had, but this guy was such a legend in his admittedly narrow field I couldn't help but be flattered he even knew I was alive.

'He did.'

'Well, that's really great – I mean, wow! – but I'm not a ghost writer. Trust me, I am not the person you want for this job and I'm just being upfront with you. I make things up for a living – that's my specialty, if you like: lying. I don't know how to write a truthful line, now that I come to think of it. My books are fiction – made-up stories to entertain people.

'A memoir is a whole other field. If what you say can't be believed – well, people might buy the memoir, there's a lot of those packs-of-lies books out there, but they're not going to take you seriously and I'm sure that's what you want. Isn't that what we all want?' I added that last bit in an appeal to her common humanity, but I could tell she wasn't listening. Her agent had given her marching orders which were to talk me into this by hook or by crook, that much I thought was clear. But all the flattery and brandy in the world couldn't make me say yes to a proposition like this. Apart from anything else it wasn't as if I had loads of spare time. I decided to voice that thought aloud at the first opportunity.

But Callie seemed baffled by my insistence I made up lies for a living.

'I'm not suggesting you should tell the truth,' she said. 'Not entirely.'

'I don't really have a lot of free time,' I said, playing my last card.

'OK.'

She backed off so quickly I should have been suspicious. Instead, she would try another tack. I was to come to understand this was another of Callie's methods. Maybe she would make a good ambassador after all. The kind who could bring everyone to their knees at the peace treaty table. Which reminded me: 'What does all this have to do with an ambassadorship, anyway?'

'I'm an unknown. My husband is famous, not me. I need to get my name out there and this is the way I'm going to do it.'

By making enemies, by revealing everyone's scandals. It made absolutely no sense at all. Which suggested there was more to this than met the eye.

'Just out of curiosity, where do you want to be an ambassador to?'

'Well,' she said, almost as if she had given this no thought up until that moment, 'there are a few possibilities. I think overall I want to go someplace that isn't like, you know, war-torn.'

I tipped my glass to her. 'Good thinking,' I said.

'Somewhere with good restaurants and apres-ski spots, like Mandrekka. Someplace with a beach would be nice, too. If Callista Gingrich can be ambassador to the Holy See, how hard can it be?'

While many would agree, I was not certain Callie could be trusted with a similar exalted position even in little Mandrekka, especially since all Callie seemed to know about Mandrekka was it had snowy mountains and maybe a beach. I happened to know it does have a beach, by the way. I was less certain about the ski lodges. Geographically speaking, a requirement for mountains *and* beaches might be a challenge.

I supposed so long as Callie didn't go to a country with experimental biolabs and nuclear capabilities it might be all right. Years of living in DC had made me a bit fatalistic, more than a bit cynical, and light years away from being a girl with idealistic notions. As Vince Foster said, DC is a place where ruining people is a sport. The beliefs I had brought with me from Maine were still in there somewhere, but they tended to show themselves in my books, where the bad guys were always brought to justice. As you and I know, that is seldom the case in real life.

Still, I felt it might have been better for appearances' sake for Callie to have said something a bit flag-wavey about the desire to serve her country. And for her to learn something about her aspirational posting apart from its average annual temperature.

'Wow,' I said. 'Mandrekka. What *is* the capital of Mandrekka, anyway?'

'I'm not sure,' she said. 'I'll Google it if I need to remember.'

At least Callista knew the Vatican was in Italy.

'I haven't met the king yet,' she said.

'It's a principality, like Monaco. Their monarch is a prince.'

'Really?' She drummed her fingernails a moment before saying, 'OK. I can work with that.'

I was reminded of something Prime Minister Edward Heath had said: 'A diplomat is a man who thinks twice before he says nothing.'

'Here's the thing,' she said, again leaning in. She looked around as if we were suddenly in a James Rugger spy novel and might be overheard by foreign agents who'd planted a wiretap in the stuff sticking out of her drink. 'I happen to know the position in Mandrekka will be up for grabs soon. The current ambassador has announced she is leaving to spend time with her family.'

That was often diplomat-speak for having a drug and/or alcohol problem or having a husband with an incurable wandering eye.

'The place is so obscure I think there will be little opposition to my becoming an ambassador,' she added, at last displaying a teeny flicker of self-awareness.

'What makes you so interested in this, Callie?'

'It's been a lifelong dream since' – and here she waved one hand about vaguely – 'since the congressional thing didn't work out.'

I wondered what in heck that meant but I was afraid to ask. I hoped this wouldn't develop into a matter of national security. It was clear her main interest in all of this was hosting Instagram-worthy dinner parties, not in passing along state secrets or trying to show totalitarian regimes the error of their ways.

'Besides, I have an inside track. Between us girls, I used to be super friendly with this guy, he said he was like a minister of Mandrekka. I'll be a shoo-in.'

Hmm.

'It may not be that easy,' I said.

'Which is why I need your help.'

'I really don't see how I—'

'I'll need your help stage-managing my rehabilitation, if you like to call it that,' Callie breezed on. 'My reintegration into public service.' She declined to elaborate on the rehabilitation part and before too much more time had passed I would wish I'd pressed her more on those annoying little details. But, honestly, at this point I was afraid she might tell me and it would probably turn out to be one of those things you're better off not knowing.

'You do see, don't you?' she asked, with a winsome smile. 'What I need to do is cultivate the media, make them remember I'm alive at this point, and get my name in the news in a good way' – she did not add 'for a change' but mentally I filled in that blank for her – 'so that when nominations are being floated my name will rise to the top.'

Like flotsam. I guessed this was how these things happened in the hallowed corridors of government. As Oscar Wilde said, 'The only thing worse than being talked about was not being talked about.'

Also, 'There's no such thing as bad publicity.' Or maybe that was Barnum, the guy who owned the circus.

Callie seemed to hew to both these philosophies. Once again I figured the less I knew the happier and longer my life would be.

'Just out of curiosity,' I said, 'how exactly did you interest Rem Larsson in representing you?'

'Well, like I said, by pulling on the strings attached to my famous marriage – Tommy is so well known and very much worth cultivating – and by promising a tale of scandalous affairs in Congress and the Oval Office. *And* beyond. You know, the usual.'

'OK.' I noticed this time she didn't mention how thrilled he'd been at the chance to have me on board as ghost writer.

'Also, Rem has ties to Mandrekka via his mother. Or maybe it's his grandmother. Anyway, that's not useful yet but it might be.'

'I see.'

'While I can't go into detail until you are committed to the project, I promise you this is something bigger than the usual "who is bedding who" on Capitol Hill. Something that may even involve national security.'

'Whom,' I corrected automatically. 'Who is bedding whom.'

I didn't know whether to believe her. I only knew I loved that bit about things being kept from me until it was too late and I was committed to the project. I did wonder, only casually you understand, if Callie, political nitwit that she was, had stumbled on to something. In spite of myself, I was intrigued.

Even her name, Calypso, meant 'she who hides.' I was rather a connoisseur of names, being a frequent visitor to baby naming sites in search of character names that are either highly unusual or extremely common. So I tended to know this kind of thing.

And I did wonder: What might Callie be hiding – or from *whom* might she be hiding?

'Grammar was never my strong point,' she said. 'You see why I need you!'

For that she could hire a grammarian. I had little doubt at this point she was both lazy and clueless, and looking for someone to do all the work for her.

'Of course, you need time to think it over; I get that. I'll tell you what. I'm having a dinner party this weekend and there are people there you will absolutely *die* to meet.'

I took another sip of my drink 'Well that sounds like fun, apart from the dying part.' I had no serious intention of accepting the invitation but again out of curiosity I asked, 'So, who will be there?'

'Doc Burke. You know, David Burke.'

I did know. David Burke, always called Doc Burke, was a celebrity surgeon specializing in facelifts for the famous. In fact, if memory could be trusted, that was his advertising slogan. As shallow as that makes him sound, he was mostly renowned for his charity work, helping children and people from battle-scarred nations who had injuries or afflictions like cleft palates which could be alleviated by surgery. That was how I knew him, from various articles about his work, most recently one appearing in the *Washington Post* Sunday magazine. He was legendary in the area and beyond. In photos he looked to be somewhere in his mid-sixties, with a worn, weather-beaten face which suggested he did not care to avail himself of the services of his own profession. He liked himself just the way he had been born, large nose, bony face, bushy eyebrows, and all.

'Impressive,' I said.

'Also, Carnegie Hilton and his wife Mary. You know Carn, don't you?'

God. Carn was a soon-to-be-former congressman who had escaped going to prison a few times for accepting bribes or persuading lawmakers to vote the way a donor with money wanted them to vote. No one had ever been able to pin anything on him. His wife I had seen on television a few times when she had been wheeled out for the obligatory 'Stand by your man' moment during press conferences.

'I can't say Carn and I are on a first-name basis, but of course I know who he is.'

'And then there is Montana – you know, the stylist – and a CIA woman with a story or two of her own to tell. She's another client of Rem's – I think her book will be out early next year. She'll be there with her husband.'

OK, now she had me. I wasn't particularly interested in a slippery politician and his deluded wife – although everyone wondered exactly how deluded she was. She was presumably savvy enough to be wise to her husband's vices, but she had chosen to stay in the marriage for whatever reasons of her own.

Nor was I much interested in Montana, although he was television-famous and probably interesting to meet just for all the people he knew and had 'styled.' It was just plain Montana, by the way: one name, like Madonna or Cher. Since his fame had been built on doing makeovers on a weekly show, 'Say Yes to (Almost) Everything,' I feared he might take one look at me, gasp in horror and wring his hands in dismay, and spend the entire evening singing the praises of Spanx shapewear. He had opened a service in Old Town that did hair and makeup and gave wardrobe and TV advice, with particular emphasis on preparing people for interviews, both live and recorded. He was the only serious game in town for that sort of preparation and I suspected he was doing very well.

The one who really grabbed my attention was the CIA woman. I knew who it must be, and she had been outed – her cover blown – and put in danger by a loose-lipped ambassador from a rogue South American nation. Felicity Overstone. I didn't know her husband's name or what he did while she was out bringing down the bad guys – getting 'dirtbags' off the street, as John Walsh of *In Pursuit* would say. But I was sure she would have quite a story to tell.

I told myself I could come prepped with an excuse to leave early. Besides, Callie's house, a mansion where she lived with her bigwig lobbyist, was a known showcase. It had been featured in fluff articles in a local magazine or two, and more than once had been part of the stately home tour during Old Town's annual fundraiser for childhood cancer. Since my husband had been a pediatrician, of course I was aware of the fundraiser and had attended a few of the featured homes myself. But I had not been inside Callie's place; it had not been on the showcase list the last time I'd bought tickets for the tour. At least I'd get to see inside it for myself. And meet the legendary Doc Burke. And

Rem Larsson. And maybe pick up some sleuthing tips for my series character from an honest-to-God spy.

'It sounds lovely,' I said. 'Saturday, is it?'

She nodded happily. She had easily got what she wanted despite all my misgivings, making me think again she might not be a total loss as ambassador material.

I tipped back the last of my drink. It was time to go before she talked me into anything more than a simple dinner party with some interesting characters.

'I have to get home to walk my dog,' I said.

'I'll drive you.'

'That's OK. It's only a few blocks.'

'It's not New York City but there are still people out there ready to drag an attractive woman off the street if she's by herself. I'm parked nearby. Come on. No arguments.'

I accepted mainly because Roscoe was a bit overdue for his final walk of the night by this point. On the way we talked of normal things like the autumn weather and how wonderful it was after the brutal summer. She gave me the address to her house and I entered it in my phone. I was certain I knew exactly where it was, even though all the houses along the river south of town were stunners.

She pulled up in front of my house on Fendall Street, waited until she saw I was safely inside, then drove off in her BMW. Perfect manners.

As she was driving away, I stood watching out one of the small windows to the left of the door, wondering how Callie Moore had known where I lived.

THREE

I Ubered to the stately home of Callie and Tommy Moore, decked out in my version of Kinsey Millhone's all-purpose little black dress – black pants with matching jacket and flats, all of which I'd had custom-made in London a few years before when I finally realized money was no object, nor was it ever likely to be unless I developed a gambling habit.

I own three copies of the same outfit which I rotate while the others are at the cleaners, copying a page from the time-saving book of Steve Jobs. All I have to do is switch out the tops I wear beneath the jacket so it looks like I at least tried. Generally, I'm a jeans and sweater person, so the pant suits often hang unused in my closet, looking like they're waiting for Angela Merkel to come claim them. During the pandemic, I pretty much downgraded to sweatpants and T-shirts and since no one sees me most days that still works out fine. I generally wear my hair in a topknot, which doubles as a pencil holder.

For this occasion, I had borrowed black and white 'statement jewelry' from my friend and neighbor Misaki Jones, who was instrumental in helping me solve what we always referred to as 'The Case of the Missing Neighbors.' Misaki, who used terms like 'statement jewelry' and offered advice like 'color makes your outfit pop' had been agog to hear Montana would be one of the guests at the dinner party.

She insisted I report back with details and arrange a personal introduction later. She's a former lawyer but her 'passion' is for design and fashion. She wears extravagant outfits *à la* Moira Rose of *Schitt's Creek* fame, and in an emergency acts as my fashion consultant. To me, nearly every public appearance is an emergency so I'm glad for that and many other reasons to have her in my life.

The Uber pulled up before the Moore house within twenty-five minutes. The place was neoclassical in style, as was common to the area, and fronted by tall columns and a long porch. The columns – I think they are called Doric; I'm not up on my Greco-Roman architecture – helped frame a wide main door with a triangular pediment. Six windows, three on each side, were spaced across the front with mathematical precision.

The Uber driver let out a soft whistle as he pulled up, engaging the brake to keep the car from sliding back down the long drive. The whistle was either for the house or for the old Bentley, restored to immaculate condition, parked off to one side. I knew little about cars except I drove an old Jeep from which I could not be parted, but I knew this one was somewhat of a masterpiece.

I would come to learn that the back of the house was equally impressive and included an upper terrace sheltering a patio and lower terrace around a swimming pool, the grounds tilting down eventually – oh so eventually, with land to spare – to the river beneath. An oversized two-car garage was hidden among the trees behind the house. There were probably seven or eight bedrooms with bathrooms of equal number in the several-thousand square-foot space. At a guess the lot size was nearly half an acre. The Moores' neighbors were decently hidden on either side by groves of trees. It didn't seem the type of neighborhood where people popped into the kitchen to borrow sugar anyway, nor would there be an HOA such as I answered to at my townhouse. Snow removal and mulch laying would be farmed out to privately hired maintenance crews.

I found I was pleased overall to have been invited and was enjoying the break in my routine, looking forward to a gourmet meal with distinguished guests followed by an Uber home and an early night. It felt like a reward because I had that afternoon finished a draft of an extremely tricky chapter containing a crowd scene. Those are always the most difficult to write and for whatever reason every book of mine tends to have one. You would think I'd learn but somehow there always comes a day when a crowd seems essential to moving the plot forward or to introducing new characters.

A man was leaving the house as I was arriving. I recognized Callie's husband, Tommy Moore, who unlike most lobbyists flew atop the news radar rather than under. Tall, polished, heavy-featured but handsome. I may have imagined he carried the air of the revival tent or snake oil salesman about him, but he concealed it behind a façade of urbanity.

'Oh, hello,' he said, clearly caught off guard. He was showing every sign of a man sneaking out of his own house and trying not to be noticed, having closed the door behind him with utmost care. 'You're the writer, aren't you?' he said in a low voice. 'The mystery writer?'

'Augusta Hawke,' I said, offering a handshake. 'Pleasure to meet you.'

'Callie said you'd be joining the party,' he said. His hand was big; his handshake warm and firm. I supposed if you were in the handshake business you would have a lot of practice getting it right. I could feel myself start to thaw in his presence. 'Sorry to miss out, but duty calls, you know.'

I didn't keep tabs on when Congress was or wasn't in session, but I supposed lobbyists never stopped working, pulling those strings so often attached by invisible threads to our elected officials.

'I admired your work on that gun bill,' I said in all sincerity. 'A few common-sense controls are long overdue.'

'I'm sure I don't know what you mean,' he said with a smile. I supposed that went with the territory: You could never really come out and say yeah, I did that; I was responsible for wining and dining and talking the right people into seeing the point of view of the often-shadowy figures who paid me to act on their behalf. The elected official would want credit when all was said and done and the legislation had passed and probably was reluctant to share credit – unless the whole thing turned into a political disaster, of course.

Just then Tommy did something strange. At the sound of someone in high heels approaching the front door from within he, taking my arm, scurried us both around to the side of the house. The sight of a grown man in his sixties, impeccably groomed in a tailored suit and power tie, skulking about in this way was incongruous to say the least. We both stood effectively shielded by a large, manicured hedge.

'Well,' I said, 'this is fun.'

He held one finger to his lips. '*Shhh.*'

I could hear the front door opening and Callie calling,

'Tommy?' She tried a few more times before giving up and closing the door.

Tommy Moore turned to me and said, 'I'm sorry. That was kind of a reflex reaction. I don't want to get into a long conversation with Callie right now. She will make me late and besides, she has guests inside to take care of – something to distract her. I thought I'd chosen my moment, but I guess not.'

'Can you tell me what's going on?'

'It is a bit hard to explain, but Callie gets these ideas and there is no talking her out of them. How long have you known her?'

'I just met her the other night when she showed up at my book signing.'

'Oh, that's right. She told me she was going to your signing. I was surprised because – please take no offense – her idea of a good read is Bridget Carlisle. I don't think there's a lot of crossover between your books and hers, is there?'

'I should hope not.'

Here was a man after my own heart.

'As for me, I don't have much time for reading, but when I do, it's James Rugger all the way. Love the guy. You ever read him?'

'No.'

'Well, anyway, I'm delighted Callie has a new friend and a good author to read, but I'm sure you know she's going to want something from you.'

'Well, yes. So she indicated. We had a drink together afterward and she mentioned wanting me to ghostwrite her memoirs. I'm not great at saying no but this time I'm going to have to be firm.' In fact, I was there at the house under false pretenses to a large extent because the chances I would ghostwrite a book for an aspiring ambassador were right up there with the chances I would swim the English Channel in winter in a bikini with weights tied to my ankles. I had, however, been quite clear about my position. I was sure of it. I was also certain Callie had listened to not one word I said but that was on her.

'Well, good luck with that. Once my wife gets something into her head . . .'

I was starting to like him. At least he seemed to have few illusions about Callie. 'Can you tell me why we're standing here behind the hedges?'

He let out a small, embarrassed laugh. *Heh.*

'My wife is a fascinating woman, beautiful and accomplished and fearless when it comes to getting her way. Unstoppable.'

'Yes, and so?'

'She's also deeply jealous of me and I promise you I've given her no reason to be. Her jealousy is verging on paranoia. She has even accused me of having an affair. Can you believe it?'

'Wow,' I said. After my time with my husband, now deceased, I did not find this difficult to believe at all. Marcus had had me completely fooled on this score.

I was astonished Tommy would confide this in me, a total stranger. Did he never hear of loose lips sinking ships? He and his wife both had a penchant for talking out of school, I thought. If she should succeed in getting a posting – no easy task, as for one thing she'd have to appear before a congressional committee and answer questions; I would pay to be there to see it – these two were an international diplomatic scandal waiting to happen.

I also wondered if Tommy had a hidden agenda for taking me into his confidence, but I couldn't think of a reason this would be to his advantage. Maybe he just had no one else to tell.

'Callie's imaginings are nonsense,' he said emphatically. 'Now I really do have to run. Would you mind waiting until I've left the driveway and am safely on my way before you knock on the door and let Callie know you're here?'

It seemed a small thing to do so I stood there hiding like a burglar until he powered up the gorgeous old car and drove off.

As I strode up to the door I thought how interesting it was that Callie apparently had everything but wanted more. I guess that wasn't such a rare trait. I had it too. I just didn't want to be part of her plan.

Knocking on the door, I decided not to worry about it and just enjoy the meal and the elegant surroundings. It's not often I dined on something other than Trader Joe's Guilt-Reduced Mac and Cheese. There would be plenty of time later to dissuade Callie about this ghostwriting scheme, I thought.

In any event, Callie seemed the type of person to move on to the next enthusiasm quickly. With any luck she would soon forget all about it.

FOUR

Callie greeted me at the door with every appearance of delight at my arrival. I was still a bit early, a habit of mine as I liked to allow for traffic contingencies, but I could see that behind her in a room to the right people were already standing about clutching drinks.

'So sorry you're going to miss meeting Tommy,' she said. This would have been the moment to mention I had just met her husband, but I'm a coward so I let it go. 'He has to work late – again. Now we have an odd number for dinner but it'll be fine.'

'I'm sure it will,' I murmured.

'He has an emergency meeting of the joint chiefs,' she went on. 'All very hush hush.'

If it's so hush hush how come you're telling me? Anyway, since when does a lobbyist meet openly with the military's joint chiefs? The media would be all over it like cat hair on Velcro.

No question, Callie was too big a blabbermouth to be a diplomat. Whatever would keep the US out of the next war – and there was always a next war – Callie Moore wasn't it.

She was freshly coiffed and wearing a Holly Golightly dress with elbow-length gloves better suited to Audrey Hepburn's lean figure but lovely nonetheless. When I complimented her on her haircut she told me she was fresh from her weekly hair-and-nails appointment in DC. She beckoned me to follow as she began teetering her high-heeled way toward a beautifully appointed room where her other guests had gathered. I stepped carefully across a highly polished parquet floor scattered with antique woolen rugs to join her. The hall was covered top to bottom in muted pastoral scenes from circa the nineteenth century, all clearly influenced by Turner, the ones at eye level discreetly lighted in gallery fashion. We might have been in the British Museum, a look which was replicated in the withdrawing room or waiting room or whatever Callie might call it. I felt certain 'living room' would not be deemed a grand enough term.

We passed under an arch into a large space heated for autumn by a crackling blaze in the fireplace. Scattered about were several chairs and sofas covered in worn plush velvet with tasseled cushions; on the walls were more paintings of English scenes. For a people who had fought the British to the death, we Americans had gone to a lot of trouble to keep its traditions all around us.

The first person in the room to catch my eye was a very tall man instantly recognizable from photos in *People* and *Vanity Fair* as Doc Burke, a man who charged enormous prices to the wealthy to fund his true avocation of facial surgery and reconstruction for the poor. I had heard him described as the Robin Hood of Botox. In person his features were large but distinguished, his bearing noble if a bit stooped, perhaps from spending hours at an operating table that needed to be adjusted for his height. I realized he resembled honest Abe Lincoln, pre-beard.

I wondered if he was aware of the resemblance to our most revered president and had cultivated it by letting his hair curl at his neck. Media photos often caught him in the wild, reminding one of the famous shots of Princess Diana tooling about some of the saddest, most war-ravaged spots on earth. He would appear in some godforsaken village and people would line up with their horrifically damaged children, sometimes having to draw a lottery number for access to Doc Burke's field operating room. He often worked in tandem with Doctors Without Borders.

I don't think I imagined the lines of worry and sadness on his face, surely there at the memory of these occasions and the many desperate people he had had to turn away. I wasn't sure if he was married. It would take a special woman, I thought, to put up with the constant absences but at the same time it would be hard for anyone to deny it was all in a good cause – and an honor besides to be married to such a humanitarian.

I'd faced the same dilemma with Marcus, of course – he would be gone all hours when an emergency arose in his pediatric practice, and I never complained or even thought about complaining. How could I? I simply learned to adapt, watching lots of movies and streaming old TV series and dining in with Trader Joe. I suspect a small part of me – a part I never wanted to examine – was often glad to have the 'me time,' even though I knew it meant a child somewhere was in distress.

And even though it said a lot about my marriage that I cherished the 'me time' so much.

It was only after I learned these emergencies of Marcus's were not always medical in nature that I felt abandoned and misused, although I seem to have been a willing participant in the bizarre and changeable boundaries of my marriage. The example of my parents' marriage was hardly a model for anyone to live by. I worked through those issues – was still working through them – with my grief group of women who called themselves the Desperados. They all had a story to tell – and how.

Across the room and standing to one side were a couple surveying everyone and everything, as if taking mental notes for later comparison. This was most likely the CIA agent and her husband. I didn't know what he did for a living, but it seemed similarly to involve a tendency toward hyper-awareness verging on paranoia. Maybe he was or had been a policeman, from the burly aerobicized look of him. Or a member of the Secret Service. Evenings at home must be fun with these two. Perhaps they played hide and seek or tossed their living room furniture about for fun and fitness. They made me think of the cartoon characters Boris and Natasha.

I tried to catch her eye but they both hung back, keeping to themselves. Like everyone else, they were dressed in black. We might have been at a funeral.

The only real-life female member of the CIA I'd ever met was Valerie Plame, who wrote a memoir about the events leading to her resignation from the CIA. She'd gone on to write spy novels. I'd come across her at a writers' conference or two.

The woman in Callie's parlor was different in appearance: dark where Valerie was blonde, voluptuous where Valerie was svelte. Both women were beautiful, but I could more easily picture Felicity Overstone vamping the Russians to beat hell until they gave up their secrets. She had that air of easy seduction about her that would make women stand a bit closer to their husbands.

I recalled Callie saying Felicity, represented by agent Rem Larsson, was writing a memoir – no doubt wanting to follow in Valerie's bestselling footsteps. Altogether, the word 'memoir' seemed to hover in the air that evening.

I'd read Valerie's book and come away wishing I'd chosen

another profession than writing – something more active, more life-saving; something with more at stake on a global scale. We all have our fantasies, but I knew while I could bluff my way out of certain situations so long as not too much was riding on it, the kind of nerveless panache required by real spies might have been a stretch for me.

Might have been. Dreams die hard.

Doc Burke appeared to be lost in his own thoughts and I decided to leave him to it. He likely attracted a certain amount of female attention – despite or because of his interestingly craggy appearance – and I didn't want to come across as one of his groupies.

As I was about to approach the Overstones an honest-to-God butler escorted another pair of guests into the room before discreetly withdrawing to polish the silver or the chandeliers or something. Callie had disappeared somewhere into the house by now, presumably on some hostessy errand.

I immediately recognized the couple being shown in. The congressman and his wife – Carnegie 'Carn' Hilton and Mary Hilton – looking sleek as seals, well turned out in a strictly conservative way. He happened to be a Democrat so by 'conservative' I mean terrified of coloring outside the lines, and the choice of clothing is the first tell. His suit fit nicely but was nothing more than an altered off-the-rack number. Bespoke tailors are not used by a man of the people, not if he's smart. The suit probably came from the Joe Banks' men's clothing store but nothing more high-end than that. It was the Democratic equivalent of Pat Nixon's cloth coat.

Mary Hilton wore a fitted dress in bright blue, a color de rigueur for Democrats since Republicans had appropriated for their own use all the red dresses produced in the US. The dress was nicely tailored to her slender shape but was not bandage style, a look she could have carried off, as fit as she was.

As always, however, Mary Hilton managed to look as if she were under duress. I say 'as always' but I had only seen the woman on television and only on occasions where her husband had stepped in it somehow. Rumors swirled around him to such an extent he could hardly leave the house without some woman accusing him of harassment.

Were the claims true? Almost certainly, in my opinion, but

that's what it generally came down to every time, despite a recent and disputed hotel room videotape. Until then, he would simply be trailed by innuendo and scandal the way Charles Shultz's Pigpen was trailed by a cloud of dust. If he were an innocent, I would feel terrible about this, but he did little to discourage this type of thinking about his reputation. He was famous for a sort of twinkly Southern charm which he may have believed made him irresistible to all women, specifically, and to all voters, in general. And history had proven him right: He had been automatically re-elected to office for many years before announcing he would be retiring because of ill health. He would soon be out of the congressional ring but old habits undoubtedly died hard. He took one look at me and came twinkling his way across the room, his arms wide open as if he had recognized in me a long-lost friend. I executed a last-minute backstep before he could swoop me into a bear hug. If he were retiring for reasons of ill health, he certainly looked fit as a fiddle now. I waited until his wife reclaimed his side before shaking both his hand and hers, sending, I hoped, a clear message that despite his undeniable graying attractiveness this just wasn't going to happen.

'Augusta Hawke!' he exclaimed as if he couldn't believe his luck at meeting me. I don't know a single author who isn't pleased to be recognized out of context – not, for a change, pallidly haunting a book fair or languishing in a bookshop or staring into space in a coffee shop but attending a dinner party like a normal person.

I imagined that this man still went nowhere without being briefed on the people he was likely to meet, for congresspeople, in my limited experience, were obsessed with working the room. Not to mention obsessed with their safety: Undoubtedly, he had received names from Callie in advance in case someone decided to make good on their verbal threats and Facebook rants. I was sure when he was no longer entitled to Secret Service protection he would have to hire private help. Creepy as it was to realize, there was undoubtedly a file on me somewhere, and my recent involvement with a missing persons case may have been a big black splotch on my dossier.

Because otherwise, trust me on this, I didn't have the kind of fame that would make me immediately recognizable to him or his wife, who stood beside him with a wan smile pasted to her face. Being next to her famous husband was probably like being a plant that thrived only in shadow, rather like deadly nightshade. There was no need for her to make much effort at being social – it was clear he would do all the talking because he always had.

I sensed movement behind me and turned to see a woman dressed in maid's uniform, looking like an actress in a French farce – a white apron over a black dress with a little white cap. You don't really see that much anymore, even in shows like *Succession* or *Billions* about the uber-wealthy. Buckingham Palace might be the last place on earth for that sort of performance. I assumed the woman was by day the housekeeper and by night the server of dinners. I would come to learn she cooked all the meals for the household. I hoped she had help with the chores and that Callie paid well but what were the chances? She smiled fleetingly at me when she caught me looking at her and quickly ducked her way out of the room, having taken several requests for cocktails. Seen but not heard. The perfect servant.

I wondered if she was married to the butler. The two were about the same age and appeared to be of Middle Eastern descent, Iranian at a guess.

Next the butler ushered in Montana. 'Just Montana.' I knew he was the star of more than one TV series, but the one I remembered most was 'Fix the Boss,' something like that, in which employees submitted their schlumpy bosses for makeovers. This seemed a senselessly brave thing to do, bordering on insanity for those wishing to keep their jobs, but apparently there were good-natured bosses in the world who appreciated this sort of input from their subordinates.

Montana immediately came over to join my little political coalition.

'Hi, Congressman Hilton,' he said affably. Turning to Carn's wife he nodded. 'Mrs Hilton.'

'Mary, please,' she said.

It occurred to me Carn Hilton may have availed himself of Montana's expertise in helping him be his best self in front of the cameras, improving his man-of-the-people schtick and teaching him how to field tricky questions about female interns he had known (Carn's name was frequently linked to an unfortunate

Twitter trend called #bimbogate). My idea was confirmed by Montana's next words:

'I caught your interview when the whole hostage crisis was coming unstuck. Very smooth, very polished. They were really moving in for the kill and you stayed calm and unruffled, as rehearsed.'

I could use some help myself in dealing with interviewers, particularly those of the school of ambush journalism. I wondered idly what Montana charged per hour and if I could stick my publisher with the bill.

'It's really not easy when you just want to wring the interviewer's neck the entire time,' Carn said. 'Where do they get these people? They all look about twenty-five years old with ridiculous haircuts, and they cannot possibly know what they're talking about. I have socks older than most of them.'

Montana threw back his head and laughed, as if he had never heard a more hilarious comment. Mary Hilton gave a little twitch of the lips, probably hearing her husband's joke for the hundredth time. Perhaps it was an allergic reaction to the scented candles set about the room, competing for attention with Felicity Overstone's perfume. There was no overhead light, so we all shimmered in candlelight, laugh lines softened, smelling great and showing our best sides for the camera.

Callie had said there would be eight of us at dinner and I did a quick head count to see if we were all there: me, Montana, the Hiltons, Boris and Natasha, and Doc Burke. Rem Larsson was either late or had cancelled.

It was an intimate group by Washington standards but Callie was probably hoping the conversation might be less cocktail chit-chat and more witty salon dialogue about books and screen adaptations. It occurred to me all these guests looked suspiciously like people who had written a book or were planning to write a book 'one day' or 'in their spare time.' I wouldn't be at all surprised to learn this included the chef and housekeeper, who might do a mean line in penning a modern-day *Downton Abbey*, although I suspected they had precious little time to spare. Callie would see to that.

If the talk was to be of books, I wondered if Montana might not be planning a self-help book or a book of fashion advice, suggested title, 'You're Not Seriously Wearing That'. Carn would be thinking in terms of his memoirs to pass along his wisdom for the ages, a book in the 'let me explain what really happened' mold. I cringed at the thought, knowing no matter what he would outsell my last book.

The CIA woman undoubtedly had stories to sell, although the confidentiality agreement all undercover agents signed would put a damper on any tell-all impulses.

I wasn't as sure about her husband, his place in all this, although he had such a furtive look about him I doubted he was a stay-at-home dad, assuming they had children. Perhaps he was part of her cover, as in *The Americans*.

Doc Burke was the only one who didn't seem to fit in at this literary soirée. So far as I knew he was still a practicing physician, though he was getting up in age. Living in some of the worst corners of the world may have added years to his appearance but I thought he was about sixty-five.

Perhaps there was no mandatory retirement for someone at his skill level. Or, rather than doing actual surgeries, he might be relegated to consulting in the surgical theatre, sort of standing by with advice on which scalpel to use.

While it was hard to picture this man of action sitting down to write his memoirs of the war-torn places he had served, the more I thought about it, the more I realized it might make quite a book.

I must ask him, I thought. Because otherwise his presence at the gathering made little sense. How did he even know Callie?

The 'French' maid appeared in a large double doorway leading to the dining room, from where she announced that dinner was served.

FIVE

Over an appetizer of shrimp avocado and a glass of Chardonnay, Callie said, 'Of course I name names. What's the point of a true story that doesn't? Otherwise, I may as well write – oh, I don't know. Poetry. Or a murder mystery like my friend Augusta here.' She gave a nod in my direction, and I waved a fork vaguely back in hers. The avocado was delicious, and I didn't particularly want to be interrupted.

'That's all very well,' said Rem Larsson, the agent to whom her remarks were directed, 'but the market for memoirs or autofiction as it's called – horribly suggestive name – is flooded right now. As I tell my clients, you must ask yourself before you even begin: What's so special about your story? That's true of any story, of course, but most especially it's true of the memoir.'

To which Callie instantly replied, 'My life story is fascinating. But it's not just *my* story. It's also the story of the many famous people I've met in my life. As well as some famous people I am descended from. For example, it's partly a memoir of my Aunt Davinia who was a mere heartbeat away from being a member of the British royal family at one point. A *heart*beat.'

Larsson, messing about with his silverware, was not enjoying this topic. Taking pity on him and hoping to distract Callie, I said, 'I agree with you about autofiction, Rem. It takes narcissism to a whole new level, doesn't it? It's probably a by-product of the age of social media.'

'Whatever,' said Callie, resenting the interruption.

'It's hard to make anyone understand,' he said, with a grateful glance in my direction. 'And I would have to give you fair warning, Callie, that nothing usually comes of this sort of writing, particularly not a family memoir. I will take a quick look if you'd like but just know that dear Aunt Davinia or whoever thinks their life was much more exciting than it probably was.'

I couldn't help but notice Larsson was miles from being as on board with this project as Callie had intimated to me he was.

It was probably a case of wishful or magical thinking on her part – if she pretended Rem Larsson was her agent then, hey presto, he would become her agent. She'd probably pasted a photo of him on her vision board.

I felt in danger of being cornered for an introduction to my own agent since Larsson was clearly so lukewarm. I hated being put in a position of having to say no or wasting Ali's time.

Hating to say no to anyone was how I ended up married to Marcus, come to think of it.

'I'd be ever so grateful,' Callie said to Larsson. 'I promise, you won't be sorry.' She put down her fork, settled one elbow on the table and, chin resting on her hand, added in an offhand tone, 'Aunt Davinia did have an affair with then-Prince Charles. Eons ago. Do you think anyone would be interested?'

Rem Larsson put down his glass slowly.

'They might,' he said cautiously. 'Yes, they might. It all depends. There's an editor at Penguin who is mad for all things having to do with the UK's royals. I suppose you have proof of this affair?'

'Oh, yes, of course I have proof if they can't take my *word* for things. Letters, a photograph or two.'

She clearly had Larsson's attention as well as mine. He resettled his tortoiseshell glasses on his patrician nose. Others at the table, one by one, put down their utensils or glasses to pay closer attention as they realized a sort of hum had started at one end of the table. I watched as Doc Burke surreptitiously fiddled with something behind his right ear; presumably he was turning up the volume on his hearing aid. It was a gesture I'd seen my grandfather do many a time. Often he'd do it to tune out his second wife, who was not quite the bargain he'd hoped when he married her.

'Was this during his marriage to Diana or before?' Larsson asked.

'A bit of both,' Callie tossed out casually, batting her eyelashes and reaching for her wine, taking a small sip, aware of the impact she was having. She put me in mind of another famous political appointee, Pamela Harriman, also an iron-hand-in-velvet-glove type. Despite all the jokes about her appointment by Bill Clinton, the British-born Pamela had turned out to be a near-perfect ambassador to France for the US.

Now Larsson, a terrible actor in comparison with Callie, said in what he no doubt hoped was a casual tone, 'Well, send it to me by email and I'll see what I can do. Again, no promises, but if you send it by tomorrow I might have time? And, can you scan the photos for me? And email those too?'

'I don't know,' she said. 'How secure is your server?'

Advantage Callie, I thought. That would make him think there was something deeply, wonderfully scandalous at stake.

'It's – never mind,' he said, backing down a bit too quickly. It was obvious he was dying to get his hands on whatever Callie was selling. 'I'll send over a courier to pick them up tomorrow.' At what looked like the start of a protest from Callie, he quickly added, 'My firm has its own private courier on call. I would trust Harry with my life.'

'Much better,' she said, now all smiles. I wondered what these photos could possibly consist of. Hopefully all concerned had kept their clothes on but Callie was being so mysterious about everything one couldn't be sure. Photos of Charles in flagrante with Aunt Davinia or with anyone else would be of value, and not only to the gutter press. The worst the world had seen so far of that sort of thing from Charles had been photos of him in his youth attempting to disco dance.

The photos would certainly speak for themselves and could be sold to the highest bidder but the whole thing had such an unsavory element to it I felt Larsson, from what I knew of him, would not want to touch it with a barge pole. There'd be money in it for sure, and he'd be tempted – who wouldn't be? – but he simply didn't need to get involved in this kind of thing, not with his solid reputation. He might have a job ahead of him, however, if he felt he needed to talk Callie out of this memoir altogether.

It occurred to me his interest might be in garnering favor with Buckingham Palace by discreetly turning over the photos. Perhaps in exchange for exclusive rights to a book by one of the royals themselves. Perhaps in exchange for an honorary knighthood. You never knew what ticked some people's boxes. I realized my mind was wandering down all kinds of tracks, but it wasn't impossible. Not any of it was impossible.

The woman I thought of as Natasha Fatale was paying very

close attention to this exchange, as was her husband. I supposed palace intrigue was part of Felicity Overstone's stock in trade at the CIA. That kind of scandal could bring down nations, always depending on the nation. The French might be blasé and *je ne sais quoi* about romantic affairs but Americans even now tended to regard fidelity, particularly of the married kind, as sacrosanct, hypocritical about it though some might be. And Charles, now safely married to Camilla following the public relations coup of the century, certainly would not welcome this kind of disclosure – even assuming any of it were true. With Callie at the wheel, dropping hints out the window like discarded cigarettes, I was doubtful.

As the butler began serving the main course, a helicopter could be heard flying north up the Potomac. It flew perilously close to the house and put a stop to conversation as it roared overhead. Living in this area one got used to this sort of commotion to a fatalistic degree. It was not uncommon to see the presidential helicopter and escort whirring by on their way to the White House lawn.

Callie, however, had a different theory.

'A helicopter is used routinely for surveillance of our house,' she said.

Even though it was the home of a well-known figure – two well-known figures if Callie got her way – I didn't believe the US military would waste resources like that when it could be engaged in bombing medieval cultures back to the stone age. Was this proof of the paranoia her husband claimed Callie had? I thought it possible she lived entirely in a fantasy world. One glance at Larsson and I could tell he was thinking the same. His lips were pursed in a small moue of concern as he busied himself with knife and fork over his prime rib.

'You don't believe me,' said Callie, looking around the table. The faces looking back at her showed various levels of skepticism, but I thought the congressman's expression was close to blasé. He wasn't going to weigh in until he had all the evidence. Which is exactly what you want in a leader isn't it? No prejudging or jumping to conclusions? His wife, on the other hand, looked incredulous, and possibly was beginning to rehearse her excuses for an early goodnight.

'My husband has been receiving death threats ever since he lobbied over the new gun laws,' Callie went on. 'Didn't you notice the Secret Service parked on the road in front of the house?'

Everyone glanced at their nearest neighbors, and all shook their heads. The Overstones looked particularly unconvinced, and they, along with Carn Hilton, would know how these things worked if anyone sitting at the table did. Added to doubts the Moores were worth a Secret Service operation was the question of whether spying from a helicopter after dark made any sense at all. Not when there were drones which could be more easily deployed against Callie and Tommy Moore.

'No,' I said. 'I didn't spot them as I arrived. I guess that's why they're secret. Wow. Those guys are good.'

I was trying for levity since no one seemed to know how to respond to her declarations, but at the same time I was wondering if anything Callie said was true. Montana looked nonplussed, as did Doc Burke, whose expression held a further element of what looked like alarm. Perhaps as a medical man his training had included a few courses in psychiatry. No doubt this was the place to apply that knowledge.

How stable was she, I wondered? Her flair for the dramatic was evident everywhere – in her dress (although she had taken off the Audrey Hepburn gloves once we sat down to the table), in her lavish pearl jewelry, and in the plush furnishings of the candlelit dining room, which could best be described as early Marie Antoinette. Everything was satiny and tufted and swathed in pastel shades of pink, green, and blue trimmed in gold. It was a distinctly feminine look, and far more suitable for a boudoir; I wondered if there weren't a room set aside somewhere for Tommy to assert his manly right to things like boar's heads and tartan rugs and club furniture. Surely the arm-twisting involved in lobbying would not be conducted at a table with such ladylike flouncy decorations.

Although the way lobbying generally worked, the target was taken out for a meal and the honest targets would pick up the check rather than be seen being bribed into changing his or her thinking. Whether in fact the lobbyists didn't more often pay was something widely known in DC and winked at as just the way of doing business. The good guys in politics, and there were a few, would not be caught dead having a meal with a lobbyist. And the truly honest just ate at home every night.

'Very well,' she said. Callie had finished her main course but looked around to see how everyone else was doing. She signaled the butler, who stood unnoticed in a corner of the room, which was deeply unnerving. How did people live with servants lurking about, I wondered? You'd have to leave your own house to get some privacy. He walked around the table offering more wine – an excellent red this time to go with the steak course. Doc Burke put his hand over his glass to stop the butler; I heard him murmur something about a dicky heart. The Chardonnay pour had indeed been generous, but that didn't stop me from accepting the red.

Callie seemed content for the moment to sit and watch us eat and drink. The conversation meandered over topics having nothing to do with wayward royals – the weather forecast, the football season. I did hear someone ask Doc Burke about his work and was leaning in to listen to the response when the congressman began talking loudly about the latest outrage on Capitol Hill. I couldn't think of anything more boring but I listened politely, eventually giving up the struggle to hear what the good doctor was saying. After about ten minutes Callie, noticing the conversation becoming as empty as the wine glasses, tapped a spoon against her water glass to get our attention.

'We will have dessert with port on the patio,' she announced, 'since the weather has cooperated by not raining. We have outdoor heaters, besides, and I've asked Antoine to light the outdoor firepit. If any of you especially feel the cold I will be glad to loan you a shawl or a blanket.'

She had regained her equilibrium and was being magnanimous, pleased to have got her way with the agent so far but perhaps less pleased no one seemed to have believed her story about the helicopter.

'How lovely,' said Mary. This little banality was the first thing I'd heard her say throughout dinner, but then she was seated across from me, it was a wide table, and her voice was soft. She did seem to have been engaged in a lively if one-sided conversation with Montana to my right, however. He was the sort of man who gesticulated wildly to emphasize a point. She sat as if spellbound, no doubt a hardened veteran of many a rubber chicken dinner on her husband's campaign trail. But I saw this brush with a TV celebrity was adding a little flush of color to her cheeks and a sparkle to her eyes that had not been there before. I realized she was quite pretty once she was allowed for a moment to stand in her own light.

Good for you, I thought. She struck me as the kind of woman whose children had finally flown the coop, giving her enough peace and quiet finally to look around and say, *Is this all there is?* She was approaching the time of life when a lot of women started their own businesses, or trained to run a marathon, or ran for office.

Or had an affair themselves.

Again, I was reading a lot of things into what I knew of the reputation of her husband and struggling mightily against that kind of knee-jerk reaction but if this woman could find any happiness anywhere, certainly it was her turn. They also serve who only stand and wait, and all that. Whatever she thought of as happiness, and I hoped it wasn't something like taking up macramé, I wanted her to go for it.

Those of us who had not finished our wine took our glasses with us to the patio, reached via a long hallway elbowing its way around the kitchen and toward a set of French doors leading outside. It was the kind of house where you needed to leave breadcrumbs and sticky notes to find your way back. Everyone was a bit tipsy by this point, on their third or fourth drink at least, and when Montana started a conga line behind Callie, we all fell into place, laughing – even Fred Overstone, who had mastered the art of blending into the background like Mary Hilton, the politician's wife. It was all the funnier to see the great and the good let their hair down. Even Doc Burke, who was definitely the serious type, had a smile on his face. He may not have been a natural, but he did try to keep up.

The best dancer of us all was Felicity Overstone. In her pre-CIA life she might have been a Vegas showgirl. I wondered what age she was. Perhaps forty-seven – young for retirement, voluntary or otherwise. She might still be on active duty. But if she was writing a book, chances were she'd have to leave the CIA before any publisher would touch it. Also, anything she wrote would have to be vetted and redacted to within an inch of its life during pre-publication review. If she'd been black ops, she wouldn't be able to write a word about it.

Her husband was such a misfit for her it was hard to say what was going on there: he was older and easier to overlook than his va-va-voomy wife. I barely noticed him at dinner and had come to think of that disappearing quality as quite likely being his cover. He truly was the Invisible Man, and I wondered if, incongruous as it seemed, *he* was the black ops guy.

Once we reached the pool and began fanning out around the firepit, the butler appeared with a tray loaded with tawny port in cut-glass crystal glasses. It seemed important later how many partook of this latest refreshment, and of course I had only the foggiest memory, thus scuppering my chances of later being a star witness for the prosecution. I knew I had taken a glass from the tray, not that I needed any more alcohol that night, but I remember reminding myself rather groggily it was OK, I was taking an Uber home. I just hoped I wouldn't talk the Uber driver's head off, as I tended to do after a few drinks.

Montana took a glass, as did Mary Hilton. I was fairly certain the congressman stayed with the wine he was already drinking, as did Felicity Overstone. I heard Carn say as he refused the port something about not wanting to mix his drinks too much. Even though wine and port were in the same family I knew what he meant.

I was less sure about Felicity's husband, but I think he accepted the port. He must have finished his wine at dinner because he didn't put an empty wine glass on the tray. The doctor continued sipping the drink he'd had at dinner. It looked like either a rosé or one of those flavored sparkling waters.

We all mingled and I took the opportunity to speak with Montana since he'd been otherwise occupied with Callie and Mary Hilton at dinner. I said something inane about how much I'd enjoyed his show, which wasn't strictly true, but I asked him if he missed filming and being in front of the camera.

'Not for a minute,' he said. 'The pay for being a coach, which is essentially what I'm doing now, is much better. It's also more rewarding on a personal level. I help someone pick out a tie, make them feel they're doing the right thing at last, and charge them $400 an hour.'

'I knew I was in the wrong business,' I said. 'Not that I have much of an eye for ties or anything else.'

'But you do something I could never do,' he said. 'I can barely sign my name, let alone write a book.'

I was about to ask how he came to be at the party when Callie pulled him away.

Making my way closer to the firepit, I next exchanged a few words with Felicity, who astonished me by claiming to be a fan.

'Are you kidding?' she said. 'I get some of my best ideas from your books.'

I was almost afraid to ask what that meant.

'You do know that at the CIA we hire writers to come up with scenarios, don't you? The crazier the better? I can put you in touch with the right people if you're interested.'

Honestly, I was tempted. To be paid to sit around and bounce crazy ideas off the wall like the *Saturday Night Live* writers? It sounded like heaven – it sounded in fact like what I did now, with only my dog to hear.

'I'll think about it,' I told her. 'Thanks.'

We talked awhile about her plans for her book before I drifted over to Doc Burke, who stood alone, close to the firepit. It was a cool night and even though the wind was still, I was glad of the warmth.

'Somehow,' I said to him, 'I didn't think this kind of party was your thing.'

He looked at me with his very kind brown eyes, the sorrowful eyes of a Basset Hound. 'You're quite right. I generally run a mile. But Callie and her husband have been very generous donors to various charities I'm involved with.'

'Ah,' I said.

'Also, it's very hard to say no to Callie.'

'I hear that.' His remark about the charities explained why he was there, because otherwise it was inexplicable. He was a man with a reputation for very little time for frivolity in his life. He was rather like the Dr Fauci of Facelifts – respected and admired for his unstinting devotion to his calling. I wondered about his private life but really couldn't think of a way to barge in there. I offered an opening if he wanted one.

'You're not thinking of writing a memoir, then, about your life? Nearly everyone else at this party is writing something or other. Certainly Callie plans to.'

If anything, his eyes got even sadder. He was fair-skinned and had spent a lot of time in the sun in climates that weren't kind to fair-skinned people. The bags and dark circles beneath his eyes filled me with pity. He really did not look well. I remembered what he'd said at the table about having a dicky heart.

'No,' he said. 'No, I'm not. At least, nothing I'd want published while I'm alive. And I'd appreciate it very much if no one wrote a biography of me either.'

'I hear that also,' I said. 'I can't think of anything worse than to have someone trying to describe my life when I have trouble myself making sense of it. Not that I'm biography worthy but I think you may be, to be honest.'

'You're very kind,' he said. 'I'm sure we all do what we can.'

'I'm sure we all don't. That's just the point. We read of these things in the news, wars and famines and poverty, and we're horrified and we're saddened and maybe we write a bigger check next time to the Red Cross or Save the Children, but there are so many calamities we know that our check is but a drop in the bucket.'

'Of course, I know what you mean. It's donor fatigue and I see it everywhere I go. We're all so saturated with bad news. We must tune it out to some extent – otherwise we couldn't go on with our daily lives. I do so myself.'

I found that hard to believe; if anything, he had the air of a man who took everything on board as his personal responsibility.

'Well, good for Callie and her husband for trying to help,' I said. 'Too bad he couldn't be here tonight.'

'Isn't it a shame,' said Doc Burke. There was some shading behind those words I couldn't interpret. 'Now if you'll forgive me, I'm rather tired. I think I'll just rest quietly for a moment.' Just then Callie's voice could be heard in the near darkness, a darkness leavened only by the low flames from the firepit. It was a setting both romantic and eerie, a setting for ghost stories. A mild breeze ruffled the branches of the nearby trees, dispersing the musky scents of autumn.

'We have a special treat tonight from my marvelous chef,' said Callie when she had our attention. 'I stole her from one of the embassies, you know. For tonight, we won't have fireworks to celebrate but we'll have the closest thing to it we can. First a toast, to my wonderful new agent. May Washington never run out of scandals.'

It was an odd toast, and probably news to Rem Larsson he had a new client, but we all raised a small cheer and drank to it.

'No chance of that happening!' said Montana. 'Why do you think I came here but for the scandals? They're my stock in trade.' Everyone avoided meeting Carn Hilton's eyes but we all laughed – all but Rem Larsson.

The butler appeared on cue, pushing a wheeled food cart directly out of the kitchen, which was otherwise shielded from view. The curtains covering the French doors fell closed behind him and I caught a peek of his wife at work scrubbing the kitchen counters.

He stopped the cart near the firepit and set the wheel locks. The cart held a rounded structure on a large plate, looking like a small hill covered in meringue. I was guessing it was Baked Alaska. I hadn't seen that dessert in ten years. Most restaurants couldn't be bothered with it and the chances I would make it myself at home were close to zero.

'Is Madam ready?' he asked.

'Light my fire, Antoine!' Callie cried with a maniacal laugh. It fit right in with the Petit Trianon vibe of the evening.

The butler poured rum over the meringue and clicked an electric lighter, continuing to pour the alcohol so the flames ran down the side like lava from a volcano. It made a lovely show lasting nearly a minute before it burnt itself out. He then flashed a large knife and began cutting the dessert into even slices, revealing the sponge cake base and three even layers of ice cream within – pistachio, chocolate, and vanilla. Antoine offered the first slice to me and the second to Doc Burke, who waved a hand in polite refusal. At the butler's urging, however, he accepted a small portion.

The sweet dessert seemed to have a soporific effect on the

group. On top of all the alcohol we were pretty much done for the evening, our bodies practically fizzing with sugar and preparing to crash. The conversation, as much as I could recall of it later, was desultory, talk of current events or legislation pending or business deals. In DC, that was normal. I suppose in Hollywood it was all business deals, too, but of a different kind, with people who slinked about looking amazing rather than purposeful.

In DC, people didn't tend to talk about their childhoods or make personal confessions – raking over those coals was not the cocktail chit-chat it might be in other parts of the nation. We loved scandal just so long as it didn't involve us. A racy anecdote about an ancestor might be told so long as the ancestor was part of very ancient history. My upbringing in Maine had probably made me a bit of a Stoic but I preferred the sort of social distancing DC went in for, even before the pandemic gave it a name.

Because of the hazing effect of sugar and alcohol on the bloodstream, I can't say even now how much time passed before we realized a tragedy had taken place right in our midst. For perhaps fifteen minutes to half an hour I floated about, social butterfly that I am, talking of nothing, occasionally throwing my head back to laugh at something Montana or Rem Larsson said, and it took me awhile to realize Doc Burke was nowhere in sight. I began to look for him, thinking maybe he had left quietly to avoid prolonged goodbyes, but then I spotted him sitting in the dark in an upholstered patio chair a few yards from the pool. He was still. The more I looked, squinting through the darkness, the more I realized he was unnaturally still. His hands were folded loosely in his lap but his head was down, his feet slightly askew. It was nothing too alarming – I assumed the poor man had simply fallen asleep. This kind of do was obviously not his jam any more than it normally was mine.

Some instinct led me to walk over and make sure he was all right. He wasn't ancient but he wasn't young either and maybe the big meal had not agreed with him. But as I got nearer the instinct told me, more loudly: *No*. No, this is not right.

Tentatively I touched one of his hands, his left hand. It was like touching marble, not precisely because it was cold but because it was no longer human flesh. I don't know how else to describe it but I knew then something was dead wrong. I squatted down beside him to peer up into his face. He sat in near-total darkness so it wasn't easy, away from the firepit which the butler had periodically prodded into life throughout the night.

But what I saw was not a man in repose but a man who had suffered a sudden seizure or collapse. I suspected a heart attack, but not having a lot of experience with that I wasn't sure. I write about this kind of thing, and I try to be accurate, but it's not something you can actively research unless you work in a hospital.

I did not suspect foul play. Even given my profession where people collapse all the time and it's always – without fail, *always* – the result of a nefarious deed. For that very reason I tend to think, illogically, that sudden death in real life must be due to natural causes since in a crime story it was always the result of a crime.

I tried to find a pulse on his ropy wrist with its big protruding veins but I could feel nothing. Thinking that testing his wrist was not necessarily conclusive, I tried his neck, feeling for that thump of blood pulsing, that blessed sign of life. Nothing. I was fighting back panic the entire time, telling myself I had to stay one hundred percent calm and if I did so, if I *did not panic*, he might revive. Surely this was my imagination run wild. When you've just been speaking with someone, having a conversation about charities and whatnot, the mind insists that he could not suddenly have died. Furthermore, I thought, if he had cried out, I would have heard him. Someone would have heard him. But in fact the party had left him to one side, in the background, forgetting his existence as we all talked loudly and gaily about nothing.

I shook him gently and that's when he collapsed to one side of the chair, scaring the bejeezus out of me. I jumped back, my own heart pounding, and I spun round, looking for someone, anyone looking in my direction. It happened to be Montana, his face registering rising alarm on seeing my frantic, helpless gesturing. No doubt reacting to my peculiar body language and the look on my face, he strode over, first putting his plate carefully to one side on a low table.

'Something is wrong with him,' I said, walking halfway to meet him. I said it in a hushed voice, as if I were sharing a secret.

I wasn't sure why I spoke so softly, but I was fighting an onslaught of reactions, some of them superstitious, some of them probably as old as time. If I didn't say it aloud, if I didn't say the word 'dead,' the poor man would still be alive and leaving soon on another mission of mercy.

In Montana I had by good luck chosen the right man of action for the job; he walked calmly over to Doc Burke's chair with me following behind. He mimicked my own actions, trying to find a pulse at wrist and neck. He looked back at me and shook his head.

Shit. I may have said it aloud. What I did say was, 'What do we do?' Obviously, the logical thing to do when a guest has collapsed at someone's party is to contact the hostess with the news, but since that would be Callie I was putting off the inevitable.

'I'll go get the butler,' I said. Montana nodded, as if understanding my preferred choice of emergency personnel. I left him where he was, shielding the sight of Doc Burke from the others, and walked toward the kitchen. I looked back and saw he had somehow lifted the doctor out of the chair and laid him flat, performing CPR.

Pulling open the door between the patio and the kitchen and pushing through the curtains, I came upon a cozy domestic scene. The dishwasher was whirring and thumping away in one corner and the butler and Zelda, as I would learn she was called, were bustling about, putting plates away in glass-fronted cabinets, slotting clean silverware into drawers, all the while no doubt hoping we would all shut up and go home soon.

'Call an ambulance,' I said. 'Someone's having a heart attack.'

Once again, I was delaying the inevitable, but logic dictated that emergency services would get here faster for someone who might be savable, even though I personally doubted the doctor would revive even if they got here quickly and applied those paddles they use to restart a stalled heart. Still, it wasn't my call to make as to his exact condition. I just knew, the sooner the better.

Remembering some ancient lesson in first aid from high school, I pointed directly at Zelda as I made this command. The advice, which I had never had the opportunity to put into action, was that you should delegate just one person to call for help while you stayed with the victim. If there was a crowd gathered and you just looked around at all the faces, their instinct would be to hope someone else would take command of things, people being genetically related to sheep as far as anyone can tell. Assigning someone to take charge, making them the responsible party even though you had no authority whatsoever to do so, generally worked. And that person would be evident without the rescuer having to give it a lot of thought. Some people just had that air about them and a gut instinct for the person who would not panic was, well, instinctive in a crisis. While Antoine seemed eminently capable, it was to Zelda that I turned for action.

Once I saw she was on the landline explaining that a guest had had a heart attack and that someone needed to be dispatched quickly, I returned to the pool area where by now a hubbub was brewing. Montana had kept people back, probably by telling them Doc Burke needed room to breathe, but I suspected he just didn't want a lot of people gawking and interfering with what might be a crime scene.

His reaction was infectious: The doctor's death was so sudden I began to have my own suspicions. Montana must have watched many of the same shows I did for his instincts were the same as mine: touch nothing any more than was necessary. Think in terms of the clues left by touch DNA. Keep people clear of the area in case of footprints that might be relevant. Keep hysteria to a minimum.

Too late for that last, however. Callie was standing back as instructed but wringing her hands and making a keening sound like a professional mourner. Interspersed with exclamations of, '*Oh my God! Oh my God!*' were speculations as to what could have happened, and many questions as to why in the world this had to happen here and now. I didn't once hear her say anything like, 'I hope he'll be all right.'

I did notice a few things, filing them away in memory for later.

First, the congressman and his wife had closed ranks, quite literally, her arm linked tightly through his as if prepared to stare down yet another crisis, another potential blotch on his Wikipedia entry.

Second, the CIA woman, Felicity Overstone, had pulled out a little gun from somewhere, probably from the dainty diamanté evening purse that dangled from her wrist. It was an open question whom she thought she might have to shoot with it, but it made me distinctly uncomfortable that her training had kicked in at this particular moment and in that particular way.

There was a third thing I noticed and that was that Rem Larsson had pulled his phone from his pocket, I assumed to make a 911 call himself. Instead, he was taking photos of the scene – perhaps a video. This was bizarre, and I wondered that no one called him out on it, but I think I was the only one who noticed. Everyone else was staring at the clearly lifeless body, unresponsive to Montana's efforts. I recalled that Larsson's was a trained legal mind and maybe his first instinct was to document the scene. Or maybe he thought it would make a great book. God only knew.

This was fast becoming my personal idea of a party from hell. I'd feared all these writer manqués in one room could only lead to trouble, but truly I'd had no idea.

When Montana sat back on his heels, clearly giving up, Felicity stepped up to take his place, expertly placing her hands on the doctor's sternum and pushing hard enough to break a rib. Presumably the gun was back in her purse.

I stood by the pool wringing my hands along with Callie. I felt an arm around my waist – it was Callie, clinging to me for dear life. Thinking she might faint, I tried to lead her over to one of the patio chairs, but she stood rooted like a tree.

What flashed through my mind was that it was a tragedy where a swimming pool had been filled in with concrete by grieving grandparents – an incongruous thought until I realized my mind had made the jump between that grandchild who could not be saved and all the children Doc Burke had helped to live healthy, productive lives. At least, lives where they were not stared at and bullied and held up to pity or ridicule. A rather homely man himself, he had found his calling in helping others who did not fit society's ideas of beauty, thanks to unlucky births or the weapons of war. To think of him gone was tremendously sad; it was as if his very large heart had suddenly decided it had given all it had to give to the world.

We stood about in that tableau of stricken grief and panic for perhaps ten minutes. The butler emerged from the house saying help was on the way. He flicked on a switch that illuminated the pool area. Now we could see the ghastly tableau in full detail, although most of us chose to avert our eyes.

Felicity was by this point ready to give up. The butler took over from her and she seemed relieved to stand down, shaking her head and wiping a tear from her eye. She was not alone in that; Mary Hilton's eyes glistened with moisture, as I'm sure mine did. Montana stood by, still guarding the space around the body.

We heard emergency sirens in the distance. They were coming up George Washington Parkway at a satisfyingly fast clip; within two minutes of the *wee-ooo* sound first reaching us, they could be heard making their way up the drive to the house. The siren's mechanical keening increased in volume to a terrible shriek, then mercifully went silent. No one was making a move so I made as if to go to the front door to let them in, precisely as if I owned the place. Then I saw Felicity was already on the way. No doubt her training had given her quicker reaction times than mine.

Our hostess Callie was in her own world. I wasn't sure where the maid-slash-chef had got to.

Just as I was turning to follow Felicity, a man's voice from behind me shouted, 'What in hell is going on here?'

Tommy Moore emerged from the doors at the end of the house's main hallway. He walked over to his wife, his hands open at his side in a 'WTF?' gesture.

'Callie?' he said. 'What is—'

He followed her shaking hand with its pointing finger to the motionless form of the doctor. His face was hidden by the butler's ministrations, that face with its rictus of pain and shock which I would remember longer than I cared too. The butler stood up. There was clearly no point in any of us trying further.

Tommy edged his way slowly past the small group to stand near the butler. 'Is he dead?'

'I'm afraid so, sir,' replied the butler.

By this point Callie had collected herself enough to walk over to her husband, still averting her eyes from the focal point of the catastrophe engulfing her dinner party.

'Why are you here?' she hissed in his ear, clearly hoping not to be overheard. It was a vain hope. The silence otherwise was complete, only disturbed by a distant commotion coming from outside the front door and the gentle splash of the river against the shore at the foot of the backyard.

'My meeting was cancelled,' he said. 'One of the key players came down with the flu and had to beg off.'

'Too bad he couldn't have told you that.'

'Yeah. Anyway, there was no reason for the rest of us to be there so I came home. I thought I'd get some work done.'

'How long have you been home?' she asked.

Before he could answer there came a pounding on the door.

When the EMTs left, they were carrying the shrouded body of Doc Burke on a stretcher. No one seemed to know what to do next.

'Would anyone like coffee?' Callie asked.

We all looked at her, incredulous.

The social awkwardness generated by this offer of coffee cannot be overstated, but it seemed to jolt her guests out of the trance that held them spellbound. They simply shook their heads, mumbled their thanks, and headed toward the door. I went to retrieve my purse from the cloak room so I could call an Uber.

The doctor had been pronounced dead at the scene. We'd all been told someone might be in touch with questions. No one was, at least not immediately. David Burke was simply an aging man who'd had a heart attack, one of probably several dozen deaths that night in the big city, one of the sad parade of victims who succumbed to either gunshot wounds or the occasional stabbing or a simple heart attack from overeating or bad luck in the gene department. I assumed the doctor had inherited a genetic predisposition because while he didn't look to be in the pink of health he didn't have any of the obvious signs of putting too much pressure on his support system – meaning his veins and arteries and his heart and lungs and liver. The only thing that looked wrong with him were those bags under his eyes. What might a good night's sleep have accomplished to avert this tragedy?

Despite my instinct and Montana's for preserving the scene, I never seriously questioned it was a medical problem that took

Doc Burke's life, for I would've said he had not an enemy in the world. He had enough star quality even I knew who he was and that he was famously a man who worked at his 'day job' only as it allowed him to serve the poor and desperate. What was not to like about such a paragon?

If this had been a situation in one of my books, and foul play had been suspected, Callie certainly would have been a suspect, if only because on closer association she annoyed the heck out of me. The doctor had appeared at her dinner because he didn't feel he could refuse the invitation from a major donor. Was there more to it than that?

But that night there was no time to ask questions, even had it seemed necessary. I would find out more later when the police got involved. Oh yes, the police got involved.

And come to find out, they thought Callie made an interesting suspect, mostly on general principles. They found everything she said to be, literally, incredible.

I learned this later from the man who had become a friend in a strange way when I – let's just say it – *totally* helped him solve 'The Case of the Missing Neighbors.' The man who had shown up at my book signing but had left abruptly. The very signing where I'd met Callie Moore.

Detective Narduzzi later came to ask me a few questions about that night. I'd provided him with information I thought he'd find interesting, and as he started poking about, he had his own suspicions.

Of course, he wouldn't tell me what suspicions exactly. Not for a while. But he wanted to take my mind as the saying goes. That was me – all give and no take when it comes to police investigations.

I told him that whatever Callie said was probably fantasy and nonsense, especially anything pertaining to the good doctor. That Callie, ever the narcissist, would obsess over how to control the media reaction to the doctor's death. She would worry in case of a full police investigation. If that happened, her plans to live in a glamorous foreign embassy, even in an obscure principality like Mandrekka, might be derailed by scandal.

There went the fancy parties and the occasions to wear elegant clothes and jewelry and the vacations on private yachts. So she might decide on a pre-emptive PR campaign, something that would make her look interesting, compassionate, and altruistic, because of the doctor's wonderful reputation. She would likely claim a close friendship, since anyone involved with him would be by association some kind of angel.

I know that's tortured thinking and pretty crazy to boot but you have to consider the source. Everything and everyone who could be used to Callie's advantage, would be used. Including a deceased humanitarian. Including yours truly.

Of course, I had no real reason at the time of the doctor's death to think it was murder or that everyone involved was a suspect, but time would prove me wrong.

PART II

SIX

I spent the next three months involved in backstage work for the little theatre a few blocks from my house. I didn't have time to try out for a role in *The Odd Couple*, which was a shame. I'd have made a perfect girlfriend for Oscar, but I had to keep my spring deadline in mind. I'd been late with the last book; I couldn't in good conscience or courtesy be late with the current one.

I'd also worked in a quick family visit for Christmas to my stepson and his wife in Vancouver. He had moved out there after his father Marcus died to become a pig farmer, about which the less said the better. Pigs, like many humans, are only cute when they're little. I tried not to ask too many questions in case I ended up milking them or something.

Callie seemed to have dropped her pursuit of me as ghostwriter. Either she'd found another writer or she'd wisely decided to go to ground for a while.

I'd committed to lead a writers' retreat in a couple of months and was very much counting on using the time away to pursue my own work. My plan was to set an assignment for the attendees at the start of each day, then send them off until the evening when I would have them read aloud their best efforts, leaving me eight blissful writing hours of my own.

Every so often I'd sit back in my office chair, distracted, pulling myself out of the Dordogne and the travails of Caroline and Claude. I was introducing a new character, an American. She was from Philadelphia and they all made fun of her accent behind her back. To paraphrase Helen Fielding: cruel race, the French.

I needed a name for the character and I knew I wouldn't get much further until I figured it out. In these situations, I generally searched online databases, births and deaths, and combined names to make sure I wasn't citing a real person in my book.

But despite my being so busy my mind kept going back to that party, to the later part of the night when we'd gathered by the pool.

To me, finding Doc Burke sitting still, too still.

To Doc Burke, slumped over in his chair.

To the awful, long minutes when people struggled to revive him to no avail.

There was no reason for Doc Burke to have died, but he had. Why? It seemed to me a little investigation was called for. Especially with a new deadline staring me in the face. Most writers take procrastination to a fine art, but I'd be willing to bet no one could hold a candle to me.

The good doctor's death had received the official 'natural causes' stamp of approval and everyone had moved on. When a victim is elderly and known to have a heart condition, no autopsy is conducted in Virginia, as in most states and countries. People tend to think autopsies are automatic, but that's far from the truth. There simply aren't enough personnel even in the larger cities, let alone the smaller ones, and the chances anything nefarious will slip through the cracks are slim. Not non-existent but slim.

Somehow my mind just wouldn't let it alone, and I started thinking of it as if I were plotting out one of my books. It was probably a way of distancing myself from the trauma. If I could only turn it into a story, the pain of those moments would subside. I could *control* the pain.

At a minimum, at least I knew the main players, the characters I would ordinarily have to create from scratch. But here they were laid out for me in living color with all their idiosyncrasies.

There were nine people, including me, at the party – eight, if you don't count the doctor. Seven suspects, then. There was also a butler and a live-in housekeeper to cook and serve the meal – a married couple. Make that nine suspects. Callie had told me she called them 'A to Z, because they do everything,' and because she could never remember their names.

Then as it turned out, Callie's husband was home. I'd add him as a footnote.

Up to ten suspects.

I made a list of names in my notebook, as if I were preparing the cast of characters which appeared at the front of my books.

1. I, Augusta
2. Calypso/Callie Moore
3. Doctor David 'Doc' Burke (Victim. Plastic surgeon to the stars and the poor)
4. Literary agent Rem Larsson
5. Carnegie 'Carn' Hilton, congressman (sketchy)
6. Mary Hilton, his wife (sketchy by association)
7. CIA woman Felicity Overstone
8. Her husband Fred, the Invisible Man
9. Montana, media consultant
10. Butler Antoine
11. Chef and housekeeper Zelda
12. Callie's husband, Tommy (late arrival)

No doubt all the dinner guests had been interviewed by someone from the police, albeit informally, briefly, by phone, and by an underling. I was sure they only bothered to that extent because of the fame of the doctor. The police were merely dotting those 'i's and crossing those 't's.

After the party, we all disappeared back into our normal lives. Since that time I had only seen one of the dinner party guests, Montana, the media consultant, whom I had run into in the street. He had offices on Cameron Street, on the second floor in the middle of a stretch of high-end shops, offices, and apartments across from the back of City Hall.

Well, to be honest, I had sought him out as being the type to notice things and be able to provide intelligent commentary on what he'd seen. Also, he had been the one to take charge during the event itself, leading me to believe he would be someone you'd want to give evidence.

Not that it would come to that, I reminded myself.

'Running into him' took quite a bit of time and effort. I walked over one morning at around eleven thirty and sat on a bench near City Hall and waited for him to emerge, scrolling about on my phone as I waited. I also managed to sketch out a new character for my book in progress, so the time wasn't a total loss. It was ruddy cold, though, and I was glad I'd remembered a woolen scarf and hat. People bustled by me, the ones headed into City Hall looking anxious or frustrated, and the ones emerging generally looking pissed off.

I figured Montana would go somewhere for lunch at one of the many restaurants nearby; he didn't seem the type to pack a paper bag with a bologna sandwich and a banana.

He came out the door of the building at noon sharp. He was alone but there was always the chance he was meeting someone. I'd cross that bridge when I came to it. I stood and followed him several blocks to the Auberge, an upscale bistro with outside seating and outdoor heaters. Since the pandemic, Old Town had taken a leaf from the pages of Europe, allowing outdoor dining pretty much year-round.

I walked by the seating area casually, then staged a double take. I thought a gasp might be too much but I did hold my hand to my chest in surprise.

'Montana?' I said, removing my hat so I'd look more familiar.

He looked up from where he had been studying the menu. It was obvious he recognized me, but he seemed to engage in a brief mental tug of war, deciding whether he wanted to invite me to join him. There could only be one topic we had in common and that would be that awful night.

In the end good manners won out. Perhaps like me he was still haunted by that night; none of us had had the chance to hash it over and put it behind us. Talking with some police underling on the phone didn't count. Believe me, those guys were not psychological or grief counsellors and that was pretty much what we all needed to lay this ghost to rest.

A waiter came over to hand me a menu and pretty much at random I selected a salad niçoise and a glass of white wine. Montana ordered the cassoulet.

As we waited for our meals, he said, 'I still can't get over it.'

'I know,' I said. 'Neither can I.'

'The strange thing is,' he said, 'I've never seen a dead body before – not like that. I mean, not outside of combat. Not at a party where everyone's supposed to be having a good time. When anyone in my family died, we had a closed coffin or cremation. Everyone is just squeamish about that kind of thing – thank God.'

'Well, you acquitted yourself very well.'

'I was in the Marines,' he said, as if that explained everything. I supposed CPR was part of the basic training.

'I see. Well, I've had one experience of a man dying in front of me but it was a completely different situation to this. The problem I'm having here is that the doctor was one of those people about whom it is always said, "He was too good, he was too young; why did this have to happen to him?"'

'Precisely. It just seems wrong. I did a tour in Afghanistan and the things I saw . . . you're never the same. Why do the bad guys get to go round killing and maiming people? People who never did a soul any harm?'

'Had you met him before?'

He shook his head. 'No. I'd heard of him of course.'

'Why were you at the party?' I sat back just as our meals were delivered, thanking the server, and giving Montana a moment to collect his words.

'Why were you?' He said it with a bantering smile, but it seemed like a bid to buy time.

'I met Callie at a book signing at Old Town Books, that place on—'

'Sure, I know the place.'

'It was weird . . .' I began and broke off.

'Anything to do with Callie Moore is weird by definition. But what was weird about this?'

Settling my napkin on my lap, I said, 'She pretended she was there by mistake looking for another author.'

'How flattering.'

'Believe me, as an author you get used to stuff like that. Well, you never get used to it but it's part of the territory and you come to understand that and offer those poor lost souls up to God's care.' He nodded solemnly so I added, 'I'm joking about the "God's care" thing, of course. Generally I don't care what happens to anyone that rude. But as it turned out, that wasn't true, what Callie said. She was there deliberately. She took me out for a drink afterward and explained what she was after. I mean, why not just be more open about it?'

He laughed. 'That's just not the way Callie does things. The word Serpentine was invented to describe such as she.'

'You seem to know her fairly well.' I was fishing, not really expecting a full answer. I didn't get one.

'Did she mention she's after an ambassadorship?' he asked.

'Why yes she did, as a matter of fact.'

I smiled and he returned a complicit smile of this own. Montana had very good teeth, probably veneered, but the dentist had made a good job of it. Sometimes people with veneers look as if the dentist had added several more ultra-white teeth to their mouths.

Given the business Montana was in I supposed it was only to be expected, the need for a highly polished appearance. It was all about image with this man. Quite a life path, from marine to Celebrity Whisperer. Generally, guys like Montana become government contractors and double dip, earning their retirement pay while also pulling down hefty salaries for selling war equipment or whatever.

I started on my salad, arranging tuna and lettuce and olives on my fork.

'She wanted me to ghostwrite her memoirs,' I told him.

'Really,' he said. 'I guess that's not too surprising. I'm not sure she can write, but if she could fiction would be her forte. Still, I'd be amazed if she had what it takes to pull a coherent narrative together. So that's why Rem Larsson was there.'

'I'm not sure if he knew in advance that was why he was there, but yes. You heard them talking at dinner about this scandalous bit of gossip she claimed to have had from her aunt Lavinia?'

'Davinia. Complete with photos and shocking letters or diary entries, yes. I didn't take any of that seriously, did you?'

'I tend to think anything is possible. I just knew I didn't want to write the thing, whatever it was.'

He lifted a spoonful of the cassoulet to his lips and blew on it before taking a tentative sip. 'Too hot,' he said, adding, 'You say you're not sure Larsson knew why he was there?'

'I only say that because Callie had told me that Larsson was one hundred percent on board and clearly at dinner it was news to him that he was one hundred percent on board.'

Montana took a sip of his wine and, nodding, put the glass down carefully. I drew my sweater a bit closer over my shoulders. It was lovely out there, sunny and bright, but chilly.

'She tells everyone she's a client of mine.'

'And that's not true?'

'We've talked about it but she balked at signing a contract and believe me that has happened once too often, especially with congressmen and senators. It's all talk and no willingness to put their name or money on the line. They don't really want people to know they are availing themselves of my services. It's embarrassing for them. They want people to think they were born with the ability to jump up and make a speech to persuade donors, to sway voters, to influence people in power. To be interviewed on TV like a natural. I get that but what tends to happen is they want to get advice and training from me and not have to pay for it. And of course, I'm not in this business for charity. So Callie came to my office and did her best to finagle me into doing all kinds of things that she wanted – free – in terms of coaching for public speaking, things like that. Also in how to do cocktail party chatter in foreign lands.'

I laughed. 'I had no idea. You mean I can come to you and say look, I'm sort of a social moron, can you help me?'

'It's what I do. Not in those words, of course, but in this increasingly digital world no one wants to be caught flat-footed, especially on tape, so my services are much in demand. From learning how to give TV interviews and video presentations to how not to offend people from other cultures. That last one is a real minefield, believe me.'

'I can see why Callie would need some help with that. She has enough trouble navigating her own culture. You have some background in this?'

'I did public relations for the US Marines for twenty years.'

'Ah,' I said. 'Makes sense. I had no idea,' I repeated. I seemed to have no idea about a lot of things. 'So anyway, Callie tried to get your advice and not pay for it.'

'Yes. As I said, it's not that uncommon, people are leery and don't quite believe me, I guess, when I tell them my services are as confidential as I can keep them. Or maybe they're just cheap and don't think advice is a real "product." But in this town, if you're seen coming through my doors, word gets out. I'm not sure if people really care much but when congressmen come to me—'

'You mean like Carn Hilton?'

'People like Congressman Carn, yes. I get lots of senators. They get elected and then realize that getting elected in Iowa or wherever is not the same as gaining the ear of the people who matter in this town. The people who get things done. A lot of the newbies just get run over like someone hit them with a truck and are never heard from again. The shrewd ones learn. They adapt.'

'Honestly I think you could help me, but we will leave that for another time,' I said. 'And I promise to pay you. Anyway, you're saying you hadn't met Doc Burke before Callie's party?'

'I had met him at some fundraiser, ages ago. I don't think he recognized me but of course I recognized him. He's very distinctive looking and famous, of course.'

'Yes, he was.'

'Was being the operative word, of course. Poor man. I still can't believe it.'

'Did you know he was going to be there? I mean, were you looking forward to meeting him?'

'No. I mean, I really had no idea of the party list. I knew that Callie would be there – well, naturally. And I knew she'd be up to something or wanting something but I had nothing else going on that night and I thought – why not? Because of her husband she's tremendously well connected. I'd love to have a photocopy of his address book. I always have to drum up new business in addition to finishing the business I have, if you understand.'

I nodded. 'You seemed to know Carn. But you didn't know he would be there. Nor his wife?'

'Yes. Poor Mary.'

'Poor?'

'I shouldn't say anything – really, it's talking out of school – but people do take bets on how long before Mary dumps him now that he's leaving public office and not likely to run again.'

'I don't think there's such a thing as a current or even former congressman who's not running for office. Not until somebody sticks a fork in them to make sure they're done.'

'I do know what you mean.' He paused, spooning up more of the cassoulet. It looked wonderful and I was beginning to wish I'd ordered it.

'How about the CIA couple? Felicity and Fred?'

He shook his head. 'Is he CIA, too? I had no idea.'

'I'm guessing there. He just has that watchful look about him. How about the agent? Rem Larsson?'

He gave an uncertain shrug and continued with his soup.

'Did you happen to notice anyone leaving the main party to go and speak with the doctor privately?'

He shook his head: a definite *no*. 'I've been searching my memory. Because if it wasn't a heart attack, and that's a big *if*, it seems obvious someone approached him and put something in his glass. It was dark back there. He had for whatever reason removed himself from the spotlight, in a manner of speaking. I don't think he was a party type, and as the party geared up people may have forgotten he was there. As for me, I spent some time talking with that CIA woman, Felicity.'

'She was talking about her book in progress?'

'Actually, no. Not specifically, at any rate. We had a few things in common, as it turned out. She'd been in Afghanistan doing God knows what and I had been there about the same time doing things they told me were going to preserve the US Constitution, however unlikely that seemed some days. So we talked about that. Did you know, and did you go? – that sort of conversation. Also about the culture and the people. They really are an attractive people with a rich heritage. It's a shame they always seem to be in the crosshairs.' He wiped his lips with his napkin and settled back in his chair, arms crossed. 'I wish we could have done more for them.' He shook his head. 'Disaster.'

'I don't suppose she talked about what exactly she was doing there.'

'In Afghanistan or at the party?'

'Either, really.'

'You know how these spy types are. She wasn't going to talk about what she was really doing and in my experience they tend to glamorize what they've been up to, anyway. And the further events appear in their rear-view mirrors the more they like to magnify their involvement. They may have been in charge of ordering office supplies and doing the coffee runs, but they make it sound as if they slept with generals, were part of every stakeout, and listened in on every wiretap.'

'Right. Did she really imply that? The "sleeps with generals" bit?'

'She implied it, sure, and I wouldn't be surprised if it were true. She may be hoping it will increase her chances of selling a book of her adventures. But her husband was standing right there, so.'

'Yeah. Awkward.'

'Why were you asking about anyone's going over to speak with the doctor?'

It was my turn to shrug. 'I honestly don't know,' I said. 'I just don't like it.'

'You write mysteries,' he said. 'Occupational hazard. The same way everything I hear is a sound bite, and every ill-fitting suit is an affront to the eye, everything you see might have been a dastardly deed prompted by greed or lust or love.'

I blushed a bit at that because it was the entire truth. I did have rather an overactive imagination. But you know what? Nine times out of ten my wildest imaginings turn out to have at least a tinge of truth to them.

'Of course, I have no proof of anything,' I said. 'Of any wrongdoing. I don't even have a strong suspicion of anything. I just have a bad feeling. Probably just because the world has lost a good man and that makes me crazy. Because there aren't enough people like Doc Burke in the world.'

'I couldn't agree more,' Montana said. 'But if the doctor died of anything other than natural causes, surely we'd have heard by now. Now, would you like some coffee?'

I was dissatisfied with the rather breezy dismissal. Yes, Montana was a busy man, and yes, there was nothing to be done now. But the whole thing rankled, and I didn't feel I could lay it to rest until I had tried to find out if my suspicions were grounded in anything but a desire to avoid writing.

I thanked him and said I had to get back to work. I began fumbling about in my purse and he waved away my attempts to pay my share.

'This is on me,' he said. 'And if you ever are looking for media training, do keep me in mind.'

SEVEN

I did get some writing done that day: I probably put in an entire hour and got another page churned out. I even polished it, taking out a typo or two and correcting the more egregious autocorrect errors. Generally, I had three more pages to go before I met my quota and could call it a day but my mind would not stick to fiction, not when there was all this non-fiction horribleness swirling around in my head. Doc Burke sprawled in that cushy chair, Doc Burke flat on the cold concrete with people pumping his chest so hard I swear I could hear his ribs break. The life-saving advice when giving CPR is to do it to the rhythm of 'Staying Alive' by the Bee Gees. Maddeningly, that song had got stuck in my mind, playing off and on since the event.

I decided to return to the scene of the crime – *if*, per Montana, there had been a crime. I chose a time when I knew Callie would be gone. She had told me she had a weekly salon appointment in DC and today, wouldn't you know it, was the day.

I didn't know what time, but I took the chance she'd be gone a good while even after a morning appointment, maybe shopping once she had her hair and nails done. If she returned home earlier than I expected, I would tell her my gloves had gone missing in all the chaos following the dinner party. Same deal if Tommy happened to be at home.

But it was Antoine opened the door and I launched into a rather gushy and scatterbrained version of my lost-gloves story. I was behaving quite unlike my usual self, I assure you – imitating the flustered version of Miss Marple immortalized by Julia McKenzie. But in vain. Antoine, his heart unmelted, stated that there had been no gloves found that were unaccounted for but that he would certainly let me know. I was equally certain he would not. He was practically closing the door in my face as he spoke, so I did not gather my presence was altogether welcome.

I did the verbal equivalent of sticking my foot in the door, dropping the flustery lady act and replacing it with my best 'Don't mess with me' look. My years with the Little Theatre, both onstage and behind the scenes, had not been wasted.

'I have to talk with you, sir. It's important.'

I don't know why I called him 'sir', but I figured he was so used to being bossed around by Callie he might respond to a show of respect for his authority. He was to his fingertips the man of action guarding the house from all comers. His hair was coal black to match his dark eyes, but it was fringed about the ears with gray hubcaps and slicked back close to his skull. His heavy eyebrows and moustache were meticulously trimmed; I imagined the upkeep on grooming was probably constant. I suspected former military, but I couldn't begin to guess what military in which Middle Eastern country. I was fairly certain that Antoine was not his given name but something adopted for his role in the Moore household.

The same with Zelda. How many people outside of Germany have you met named Zelda?

I had exactly two seconds to convince him talking to me would not only be a great idea in general for all mankind but might help him in some way.

It seemed like an occasion for the biggest lie I could pull from my repertoire.

'I'm assisting the police,' I said, donning a mantel of unimpeachable authority. Well, it could have been true. Now I mentioned it, it *should* have been true. Detective Steve Narduzzi of the Old Town police should have been in constant touch with me and I was certain he would have been had there been any cause for concern over Doc Burke's passing. I had been essential in solving 'The Case of the Missing Neighbors' and if I didn't yet have Narduzzi's undying gratitude I would eventually.

I didn't elaborate on the statement, but let it float in the air between us. The Jekyll/Hyde nature of my transformation may have helped throw him off guard.

He didn't question it. On the contrary, he seemed to react with a sinking heart, as if he had been waiting for this moment, this knock on the door, ever since the saintly doctor had been taken ill under his watch.

He opened the door wider.

'So there are questions?' He stood back, allowing me to pass.

'My wife is in the kitchen. She will want to know what's going on. I must urge you to act with discretion, however. It is lucky my employers are not here at the moment. But I have had concerns. Grave concerns. I'm glad you're looking into this.'

Wow, I thought. I'll be running the entire Old Town Police Department before long. I was beginning to wish I'd gone big with the lie, claimed to be a chief superintendent or something.

As I followed him out to the kitchen, I wondered at his reaction. It was so extreme – the crumbling to my authority, however fake – I began to suspect they were in the country illegally. It would be just like Callie to try to save a few dollars and have two people at her beck and call, too afraid of deportation to challenge her on anything. The interview would have to be softly, softly done or my being there asking about that night might alarm them into silence.

The likelihood of their insecure legal status became evident moments into my conversation with Zelda. We found her studying a book of recipes, no doubt trying to tempt Madam's palette that evening. Zelda, I knew from my own experience, was really quite a good chef and was wasting herself and her talents here with Callie and Tommy. I wished I knew the reason, but I quickly saw the effect my presence was having. I asked a simple question – Did she know anything about the events of that night? – and the response was firm, immediate, and rather loud.

'I don't listen at doors,' exclaimed Zelda. She was wearing street clothes – exercise clothing – the starched maid's outfit no doubt being only for special show-offy social occasions. 'It is despicable to do that. Where I come from—'

And she broke off there. It was clear where she came from the punishment for listening at doors in certain circles was severe.

'Of course you don't!' I cried. 'But people under the same roof, it's impossible for you not to have heard something of what goes on. Do you live in the house with the Moores?'

'No,' she said firmly. 'There is a guesthouse on the property and we live there.' She pointed vaguely in the direction of the trees beyond the pool.

'Well, that sounds nice,' I said. 'Convenient. A short commute! That's worth a lot in this area.'

'It is not so nice. It simply means we work every hour God sends.'

'Yes, yes, I see, that could be exhausting.'

'You have no idea,' she said.

I was searching for a way to break down her defenses. As it happened, I chose the wrong way. The pushy, none-of-my-business way.

'Zelda is an interesting name,' I said. 'Is it a family name? I was named for my grandmother, Augusta. She was a real tartar. "Tartar" means kind of a battle-axe.' Of course, in blathering away I was angling for her real name, trying in a heavy-handed way to establish rapport.

And of course, that was the last thing an illegal immigrant, if that was what she was, wanted to discuss. Mentally I kicked myself when I saw her expression. Fear, wariness, panic.

I turned to Antoine and his expression was identical. I had overstepped by a mile.

'I know what "tartar" is,' she said crisply. 'It means someone who is formidable. As to my name, my mother was a fan of the books of the Fitzgeralds. You have questions about what happened to the doctor? Because I have dinner to prepare now. Right now.'

Yes, as a matter of fact I did have questions, but I may have reduced the trust levels to zero and I needed to try to claw it all back. Before she could shut down completely, I said, 'Look. I know lawyers who can help you. In this area there are nothing but lawyers, you can't swing a cat without hitting one, and I know many of them. I can at least get a good recommendation for you to an immigration lawyer. I promise you there is nothing to be afraid of. It would free you to—'

But I could barely get the words out before Zelda, blood draining from her face, said, 'I do not know what you mean.' She and her husband exchanged glances. 'I was born here. I am a naturalized citizen of this country. I am honest woman. I do not need help.'

At least one of those statements was false, I thought. A person born in the United States has no reason to become a naturalized citizen.

'Of course, I'm not saying you're dishonest,' I said. 'I'm saying if you come from a country where the regime is repressive you may not be willing to talk. And the truth is, you probably should not talk with the police without getting counsel. And I will help you with that. Just keep that in mind.'

'I thought you were from the police,' said Antoine.

Shit. 'I'm assisting the police, yes,' I said. 'Detective Narduzzi of the Old Town Police Department.'

I was thinking not only would Narduzzi not be pleased if he came to hear of this conversation, but whatever Zelda knew might be lost forever to her fear of officialdom. His beat was Old Town anyway and I was fairly sure the Moores' house was far enough down the parkway to be in Fairfax County, not within the city limits guarded by Narduzzi.

Much to my surprise, I saw I had got through. Again these two exchanged glances, transmitting their equivalent of the secret handshake known to married couples everywhere. She had been designated the official spokesperson and I suspected it might be because her English was better than his.

'I can tell you are just trying to help,' she said. 'But whatever I tell you could get innocent people in trouble. I've had enough of that where I come from.'

'Where exactly is that please?'

'You did not know? We are from Mandrekka.'

Of course they were. Somehow, I felt I should have known this. Had I known more about the country I might have guessed but at best the goings on there rated a page-thirteen mention in the *Washington Post*. It was no doubt from Zelda that Callie had come to hear of the place. If it were one of the repressive regimes which seemed to have sprouted all over the world, all the more reason to keep Callie Moore away from it, but that was a worry for higher-ups than me.

'I have heard of it,' I said neutrally. 'I had no idea it had these problems of repression.'

'How do you think they get away with it?' she asked. 'They are not so stupid as to brag about it.'

'Right. Of course not.'

'Look, I think you are a nice woman, innocent and naive like most Americans. *Safe*. Being safe can make you – how do you say it?'

'Complacent.'

'Yes.' She looked as if she might add, 'stupid,' but did not.

'So, you have been happy here?' I asked. 'Happier?'

She shrugged. Her expression said, 'No,' but she said, 'I can only tell you that my husband and I have been planning to leave this house for some time. But it's not so easy to leave.'

'Why is it not easy?' But I guessed the answer before it came.

'I am not sure if we got another position Mrs Moore would give us a good recommendation. And then we would be well and truly stuck here. Having raised a fuss, you understand? And then we have to live with the fuss.'

'I understand completely,' I said. 'And I can guess why you want to leave – Callie might be . . . difficult – but was there one particular thing that was driving you out?'

'It is not a happy house.' Zelda looked over her shoulder before continuing, gesturing with one hand to draw me to one side. We stood nearer the refrigerator now, listening to it hum. When it suddenly disgorged a load of ice cubes into its bin I jumped about a foot.

'There are arguments,' she whispered. 'Madame is threatening to leave. However, this is not having the desired effect.'

'I don't follow.'

'She thinks he will beg her to stay.'

'Oh, I see. She is overplaying her hand.'

'I think that is the expression, yes. She overplays the hand. It is a poker expression is it not?'

'Precisely that. When you play a game, sometimes the risk you take is not well thought out in advance. Nor the next move.'

'And now this.' Zelda swept a hand around the room. 'Now this *murder*.' The word 'murder' was said in an even lower note, almost a hiss. 'Now Antoine and I are well and truly stuck here. Because if we leave now, how will that look to the police?'

'That will look very bad to the police, I must admit. But why do you think it was murder?' At least they had the common sense to stay put and available for questioning. But at what point might she and her husband decide the Immigration and Naturalization Services were a bigger threat than the local police? Truly they were between a rock and a hard place, especially if you add their markedly unstable employer into the mix. If Callie were overbearing to begin with, now she had an added threat to hold over their heads. If she wanted to cast blame somewhere, Antoine and Zelda might be the first place she'd start.

'We're not sure yet it was murder,' I said. *We* being me and my pal Narduzzi, of course. 'But, what did you hear exactly?' I asked this in the gentlest, calmest voice I could muster, fearing the wrong tone would frighten her into everlasting silence. 'If this helps the police, I will make sure they know you helped. I happen to be, well, rather well acquainted with Detective Narduzzi. I've helped him before, you see. I promise you he is a reasonable type and if you are cooperative, I will make sure he knows this. You will have no trouble if you tell the truth.'

'How many times I have heard that in my country!' she said, causing me to wonder just what she had been accused of doing in her country, rightly or wrongly. 'Look, it is no good. What I know – even if I thought it would help the case – what I know, it's not much.'

'Tell me,' I said. 'Let me decide if I think it's worth passing along. Maybe I can keep your name out of it.'

'And maybe you can't.' Seeming to regret the snippy tone she sighed, adding softly, 'My husband – this concerns him too. I can promise no more than that we will discuss it. Perhaps you have a card you can leave with us.'

'Actually, I—'

'Just tell me the phone number. I will memorize,' she said, saving me from having to explain why I didn't have anything identifying me as being in any way attached to the police unless you counted several old paid-up parking tickets.

During all this the butler stood slightly to one side and behind his wife. Very much melting into the background. I was reminded of Fred Overstone, with his ability to vanish at will into the wallpaper. I realized my focus had remained on Zelda rather than Antoine but that was no doubt because he was such a good man at his job, seen but not heard.

Today he was in casual clothing like his wife, in jeans and shirt instead of his formal butler's gear. The relief showed in his body language. He was, however, on alert. In his shoes, so would I be. 'The butler did it' may be a cliché but those with total access to a household are bound to be suspect. They're also bound to be terrific sources of insider information, rather depending on how indiscreet they're willing to be. A ticked-off butler is probably a fountain of information during an investigation.

I decided to try a slightly different approach. 'I'm glad you're here together,' I said. 'Because it can help me clear up a few questions I had. Antoine, you were serving the drinks throughout dinner, as I recall. But your wife served the cocktails before dinner.'

'That is correct,' she said.

'Were there any special requests?'

'They were all special requests, Madame. I mean we didn't offer, for example, a bottle of wine to share. Everyone was drinking different things before the meal. Cocktails, you know.'

'So in addition to your many talents, you are bartenders,' I said.

'Yes,' he said. 'I worked many years in the restaurant trade.'

'And that was here?'

'No, in Europe. Anyway, during the meal we had the various wines, as you know. After the meal we had port to go with the Baked Alaska.'

'That's a bit unusual, isn't it?'

'I don't know what you mean, Madame. The mistress of the house liked to serve a tawny port with every kind of dessert. It was, she liked to say, her signature.'

'There's no need to call me Madame,' I said. 'Do you recall any of the cocktails that were out of the ordinary? Any *really* strange requests?' I wasn't sure why I was asking but I thought poisoning an individual drink would be easier than poisoning the food: Everyone had a portion of the avocado shrimp and the prime rib and vegetables. Except for me, the vegetarian – I had whispered to Antoine when he tried to serve me the prime rib that I'd have only the vegetables.

Thinking this through, I realized how much the butler had control over who got what portion of what. No wonder the butler was often the prime suspect, so to speak.

One other option was the bread rolls. Antoine had portioned those out, as well. But directing one particular poisoned bread roll to the doctor, while not impossible, seemed most unlikely. Poison baked into the roll? That certainly put the onus directly back on Zelda, the chef, if so.

The Baked Alaska had been portioned out by the butler and shared by all. It would be impossible – or nearly – to poison just one segment of it. And only the butler would know which portion was tainted.

Which wasn't exactly true, I realized even as I thought it. Zelda could have made a mark on the meringue, for example, to show him the portion where, say, the ice cream inside had been poisoned.

As all of this went through my mind, Antoine was continuing to answer my cocktail question. I dragged my mind back to attention.

'The mistress was having a vodka martini, Madame. She always has a vodka martini with just the slightest soupçon of vermouth in the evenings before dinner. She is very particular about that tiny amount of vermouth. "Just set the bottle of vermouth next to the vodka bottle and that will be enough," she will say. It is her little joke, always.' He pulled back his lips in a rictus of a smile. I answered with a grim little smile of my own at the old joke.

'And the others? The guests?'

'Someone had a Manhattan. Two Manhattans, I should say. That was the Stoneovens. I am not sure about the agent.'

'The Overstones. Yes.'

'And then the congressman and his wife had sherry. I remember particularly because I had to go into the cellar to retrieve some. Very few people drink sherry anymore. It is out of fashion.'

This fit with my memory, as well as my impressions of the couple as being rigidly conservative. At least for occasions of public display they would drink not what they liked, but the most refined, Old World, Oxford-donnish drink they could think of.

'And Montana?'

'He drank a flavored sparkling water. As did the doctor.'

'Had you met the doctor before this evening?'

He shook his head as she said, '*People Magazine*.' I knew what she was referring to; I happened to catch the issue where a reporter followed the doctor around somewhere in sub-Saharan Africa.

'And was there anything about the evening that struck you as unusual?'

'I'm sure I couldn't say, Madame.'

Again, he and his wife exchanged glances. This time I was sure their glances relayed that they had talked with me long enough. I had to step up my game or I'd lose them.

'There was a lot of wine and alcohol flowing,' I said quickly. 'Was that normal in your experience?'

'Sometime,' he said. 'Sometime normal.'

It seemed as if we had entered an area these two really did not want to go.

'Did you pick up on any particular tensions in the room? People who seemed to be avoiding other people? People who were oddly friendly?'

'The only one who was oddly friendly was the congressman,' said Zelda, surprising me. 'He is a pig's ear that one. We have them in our country.'

I knew what she meant. Of course the old saying is that you can't make a silk purse out of a sow's ear. I wanted to follow up on this outburst of honesty but Antoine gave his wife a small shake of the head: *We don't talk about this here.*

That topic having become radioactive, I decided to try another tack.

'It was quite chilly on the patio. Was it normal for Madame Moore to want dessert to be served out there?'

'It was because of the Baked Alaska,' said Zelda. 'For safety's sake she didn't want the flames in the dining room. There had been an accident one time. The memory of the wallpaper, it made her very nervous.'

I thought the person who was very nervous was Zelda. She was lying about something; I was sure of it.

'It was a beautiful dessert,' I said, feeling my way through this possible minefield. 'I haven't seen it made in an age. My mother used to make it.'

This happened to be true. It was also true she caught the dining room drapes on fire one time when she'd been drinking.

Zelda softened enough to say, 'It is very tricky pudding to make.'

'But it was what Madame wanted.'

She nodded. 'It was what Madame insisted on. She said one of the guests was from Alaska and this was to honor them.'

'You have been in England it would seem?' I observed. 'No one calls it "pudding" over here.'

'At one time,' said Zelda. 'If there's nothing else, we must get back to work.'

'Keep in mind what I said. I can help.'

'Thank you. We will be fine.'

And the interview was at an end. The butler showed me to the door, closing it behind me with perhaps a bit more firmness than was necessary.

EIGHT

My interview with Antoine and Zelda left me unsatisfied. Clearly, they thought there was something more to the doctor's death. And we had barely scraped the surface of their thinking.

Why had their minds leapt to thoughts of murder, when I had been careful not to introduce the word?

I might have written it off as the natural paranoia and twitchiness of two people in the country illegally who were clearly the products of tyrannical regimes, but it seemed other people were uneasy with the situation as well. The next day I got a call from, of all people, Rem Larsson. Could I come to his office to talk about some project, unspecified?

Sure, I said. I could carve out time for Rem Larsson, the most famous agent in DC if not New York. We settled on a late morning appointment for the next day at his offices on 12th Street.

I tried very hard not to fool myself into thinking this man was showing a sudden interest in my work and wanted to dangle a Netflix deal in front of my eyes. There's nothing wrong with my work, mind, but it was not the sort of thing he would care about representing. He was probably not all that thrilled about representing thrillers written by former politicians but that was a well-paying gig and maybe it went to support pro bono work. For all I knew he was another version of the good doctor, doing things that made him metaphorically hold his nose while the income from those projects went to help the unjustly unpublished.

I paid a visit to his firm's website, where I was reminded he is first and foremost an attorney, literary agents having evolved over time, expanding their expertise as the publishing industry morphed from gentleman's pastime into something more resembling the dark satanic mills of the Industrial Age. Agents had had to adapt, swimming as they did in the increasingly murky worlds of finance, politics, justice for all, and the Internet. I learned from the website that his pro bono work as an attorney focused on cases where there was question about the evidence and tactics used by the prosecution. His work was not confined, then, to copyright disputes and so on but on occasion wandered into the shadier streets of the criminal law. He furthermore had served an apprenticeship with a justice of the Supreme Court.

He was sounding more and more like quite a guy. There was no grass growing under the feet of Rem Larsson.

His office was on 12th Street, one of those corridors of power that evolved seemingly overnight. No one quite knew how but like immigrants, lawyers had been drawn to the same area by ties of acquaintance and familiarity, not to mention the ability to speak the same language of torts and testimonies. Uber-agent Bob Barnett's law firm offices were nearby, along with the offices of a dozen other members of the same or similar professions, housed in massive buildings of polished steel and marble.

I parked at the nearby public short-term garage and entered the building by the 12th Street entrance between G & H Streets.

Security cleared my visit with someone on the phone and I was directed to a bank of elevators that would transport me to Book Nirvana on the 14th floor. There I was grabbed and handed off by various lackeys (the first a rather severe-looking woman I pegged as a graduate of Bryn Mawr or Wellesley, Women's Studies) before I was discreetly shuffled into Larsson's office, announced by a fourth lackey (Vassar, English Literature, possibly nineteenth-century Romantics) as Ms Augusta Hawke. He rose from behind his mahogany desk to greet me. The desk belonged in a museum along with other artefacts of the Vanderbilt family.

He looked smaller than I remembered in his grand surroundings. Even though at Callie's house he had stood beneath tall ceilings laced with crown moldings that had to be a nuisance for Zelda or Antoine to dust, here the massiveness of the glass picture windows overlooking 12th Street distorted his proportions further. He was still, in any setting, impressive. Sharp of eye and a sharp dresser, aging but gracefully. Graying hair grown just to meet the top of his starched shirt collar, the tortoiseshell eyeglasses giving him a scholarly look.

No bright yellow Porsches in his garage to ease him through his mid-life crisis, was my guess. He seemed too confident by far to need all that. Not surprisingly he was surrounded by books, which lined every wall. I glimpsed the titles of nearly every political biography or autobiography of the past decade, the ones not snatched up by Bob Barnett, all with glossy covers – mostly black, for some reason – and that ever desirable embossing.

In *gold.*

Callie's house, now I came to think of it, had been devoid of books, at least in the living room. Perhaps there was a library somewhere down one of the long hallways, but the place seemed more pleasure palace then literary salon.

Perhaps I was just attaching my not-impressed views of Callie to her surroundings and props. For an investigator that was an easy trap to fall into. For this I needed to keep an open mind and that included assuming that despite appearances Callie might be far brighter than she let on.

Larsson let my eyes rest for a while upon the majesty of his empire but after offering me coffee, which I declined, he quickly came to the point of our meeting. Folding his hands atop his desk blotter, he said, 'Callie has sent me some of those documents of which she spoke.'

No Netflix deal for me, then. But this sounded interesting, nonetheless.

More interesting was the question of, why tell me? From my perspective it was as if he had struck up a conversation with some random person on the Metro.

'The interesting thing about Callie,' he began, 'is that just when you feel she is full of total nonsense and it's safe to ignore her, she actually comes through.'

'Aunt Davinia's memoirs,' I said.

'She's hinting at something a bit more, well, alarming than the whole business with the then-Prince. Although there are publishers who would sell their grandmothers for the chance to publish those bits.'

'Wow,' I said. 'I mean, like you I had my doubts but . . .'

'She's only hinting, mind, at some fantastic further disclosures. Some fly-on-the-wall stuff. I'm not sure whether to believe her.'

I felt doubt was a good policy in this case and I said so.

'Let me ask you this,' I said. 'How well do you know Callie?

I didn't get the impression your relationship went back a long time.'

'No, no, it does not. I had my assistant do a general Google search on her. She's from Louisiana originally, did you know?'

'I did not know that. Interesting. She's managed to sand off that accent pretty well, assuming she had the drawl.'

'Her family owned what we would have to call even these days a plantation. Acres of cotton or coffee beans or whatever it was. When the market for what they were selling dropped they got by selling off acreage, generation after generation, acre after acre, until they were left with basically the mansion and some surrounding fields that had been exhausted of any nutrients. At which point, her parents decided it was time to get their only daughter educated and married off to a wealthy man and for some reason they felt a good hunting ground would be Washington DC. Probably by that point Callie was too notorious to be married off to any of the local swains. But I'm extrapolating there; I don't really know. She went to Hollins College in Virginia, scraping out a diploma in agronomy or whatever, and managed to get herself a job on Capitol Hill as an intern. It all made a sort of sense. She is nothing if not cunning and manipulative and the Hill is the best place in the world for such talents to take root and flourish. She met Tommy while she was busy selling access to her congressman.'

'Gosh,' I said. 'And here was I, thinking that was illegal.'

'It is if you get caught. You know how this town works and you've spent enough time in her company to know what she's capable of. I would not care to get in her way when she wanted something. Anyway, in Tommy she spotted a kindred spirit.'

'O-kaaay,' I said slowly. 'But as to these memoirs of hers, I do wonder why you are talking with me? I mean if the memories are too hot to handle, slander-wise, I would expect you to know a lot more about putting out that fire than I would.'

'It's all a matter of careful phrasing,' he said complacently. 'Believe me, the entire thing would be carefully vetted, not just by me but by several legal experts in this office.'

'Again, I don't see how I can help.'

'You are published by Traitorsgate in New York.'

I acknowledged this was true. 'Julia Swanson is my editor.'

'Yes. I know her but only slightly. I did wonder if she might not take a look, since I don't really know much about fiction – I deal almost exclusively in political memoirs these days – and I am assuming the notes Callie sent me might be for a fiction book.'

'What makes you say that? I thought she was writing her memoirs.'

'It's too crazy to be real.'

'I don't think Callie knows how to tell real from crazy, let alone how to write fiction,' I said.

'I would have said Callie Moore specialized in little else.'

'Yes, of course, I do know what you mean,' I said. 'She is given to drama and exaggeration, based on what I know on short acquaintance. I would add that she's pushy. However, I would *also* say her stock in trade, her currency, is gossip of the real-life kind. Knowing people's secrets, being able to leverage those secrets into getting what she wants.'

'Yes,' he said. 'I can see that, yes.' His eyes shifted. He seemed to be studying the rows of books on his shelves. Surely he knew those contents by heart. 'A propensity for finding, shall we say, a person's pressure points, the things they might not want known. Based just on gut feeling, not on direct experience of her, of course.' He threw up in his hands self-deprecatingly. 'My life is an open book.'

I smiled. 'I almost wonder, given what happened at the dinner party, if she knew more than she was saying about Doc Burke and whether that knowledge had something to do with his death. If it was murder, as I'm thinking. Without a shred of proof, mind.'

'You thought so too, then,' he said excitedly. 'You thought something was off that night, too.'

I said, 'But murder? Doc Burke? That doesn't make any sense, does it? Callie should have been the one to end up murdered by – well, not the Doc; it's hard to see him as a killer. But by whoever she had information on.'

'And was blackmailing, you mean.'

I hesitated. 'Not for money, surely she had plenty of that if the house is anything to go by, but for what she wanted, yes. That makes perfect sense. Getting her to admit it, though . . .'

'Maybe the police will have better luck. If it becomes a murder investigation.'

'They don't seem to be actively investigating the doctor's death.' Unless you count me showing up at the house pretending to be affiliated with the police, of course. I was certain there were penalties for that sort of thing. Best not dwell on that now.

'What happened to the photos? She said there were photos. You were going to send a courier to collect them.'

'Photos and letters, maybe a diary of sorts. With all that happened that night she just sent the man away the next day, said she was too busy to be bothered. But she emailed me later that night with a brief summary, heavy with dropped hints of what was to come. I'm not too surprised she went all coy on me but I haven't heard from her since. She's keeping a very low profile since the doctor died.'

'So, you don't know how true her story is. Or even what her story is.'

He shook his head. 'Photos and letters certainly would have helped me believe. Now I just don't know. Hints and allegations don't amount to anything but a possible lawsuit for slander. But I'm wondering: Was the doctor mixed up in this somehow?'

'With Callie's memoirs? I doubt it. He told me he was at the party because the Moores had donated generously to his various missions. I got the impression he had made an appearance a bit under duress, a bit in search of a nice meal. Those were also my motivations, so we had that much in common.'

'Nothing more than that?'

'I'm sorry?'

'The doctor. Was he coerced into appearing, do you think?'

'I doubt it,' I said finally, wondering why Larsson would care. 'I can't really see it happening. I'd say if Callie were holding something over his head, he'd be the "publish and be damned" type. It's not as if he had something to prove. He wouldn't lose clients over it unless . . . I don't know. Unless he'd been sued for malpractice somewhere in the past?'

Cupping his chin in one hand, he seemed to give this serious thought. 'I guess. Anything's possible.'

'At his age, and given his renown, a revelation like that might've been embarrassing but it wouldn't necessarily have cost him customers. I doubt people would believe it, for one thing. Being sued doesn't mean there's any truth to the lawsuit.'

'Too true.'

'The kind of paid work he does – I mean did – wouldn't grind to a halt if he was consulting or something like that. His charitable work certainly would continue. I don't know if he was still actively practicing medicine for his wealthy clients, do you?'

'No. Not that I'm aware.' He paused. I had a feeling we were skirting some issue and I was just about to ask what it was when he said, 'Do you think he was there to meet someone?'

'An arranged meeting, under cloak of darkness? Is that what you're suggesting? OK, maybe. I guess. Although I'd call that kind of clandestine carry-on outside his usual range.'

'I'm looking for some reason beyond the obvious for his being there. It's a wild idea but maybe Callie was trying to put him together with someone.'

'Romantically? I would think he had little time for romance and besides, there were few likely candidates at the party.' I began counting them out. 'There was Mary Hilton, Felicity Overstone, and me, representing the female side. Callie herself, but I would be amazed. On the male side, if Doc Burke was that way inclined, we had Fred Overstone, Congressman Hilton, Montana, and you. Not impossible, any of it. I suppose I could ask Callie if she had some matchmaking thing in mind for the doctor. Who knows? She might tell me the truth.'

He rubbed one hand across his clean-shaven chin, nodding in vague agreement. He didn't appear to be listening.

'But he sat apart most of the night, did you notice?' I asked, crossing my legs and sitting further back in the old leather-upholstered chair, which creaked alarmingly under my weight. 'Once we were out by the pool. He said he wasn't feeling well – he told me he was tired – so he wasn't mingling like most of the rest of us. Did you see anyone talking with him?'

'I've been trying to remember. I was having rather a good time at the party once I got away from Callie. I don't normally drink that much but somehow the mood was festive. I'd just closed rather a large deal with Random House for an author making a comeback after several years away from the business, so I guess I was in the mood to celebrate.'

'Congratulations.'

He acknowledged this with a distracted nod. 'Let's see . . . I spoke briefly with you; I spoke with the spy couple – you know who I mean – Felicity and Fred. Of course, they have a book they're trying to sell, something they were co-authoring, and I think I ended up promising them I would take a look or someone in my office would.'

'I thought it was just her.'

He shook his head. 'Both of them. They didn't seem to have an outline or a hook, just a wodge of random notes, and just the fact they were in the CIA isn't enough to sell a book.'

So Fred *was* CIA, after all.

'You can't cross the street here in DC without tripping over former FBI or CIA people thinking they've saved mankind,' he continued. 'But I've noticed in these situations it doesn't matter what I say; people with a book idea hear what they want to hear.'

'I'm familiar with the phenomenon,' I said. 'And I'm less sought after than you, I'm sure.'

'The trouble is, while I'm always up for a good spy novel – that's my favorite read when I have time to read for pleasure – they really are a dime a dozen and few spy novelists rise to the standard of John le Carré, may he rest in peace.'

'Amen,' I said. 'I'm not sure what it is you're asking me to do.'

It pretty much beggared belief that if Rem Larsson wanted to speak with my editor, he wouldn't just call my editor already. He didn't need me to run interference: She would certainly know who he was and be happy to talk to someone of his renown, for whatever reason. Julia Swanson was herself far from being an unknown in the publishing world. In fact, the wonder was that these two hadn't crossed paths before.

'Well, I was going to ask you to soften Julia up for an idea that I'm having,' he said.

'Soften her up,' I repeated.

'As I said, I don't know anything about novels, even mystery novels. I don't represent anyone writing that sort of thing.' Perhaps hearing how breezily condescending that sounded to a person who earned their living writing 'that sort of thing' he rushed to add, 'It's a genre that's saved the entire publishing industry, and much of it is of a very high quality. Even literary quality.'

I felt he should stop while he was drowning, but no.

'Don't get me wrong,' he said. 'It just doesn't happen to be a field in which I am knowledgeable.'

I raised my eyebrows, hoping that would convey eagerness for him to go on mixed with puzzlement over where we were headed with this.

'And you want me to talk to Julia about Callie Moore's memoirs, which you think may actually be fiction. Even though you have serious doubts about the authenticity of said memoirs without documentation, preferably photographic evidence.'

'Um. Yes.'

Curiouser and curiouser. I hazarded a guess. 'You're thinking whatever Callie's writing might be more palatable as fiction? More saleable?'

'Yes,' he agreed, almost as if I'd offered him a lifeline.

He seemed to be going to a lot of trouble over this. Since blackmail had been a very recent topic between us, I wondered if Callie hadn't been putting the screws to him. Over what, who could say. Through her lobbyist husband, she might know where the bodies were buried in DC. She also probably knew what all the live bodies were getting up to. Was it something like that? A little local scandal that for whatever reason Rem Larsson wanted kept quiet? So much so that he would engage in this rather heavy-handed and implausible bid to get me on board by helping him connect with Julia?

He so obviously could call Julia himself and say he had this great new hot property he wanted to send her. But the fact was he had only the promise of something that might be shocking but the project was tied to an untried writer of doubtful reliability. My role was to convince Julia to take the thing, and Callie, on board.

I suddenly felt very sorry for him. Whatever was going on he was clearly not in a good place with this. He had to get back to Callie, sooner rather than later, with at least the hope of a deal. His only way out was if she failed to live up to the terms of that deal, as she might well do – miss the deadline, fail to pass the smell test with the publishers' lawyers. He just didn't want to be the one to tell her that.

I said: 'If you'd really like to be let off the hook for this with Callie, I could try to bung her off on to Julia.'

He smiled, and a weak, sickly smile it was.

'She's decided she wants you to co-write the book. Not just ghostwrite it.'

'Oh.'

'She wants both of your names to appear on the cover. Hers in slightly bigger font, of course.'

'Naturally,' I said.

'I must admit she's thought it through. She knows her own name alone won't carry any weight. Not to mention, she suspects in her more honest moments she's not up to writing an eighty-thousand-word book. In an ideal world, she wants me to represent her, and your agent to represent you, and she wants your editor to edit the book.'

'What happened to the editor at Penguin who was mad for all things royal?'

He hung his head slightly, staring at the gleam of his mahogany desk.

I took a wild guess. 'You already tried. And the editor said no.'

'Yes.'

I was stunned at the level of confidence he was placing in me.

'The editor at Penguin seemed to know Callie by reputation. He said there wasn't enough supporting evidence, even for a *roman à clef*. It's a catch-22. I don't honestly know what to do.' He looked up at me, distraught. The sight of this urbane man before me, a man sought-after and admired and now reduced to asking me for favors, moved me to pity. But I didn't honestly think I could help.

'I have no special pull with Julia,' I said. 'I could organize a meeting but then I would have to step back.'

'Please, it's all I ask,' he said. 'Well, there is one more thing.'

Our eyes locked, meeting in perfect understanding across the vast expanse of his desk. I knew what was coming.

'I need those documents from Callie or I'm going to get nowhere with anyone,' he said. 'Not with Julia or anyone. And you have a certain reputation for . . . well, for getting things done.'

Well, that was nicely put. It feels odd to hear one's reputation mentioned in conversation or see it in writing. We all have precious little idea of how we are perceived by the rest of the world. I felt I could live with being known as someone who got things done.

Even though what he may have meant was, someone known to bend the rules to get things done. Whatever. I was intrigued. I pictured in my mind a calendar, the pages flipping in the breeze as in some old movie to suggest the passage of time. The pages blew right past my deadline. Oh, well.

'What if there are no documents? What if this is all, you know, a Callie fantasy?'

'I need to know that, too. She thinks withholding the documents, if they exist, is a negotiating tactic that will drive up the price. I have to make her understand that without documents there is no deal.'

'Right.'

'But for now I have to stall her. Make her think something is happening, or . . .'

'Or?'

'Or my career . . . I don't know what she's capable of. I think she's trying to make Doc Burke's death part of her publicity scheme instead of the tragedy it is. Suddenly she wants people to believe they were "incredibly close," which of course is complete nonsense. Anyone that cold-hearted is capable of anything.'

Right about then I was thinking Larsson's misdeed was likely financial, if Callie was indeed holding something over him. Also that Callie might not be above making up a lie to damage someone.

No one gave a monkey's about an affair in Washington if the affair didn't involve at least one person in high office. A literary agent, even one as high-powered as Larsson? He could do pretty much what he wanted, so long as he didn't frighten the horses, as the saying goes. That sort of scandal would be one of those three-day wonders, if it even made the paper at all. It wouldn't be enough to wreck his career.

A financial misdeed was something else, though. Accusations of skimming, of cooking the books? I didn't believe that of him but I had seen what lies like that could do in this town.

Every nerve in my body was shouting, 'Mind your own business, this is his problem, stay out of it, you can't help anyway!'

I looked at him, his aristocratic face crumpled in despair. He had removed the glasses to wipe his eyes, and he looked at me with such naked fear my will disintegrated.

Not only did I find it difficult to say no, at the back of my mind was the thought it might not hurt to have a major agent beholden to me.

Also, I was curious.

And you know what they say about curiosity.

I found myself saying, ‘I’ll see what I can do.’

NINE

Meanwhile, in the Capitol Hill area, several conversations were taking place. I was not present at these events but I'll do my best to reconstruct what happened so you can get to know the key players in the mystery surrounding Doc Burke's untimely death.

The setting: the offices of Tommy Moore, a man for hire to the highest bidder. The phones are ringing non-stop. The business of lobbying is booming.

No one quite knows how lobbyists had come to claim so much territory in Washington DC. It was as if they had been there from the beginning of time. Lobbyists, simply put, made their money helping influencers influence. Businesses, unions, public interest groups, and individuals paid them to make sure Congress was won over to their particular hobby horse, whatever it might be. Selling influence is supposed to be a crime, and it is under normal circumstances, but lobbyists operate quite legally, their ability to change the world compromised only by the occasional conflict of interest.

Lobbying is legal; bribery is not. Good luck drawing a line between the two things.

Tommy Moore leaned back in his leather swivel-tilt chair and folded his hands over his stomach. At sixty his abs may have been less six-pack than one-pack, his midriff starting to bulge, but it wasn't from lack of trying to keep gravity at bay. Tommy was often first to arrive at the nearby gym to meet with his personal trainer. Unfortunately, Lucas liked to talk as much as he liked to train clients but at least Tommy got a bit of exercise in before the workday started.

Now he looked across the desk at his administrative assistant Barbara Keller. Other people in the office called her Barbie as did Callie in a rather derogatory way, but he preferred to keep things on a professional level.

'Thank you, Barbara, for handling that grape thing. It's not the kind of small concern we can take on right now.'

'The vineyard.' She nodded. Over the years they'd developed a sort of shorthand for the various projects passing through the office. 'Maybe in a few years but when you think of Virginia right now you still don't think "famous vineyards," do you?'

'They're getting there. With global warming they'll be there before we know it. Virginia and the UK both will be as famous as the South of France for wines.'

'Right,' she said, crossing her legs. Barbara never wore pantsuits. She was rather too obviously hoping he would notice her legs. He did. With her small waist and wide hips she cut a fine figure, always perfectly coiffed, flawlessly turned out. Kind of scary-perfect in everything she did.

But Callie would kill him. Besides, she had to be fifty, and he had other fish to fry. Wealthy, younger fish.

From his school days, he had known he wanted to be a power broker but had no interest in running for office. He was much too sensible to invite that kind of scrutiny. What he enjoyed was pulling the levers behind the scenes and watching laws get passed, laws he knew would not exist without him. That at times these laws were to the benefit of 'the people' was beside the point. If lives were saved or pensioners were not forced to beg on the streets for their medications, all to the good. But knowing he was in charge was what mattered, in this imperial city arguably at the center of the known universe.

It was heady power to have and for that he knew exactly the kind of people he wanted to surround himself with. *With whom* he wanted to surround himself – he often corrected his own grammar. He still struggled to hide an old boy drawl, although people often found it attractive.

He also tended to misuse the English language, which made people think he was stupid. That was only useful when he wanted it to be useful.

For her part Barbara, as she watched him go on about global warming and which side it would be safest to side with, the deniers or the alarmists, and shouldn't Greta Thunberg be in school, anyway? was thinking: He's so *handsome*. What must he have looked like at twenty or thirty? And they had so much in common. Both had raised themselves out of hardscrabble Oklahoma childhoods by pure grit and determination. She and her older sister had grown up in a double-wide trailer and had taught themselves to read, a fact they hid from nearly everyone, out of shame and embarrassment. If it hadn't been for her sister's help she'd have been illiterate. Meanwhile, her parents pretended to be homeschooling them, a good cover for what was basically free child labor. Her first job out of school had been as far away from them as she could get, as secretary to the boss of a Virginia winery. But the bright lights had called. Not New York – too fast, too scary – but DC. Just right and full of single men. But once she met Tommy Moore, married or not, there was no other man.

One night working late she confided some of her past to him. And he confessed he came from the same background, complete with drunken father and Bible Belt mom and more kids than the neighbors could count. From that moment on her slight infatuation with her boss became a fixation. She scoured the news sources daily for word of him or his wife, googling him obsessively, not even pretending to tell herself it was part of her job. She regarded his wife as a nincompoop, but Callie also took advantage by getting her to run a lot of her personal errands. She was afraid to complain, much less to declare her love to Tommy, knowing it would be a huge mistake. For whatever reason, Callie Moore had a hold on this man. Barbara went through every day teetering on the edge of making a complete fool of herself, returning each night to an immaculate one-bedroom apartment in Cleveland Park and working on the scrapbook she was keeping of Tommy's many behind-the-scenes political triumphs.

Barbara knew instinctively that although Tommy Moore had everything in common with her, that they were in fact made for each other, what he wanted to escape most of all was anyone from a similar trashy background to his. Anyone who even reminded him of it.

She would have been better off never telling him about her upbringing; she knew that now. If she'd said her family had summered on Martha's Vineyard and her parents had met at Harvard, she would have been in with a chance, and he might never have known the difference. Well, she'd have to finesse the Harvard bit, for if he remembered her employment application, he may have wondered why she had only a high school diploma and a certificate from the Secretarial School of Tulsa (Motto: 'UPPERCASE YOUR DREAMS'). Just like Tommy she had unhoneyed her drawl and neutralized her wardrobe so no one would suspect who she really was.

'The drug company,' she said. 'How did you want to handle that?'

'Now, that is much more worth our time, don't you think? If their lab results are anything close to accurate, we need to do everything we can to get that drug to the public.'

Thrilling to his use of the word 'we,' she said, 'Absolutely. If we can send billionaires into space we should be able to treat male-pattern hair loss.'

Running his fingers through his graying but still-abundant hair, Tommy said, 'So they settled out of court, right?'

'Right. Undisclosed amount. These labs can't be expected to test for everything. Now they think they've found a treatment for the kidney cancer, as well.'

'But who are we kidding? It's saving follicles that will be our main selling point. You can get by with one kidney. We really must push on the hair thing. Lead with that.'

'With you, Tommy,' she said. 'All the way.'

Forever.

Only a few blocks away in the Longworth House Office Building, located conveniently near the Capitol South Metro, sat Carnegie 'Carn' Hilton.

Not that Carn would ever be caught dead taking the Metro. In fact, there was still some rather hard feeling on his part that having worked so hard to get elected so many times, and having done so much for the little people, he still wasn't assigned a private car and driver with a Secret Service escort.

The fact that the Secret Service only guarded the highest echelons of government did not make a dent in his thinking. As far as Carn was concerned, he was an echelon unto himself.

But after announcing his plans to run for office again, he had been forced to see the writing on the wall. Simply put, he hadn't a snowball's chance of being re-elected after that unfortunate episode with the female lobbyist in a hotel room of the Willard

Intercontinental. No one believed his claim of mistaken identity, since he was filmed wearing his Longworth House access badge, which bloggers had helpfully magnified to a clear view, leaving no doubt. Carn's name, Carn's badge number. Carn in a place he did not belong. Carn alone in a hotel room – a top floor suite, no less, paid for by taxpayers. Carn sharing drinks and more with a person he should not have been with.

He still had no idea who had filmed the encounter, or why.

He had quickly announced his retirement at the urging of his staffers and various hangers-on. His wife stood by him, as always, for the children's sake, but even Carn could see this was for Mary the absolute last straw. He had married her in part because she was so ambitious herself, ambitious enough to look the other way. But he suspected they were in new territory now. The children would soon be grown and gone.

Carn, to give credit where it's due, had not got to where he'd got without surrounding himself with the best and the smartest people and mostly being wise enough to listen to what they had to say. He had his speechwriter compile a moving speech announcing he would not seek re-election and would in fact be retiring for health reasons. It was thought best to keep the health reasons vague, but treatment for a rare disease he'd picked up while visiting orphanages in the tropics might have to be invoked should there be questions.

The chances were, however, there would not be any questions, his constituents being delighted by this time to see him go and replaced by someone younger and, with any luck, more honest.

Like Tommy Moore, Carn sat across a large desk from his own administrative assistant, having her jot down the various items that needed to be tidied up before he could decently leave without giving either the appearance of haste or a sudden bout of good health. Matters which really should have been seen to months before could not be left behind for just anyone to find and attempt to deal with or worse, complain about to the media. He was very tempted to throw all the folders in the rubbish, but some snoopy reporter might find out and start asking questions about that whole supply chain thing he'd promised to look into.

Flipping through the stacks of files and folders on his desk, most of which had sat untouched throughout his incumbency, he wondered: Who would be a public servant? He could have made a lot more money in the private sector but too late to think about that now. The best he could hope for would be a book about his time in office and his hard-won wisdom. He might have to address the little fiasco in the hotel room but that could be finessed with the right ghostwriter. He wondered idly if that Augusta Hawke woman from the party might be interested.

Maybe he'd take a swing at fiction, perhaps a detective story or a spy thriller. Why not? Everyone was doing it. Avoid the whole . . . His mind reared up against the word 'scandal.' Avoid the whole *question* about the video. Had no one heard of deep-fakes, as he thought they were called? He'd have to get someone on that.

Someone who was still working for him, that is. So many of them were slipping away. Traitors and ingrates, all of them.

What the public didn't understand was that the temptations were many. So many. And not just the interns. The administrative assistant sitting across from him – he thought her name was Marge, Marjorie, something like that – crossed her legs, looking across at him expectantly. Unfortunately, she was wearing a pantsuit. He'd never even seen the legs on this one. He'd meant to talk to her about sprucing up her image, loosening up a bit, letting her hair down, smiling more, but what did it matter now?

For her part, Margaret was feeling like the janitor assigned to clean up behind the elephants after the circus has left town, but although she'd put out numerous job feelers (and would be gone like a shot at the first opening) she hadn't yet been able to find another position on the Hill. It was rather assumed working for Carn meant you were as sleazy as he was. That wasn't necessarily a drawback in many of the public sector jobs, as they assumed you were connected and could pull strings, but she'd come to Washington DC, top of her class, to make a difference in the world. A *positive* difference.

If Carn had been set up as he claimed (and he almost certainly had been set up by the opposing party) she wished she'd known what was going down. She would have ordered champagne sent up to the room.

The sooner she and the voters got rid of this guy, the sooner she'd be able to ditch the navy-blue pantsuits and flats. She only wore them at work (and a fake engagement ring and a little gold cross necklace) as no-trespassing signs, and only around Carn Hilton. (In hindsight, the engagement ring may have been a mistake, because every Monday he'd ask, a lascivious twinkle in his eye, what she'd done over the weekend. The #MeToo movement didn't begin to address the depths of this kind of thing.)

Margaret wondered if he'd never noticed that his entire female staff dressed pretty much in the same vaguely Amish way to try to dampen Carn's interest.

Another term with him and they'd all have been wearing prayer bonnets.

At a restaurant a few blocks from the Capitol building, at an outdoor table with a patio heater burning off the chill of the day, sat the Overstones, Felicity and Fred. Spy vs Spy.

First making sure the waiter was out of earshot, she said, 'You said you'd heard from our friend,' she said.

'In Mandrekka. Yes,' Fred said.

'Jesus Christ.' She swiveled her head to see if anyone could overhear. 'Would you keep your voice down?'

She peered inside the fake flower arrangement on the table to see if a microphone was hidden among the leaves. She rifled through the packets of sugar in the white holder, then ducked under the table to see if a mic might have been taped there. The Amendment wasn't a place known as a spy hangout, that was The Exchange, but you never knew. Times change.

She looked up at the umbrella heater. It wouldn't be there, she decided, or it would melt.

There was no one else on the patio but that meant they had to talk fast before anyone else got seated or the waiter returned to check on them. Sometimes you longed for good service and sometimes you did not.

Fred was a complete idiot when it came to this undercover kind of thing. He was lovable and he was *her* idiot but he was well out of his depth.

She couldn't go to her boss just yet. Maybe not ever. She was probably breaking a few rules by having kept it to herself this long. But she worked surrounded by glory hounds, male and female, and she didn't want to share the limelight. This was *her* baby.

'Sorry,' said Fred. 'I'm in IT. I'm not as trained for covert ops as you are.'

Slowly, deliberately, she set down her water glass on the table. 'Why don't you go tell the maître d' where we work? In case there's a ten percent discount or a Groupon coupon or something? Maybe see if there's anyone in the restaurant who would be interested, someone needing some tips they can't get at the spy museum.'

'I said I was sorry.'

'For God's sake, Fred, we can't talk at home. That's why we're here. I don't trust them not to have – you know.'

'Bugged the place?'

Arggghhhhh. If she hadn't had a full plate of food in front of her, she'd have dropped her forehead on to the table. This was a mistake. They should have met in the park, the traditional spy meeting place. You saw it in all the movies because it was true. No one worth his or her salt in the spy game met in restaurants.

But she had been hungry. And those park benches could be freezing cold, as she well knew from experience.

'Let's eat our lunch and then we'll talk,' she said. 'Somewhere else.'

Somewhere where they could freeze their behinds off, she might have added, but it was the only choice. Giving Fred a job above his pay grade had been a mistake.

Once they finished their meal, they asked the waiter for go-cups so they could take their coffee to the park bench and drink it there. It was, as she had predicted, unmercifully cold. They should warn you when you join the service, she thought, to always carry a pillow to sit on.

'OK,' she said. 'What have you heard from our counterparts?'

'In Mandrekka?'

'No, in Disneyworld. Of course, Mandrekka.'

'We know that one of her passports has been activated and she's headed for the US. There's a stopover in DC before she heads to California. It all looks like a normal holiday.'

'Anything for us to do?' Felicity asked.

‘Just keep an eye out, tail her while she’s in DC.’

‘Easy.’

‘And keep an eye on Callie Moore,’ said Fred. ‘Find out if we can what her interest is in Mandrekka. If we can’t control her, we may have to shut her down.’

‘You don’t mean . . .’

‘Nah. Just find out what she knows and if she’s dumb enough to try to publish it. She’s telling everyone who will listen she’s writing her memoirs. And if that’s true, depending on what’s in them, she may be an international incident waiting to happen.’

‘She’s set her mind on Rem Larsson to represent her.’

‘That’s perfect. We can easily apply pressure to his weak spots.'

‘He’ll be easy to shut down, too, if we have to.’

TEN

Getting home took longer than usual. A fender bender on the parkway held me up and it took the police half an hour to clear a two-way path on the now one-lane road.

I never saw a policeman any more without thinking of Detective Narduzzi but if he was in uniform directing traffic, it was probably my fault. He'd let me run with my instincts and even though I'd brought him results, you never knew how those in charge were going to react, with gratitude or punishment. Writing up his report for 'The Case of the Missing Neighbors' must have been a literary challenge, to say the least. I could have helped with that if only he'd asked.

I was also driving slowly because I was distracted, turning over in my mind how I could get hold of the documents from Callie Moore. If there were documents. My natural reluctance to deal with Callie any further had to be overcome in the greater cause of the promise I had just made to Rem Larsson. While 'I'll see what I can do' was an open-ended promise, I didn't feel in good conscience I could go back to the man without having given it my best shot.

I didn't tell him the chances were not good I could get results of either a negative or positive kind. I think he knew that already.

I wondered if Callie couldn't be forced to set aside her plans for an ambassadorship, which would probably be for the best. For the good of the country if not the entire globe, not to mention the good of a galaxy yet to be discovered. Surely someone would see through her schemes. Perhaps if I could establish that her evidence was lame to non-existent, I could scuttle this whole book nonsense and convince her if she wanted to be an ambassador, she'd have to find another way. Preferably an honest one.

I was confident finding *some* way would not be a big problem for her. Not for nothing was she married to the well-connected Tommy Moore.

The thought she might use the tragedy of the doctor's passing in her schemes for world domination was annoying, to say the least. I knew from a small news item in the *Post* the coroner had delivered a verdict of death by natural causes, and no doubt investigators had moved on to other cases. Real cases with real victims of foul play, however famous or unknown to any but their families. Three months in investigator time would mean a hundred other crimes had cropped up to grab their attention. Doc Burke would live on in memory for his good works but not as a topic for *Investigation ID*.

Callie, I reflected, as I inched my way toward Ye Olde Historical District of Olde Towne, must have been deeply torn between a desire for a scandal that would put her name in the lights and a desire to have the whole thing go away in case it affected her ambassadorship. The verdict of death by natural causes had served her well, had she but the sense to realize it, since she could hardly be blamed for the loss of one of the world's great humanitarians. His death may even have garnered her some pity among the housewives of DC at having her party end in such a spectacular way. I had to factor this sort of deranged thinking in to however I approached her. I was pondering this dilemma as a Volkswagen in front of me suddenly hit the brakes for no good reason and I narrowly avoided being rear-ended.

I arrived home safely, parking the Jeep in the garage beneath my townhouse and letting myself in to the sound of rapturous barks from Roscoe. I threw my purse on the foyer table and gathered his leash to take him to the nearby dog park.

The dog park is one of the few places where I get to interact with my neighbors, although I recognize most of them by their dogs and know very few of the dog owners by name. There's a large grassy area where the city allows us to let our dogs off their leads so long as the animals are trained to heel on command. And while they gambol about, we owners sometimes chat.

There are certain unwritten rules to this chat. One of them is 'no talk of work' – a good rule – and another seems to be that no last names will be exchanged or recalled, thereby taking the 'social' out of 'socializing.' The talk itself is on the superficial level of the weather (unseasonable, always), veterinarian recommendations, and the quirks of the various breeds. Bet you did not know boxers have an affinity for burying Keds in gardens. Me neither.

I had left my phone back at the house and had not checked messages since leaving Larsson's offices. It wasn't until I led Roscoe home and got him settled with a snack and some fresh water that I looked to see what had happened during my absence from the World Wide Web.

I only checked Facebook once a week as a matter of principle, the principle being that they were making a fortune off my publisher and they didn't need my data, as well. But I was a bit of a fanatic about checking my email every day. I wasn't sure what I was hoping would happen there, but I was addicted to it and to my texting app.

There was one email from my agent and another from my editor. I could guess the content – 'How far along are you in the book? No rush, just wondering. Talk soon!' – so the one message from a person I didn't recognize caught my attention. Nell Campbell was writing via the 'Contact me' form on my website which had a standard subject line: 'A Message from the Augusta Hawke Website.' I clicked the email open and was confronted with a rather cryptic message – a message unexpected and mysterious.

Nell Campbell was writing to say she was the niece of Dr Burke – the daughter of his sister, who was deceased. She had heard through various online news outlets that I had attended the party where her uncle had been taken ill.

I was not thrilled by that – how had it come to pass that my name had been released to the media? It was not reported locally or in the *Post*, of that I was sure. Was I part of Callie's evil PR plot to get herself posted to Mandrekka?

Nell went on to say:

> My uncle left behind a will in which he left me this handwritten manuscript. He said it was important, that he'd worked on it for years, and he wanted it to be published. He had an executor named Drake who handled everything and Mr Drake got in touch with me about this bequest. Everything else would probably go to charity. If you knew my uncle, you would know how typical that was of him. If there is a heaven, I know he is there with my mother and all the children he helped will join them there, not yet but

very soon, because despite all his work children don't live long in those awful places.

Anyway, the manuscript was mailed to me here in the UK where I am in school, supposed to be working on my A levels [she inserted a smiley face here; a girl after my own heart] and I can't really make heads or tails of it. But I have a layover in Washington on my way to San Francisco to visit old friends of my mother's from when she was at Berkeley and I'm writing to ask if you would take a look if I leave the manuscript with you.

I spoke with a Detective Steve Narduzzi of the Old Town Police Department – super nice guy – and he told me that you were one of the people who tried to save my uncle when he took ill. I looked you up online while I was on the phone with him and I saw that you were a crime writer and I knew that this was meant to be. My uncle was super insistent that this work was important and that it needed to reach the right people *if anything should happen to him*. By that I guess he meant the right people in publishing and to be honest I don't know any people in publishing except you, Ms Hawke.

And then something did happen to him.

I feel a special connection to you because you were there when he passed. Also, there is something super odd that happened later and I can't put it into an email. I need to talk to you in person. It is a real-life mystery so I know you are the person I should trust with this. My uncle was very special.

Thank you very much in advance,
Nell Campbell

P.S. I told Detective Narduzzi about this manuscript of my uncle's and he said it would be right up your alley.

Well, *super*. I must be sure to thank you for that next time I see you, Detective Narduzzi. Way to clear your own desk by shoving stuff on to mine. Especially since, technically, the 'case' – if it can even be called that – is probably not in your jurisdiction. Nell may have called him mistakenly, thinking if Doc Burke lived in Old Town, the case would belong to Old Town PD.

I read this missive several times, scrolling back and forth and up and down, not wanting to answer right away. There seemed to be a lot of room for this to go wrong. For it to be a scam, first of all. But try as I might, I couldn't see how it would enrich anyone to contact me with such a story.

Since she mentioned 'A levels' I put her age at anything between sixteen and eighteen, and because of that I did not want to encourage or mislead her in any way. Why wasn't she in school anyway, rather than jetting about?

I supposed if this Nell person showed up demanding money for this precious manuscript all I would have to do is say no. She was much more likely to ask me to contact my agent about it.

Meanwhile, I hadn't had a minute to deal with Rem Larsson's fond hope that I could bail him out of his situation with Callie.

Let alone work on my book.

My first impulse, of course, was to ignore the email, quickly followed by the impulse to say, 'Sure! Let's get together when you're in town' and hope something would derail her travel plans. But this was a girl who had just lost her uncle and had also lost her mother somewhere along the way.

I didn't have the heart to not at least hear her out.

Deadline? What deadline?

One late afternoon a week later Nell Campbell arrived at my front door, carrying a large tote and a gift bag of quite good chocolate chip cookies from the Temptation Station down the street.

I welcomed her in and pointed her the way upstairs to the kitchen, offering coffee which she accepted.

While I fiddled about with the filters and settings on the coffee maker and she settled herself at my kitchen table, I took the opportunity to size her up. She was, I noticed, careful to place her tote bag nearby, within reach. She looked closer to sixteen than eighteen, with a charming little smile, and she was pretty in the way all young girls are pretty if they but knew it. Minimal make-up on even features, shiny brown hair knotted at the neck. She was wearing ripped jeans that made her appear as if she had been attacked on the way to my house by rabid dogs, a fashion trend which I heartily wish would go away. She also wore a lumberjack's red plaid shirt over a plain white T-shirt – a very American touch – and a denim jacket over it all against the chill of the day. Wrapped around her neck several times was a tasseled red woolen scarf, which she began to unwind against the heat of the house. I offered to turn down the heat and she shook her head.

'I'm fine. Really, it's lovely. At school they think it builds character if we all freeze to death half the time.'

From over my shoulder I asked, 'This is boarding school, right?'

'Right, in Scotland.' And she named a famous school for girls. It was somewhere in the Highlands, I thought. It was well known enough that I had heard of it and I was not really up on my Scottish schools.

She did not speak with a Scottish burr, however. She sounded a bit like Kate Middleton in the rare recordings I had heard of her, speaking in a soft, well-modulated, middle-class English voice.

Altogether this girl Nell could pass for any American teenager but for the accent and the little extra poise and polish of being British educated. How that showed itself, I can't really say, but she had an innate politeness and a sober demeanor around an older adult – me – which was impressive. I don't think I imagined her schooling was preparing her for a better and more literate future than what I saw going on in some American high schools.

I got out a small plate on which to arrange several of the cookies (which she called biscuits). I poured out the coffee and she helped me carry the mugs and napkins (serviettes) to the table.

We settled across from each other at the table of my small kitchen nook, overlooking the doings one floor below on Fendall Street, which at this time of day, ten a.m. on a weekday, consisted of mommies and nannies pushing and pulling their screaming children to the park. More often than not they had a dog or two attached to the stroller.

A recent trend was Mommy Yoga classes along the water, so a rolled-up yoga mat stuck out of many of the strollers.

'Nell,' I said. 'I always thought that was a pretty name. My grandmother on my mother's side was named Nell, although they called her Nellie.'

She smiled and asked if I minded if she took one of the biscuits.

'No, of course I wouldn't mind. Please help me not consume all of them right here and now. It was kind of you to bring them.'

'I read somewhere you have a sweet tooth.'

'That is not in the least bit true,' I said. 'My publicist plants these horrible stories about me to make me look bad. I'm more into broccoli, bean sprouts – anything fresh from the garden I've planted myself. Also, it's not true I'm dating Brad Pitt, although I'm sure he wishes it were.'

She took a mouthful of cookie and chewed and swallowed politely before asking, 'Who is Brad Pitt?'

'Who is Brad Pitt?' I repeated, dumbstruck. Was it possible someone her age would have no clue? I supposed it was. Online I was forever coming across the name of some actor I'd never heard of who was apparently everything a younger woman could hope to meet.

Furthermore, I realized I had no idea who would be the equivalent heartthrob of today's teenager. Douglas Booth, perhaps? He was only about fifteen years my junior and while I was hardly up on the latest *Variety*, he was the only one of that generation who had made enough impression on me I'd noted his name. I tended to view actors of any age in terms of whether they could be cast as characters in my books, should the happy day come to pass that my books make it to film. Nagging my agent on this topic had led to nothing to date.

Nell was looking horrified as if she'd made a terrible *gaffe* – not about Brad; Brad obviously did not move the needle on her kid-o-meter – but in believing the cookie lie spread by my evil publicist. I rushed to apologize, having forgotten for a moment how literal-minded the young can be. I had to look back to my own youth to remember, which really was a long stroll down memory lane.

'I was kidding. I love cookies – *love* them – and these look especially yummy. And I've never met Brad Pitt. Would you like milk for your coffee? Sorry, I forgot to ask. I don't use it.'

Her mouth full of another bite of cookie, she shook her head no.

I waited a moment before saying, 'Nell. Is it short for Eleanor?'

'Yes.' She stopped to dab crumbs from her mouth with the

napkin. 'Eleanor was my mother's name. She was the sister of Doc Burke. Half-sister, but they were close.'

'There had to be a large gap in age between them.'

'Un hum. Twenty years between her and David. Well, his name was David but no one called him that. He was Doc Burke to everyone. The memoirs or whatever they are, are his.'

'Right,' I said. *Memoirs. Great.* 'Let's get to those in a minute. Now, from your email you're hoping I can help you get these published?'

'Oh, I'm certain you can,' she said, casting all lame and wishy-washy thoughts of 'hope' aside. 'It's like a sacred trust, you understand. The last thing he ever asked of me. Come to think of it, he never asked *anything* of me. He just gave and gave. Money, presents. He always sent a birthday card. I mean, I always knew I could go to him for help if I needed it. And I feel awful now. I should've done more for him when I had the chance, you know?'

'I think we all feel that when someone has passed,' I said.

'But now I have the chance to make it up to him. I know he's up there somewhere. Do you believe in an afterlife? I think I do. I really do. And I believe he's watching me fulfil his request.'

There was no stopping her now. She put down the last of her cookie and, dusting off her fingers, pulled a cardboard box out of the tote – an old-fashioned cardboard box of the kind they used to use for a ream of typewriter paper. 'As I told you, he left this to me in his will. There was a note enclosed. It says – at least I think it says; his handwriting's rubbish – "Guard these pages with your life." Or maybe it says "knife," which sort of amounts to the same thing when you think about it, doesn't it?'

She handed the box of pages across the table. Reluctantly, I took it from her. The box weighed a good ten pounds. I felt that in taking physical possession, I was duty-bound to do something for her. Something for Doc Burke.

'Did he never tell you he was going to do this? Leave this to you?'

She shook her head. 'I think he thought he had years left.'

The box was secured by brown string tied in a bow like a Christmas package. I undid the bow and removed the lid of the box. Inside was a manuscript in the original meaning of the word, composed in the spidery hand known well to anyone who has ever had medicine prescribed to them by a physician. It had been written with an ink pen and here and there the words were splotched with blue-black ink where the pen had caught on a defect of the paper. He had paid someone to bind the pages together, the absolute worst thing a writer submitting a work for consideration can do apart from writing a twenty-page cover letter comparing their work to Moby Dick. My heart sank.

'He told me in the note he thought a major publishing house would be interested in it. He said I should first get an agent to handle the sale.'

A major publishing house. Sure.

'That was good advice. There are a lot of scammers out there, preying on hopeful or needy people. It's worse than the reverse-mortgage industry.'

I saw I'd lost her with 'reverse mortgage.'

'Never mind,' I said.

We both took little sips of our coffee, she no doubt to fortify herself for the next barrage of calls to my better nature, and me to fortify myself to resist her. She began describing her attempts to garner the attention of the publishing world.

'I've run into some trouble,' she said. 'I got the emails of agents from this online site. That part was easy enough.'

I nodded, carefully putting my mug down on the table. A set of four different white mugs had been a gift from my friend Misaki for my birthday. Written on mine was a quote from Oscar Wilde: 'If you want to tell people the truth, make them laugh, otherwise they'll kill you.' On the cup I'd given Nell was a Mark Twain quote: 'Never miss an opportunity to shut up.'

'Nothing happened for the longest time,' she said.

'It's a tough business.'

In short, she had discovered this assignment to be more difficult than she had ever imagined, and she had collected one hundred rejection emails from agents. She had promised herself that if she hit the magic one hundred number, she would enlist the help of a professional author.

'Some of the agents didn't even bother to reply within a month,' she said.

A month. 'Actually, Nell, that's not at all unusual. Sometimes they take up to a year to get back to you. If they get back at all.'

'I don't have a year,' she said.

She's all of maybe seventeen and she doesn't have a year. *Right.* I remember at that age being unable to believe I'd live to be thirty.

'Why not just self-publish?'

She must have been primed for this for it got an immediate response.

'No. No, I can't do that. Doc Burke has expressly forbidden it.'

'You spoke with him about this?'

She nodded, then said, 'Well, no, it was in the note that came with the manuscript.'

'How long before he – before he passed did you speak with him?'

'I think it was about a month.'

'I see.' A silence settled between us. I didn't want to say anything that might encourage confidences that might knock down my defenses. I could guess what was coming, and given her hesitation, she knew the next question was a big ask.

'I don't suppose you could just send it to your publisher?' she said.

I could just imagine the reaction of my publisher, a man who looked less like the swashbuckling literary trendsetter of the public's romantic imagination and more like Ebenezer Scrooge before his three miraculous holiday visitations. I personally found Ebenezer's overnight transformation into a man manic with bonhomie rather terrifying and preferred the stingy old curmudgeon, the loneliness of whose childhood I could appreciate.

Even though I saw it coming, I was dismayed by Nell's bald request. Not by the request itself but by the chance I might knuckle under and find myself promising to send the thing, if not to my publisher, to my editor or agent. That would only be to delay the inevitable rejection, I was certain.

At the same time, I felt a sort of obligation to the girl. After all, I had been present at the death of her uncle and remained unable to resolve in my own mind, to my own satisfaction, what had happened to him. To uncover the crime – if it was a crime – and put it right. This felt like a second chance somehow.

I did have one question of my own. 'You say you spoke with your uncle on the phone. How often did you usually speak?'

'Not often. He called me as often as he could. Every month, maybe every two months. It was hard for anyone to reach *him* because he was always off in some dark corner of the world where getting food was difficult, let alone mobile reception.'

'Did he have some kind of premonition? I mean did you get that feeling that he . . . you know. Felt something was going wrong in his life?'

'You know what? I *did*.' She scooted in closer to the table. 'I really did feel that something was up. But he never said anything about his heart. He wasn't one of those old people who go on and on about their ailments and their medicines and what their doctor said. But to have the manuscript sent to me only after he had passed – I don't get it. I mean why not just get his writings published himself while he was still alive? Why prepare to have them sent to me so far in advance? Because to be honest, I thought he'd live to be a hundred.'

'Maybe he thought he would, too, and that you would be quite grown by the time the whole subject came round. He was only sixty-five.' That was the age reported in the paper. I saw no reason to mention he looked haggard, older than that.

'Yeah.'

From her expression, sixty-five was an unfathomable age, an age to which the qualifier 'only' did not apply.

'How did he sound?' I asked. 'On the phone last time you spoke, I mean?'

She thought for a moment. 'Stressed. Distracted. That's the best way I can describe it. His voice was low as if he was afraid someone would overhear. In fact, I asked him where he was calling from and he said he was in a hotel lobby in Bangladesh – I think it was Bangladesh. He travelled a lot for his work, you know, but I think this time he was at a convention. Maybe it was Buffalo.'

She ended the sentence with an upward inflection, a habit of speech I had noticed was becoming universal among young English speakers.

There's such a world of difference between those two places, I thought.

Gazing at her open, heart-shaped face, I found myself agreeing (*damn it*) to see what I could do about her uncle's memoirs.

'But no promises,' I emphasized. I really was quite firm with her about not getting her hopes up, for I knew nothing was going to come of this but her own disappointment.

'I know you can do it!' replied Nell.

With a sigh, I put my hand on top of the manuscript as if I were swearing an oath. It was a symbolic surrender to the inevitable. Why did I always cave like this? It wasn't because I wanted to be liked. I didn't care about being liked – well, not much. Because I wanted to be useful? Or, slightly darker: because I wanted to feel important, inserting myself into lives and situations where I had no business being?

Flipping through the pages, I saw all of it was handwritten, page after page – about three hundred of them – of tiny illegible spidery print, dashing my hopes that at least some of it would be typewritten. It would be, I thought, like trying to read an original screed by some maiden aunt of the Bronte sisters, who themselves wrote in teeny-tiny script, adding insult to injury by cross-writing to save paper. They probably had to because their brother Branwell drank up all their profits.

But no wonder Nell couldn't interest an agent. Of course, she hadn't mailed the actual pages to anybody by post, not given the short submission timeframe she'd mentioned. Besides, no agent living would welcome a book written on actual paper; everything these days was done by email and email attachment. I surmised the rejections were based on a summary Nell had emailed *en masse*. The query letter is an art in and of itself.

Rifling the pages, I was just about to tell her the first task would be to hire someone to transcribe the document into something more legible when something on one page caught my eye. I flipped back until I found it again.

It was the word 'murder' and it made me catch my breath. If this were a movie, the camera would zoom in on the highlighted word and eerie violin music would start to play in the background.

Also, on the same page, a name that jumped out at me as if in bold type was Calypso.

Calypso? What were the chances? It would be easy enough to verify if was talking about Callie.

Still, as I valued my time and my eyesight, I decided to hand off the manuscript to a professional transcriber. I knew just the person: Edgar Montesquieu. He worked at the National Archives and in his spare time took on what he himself described as weird and impossible projects. This one certainly qualified.

'I have a friend who can turn this into typescript,' I said. 'We'll have to start there. It may turn out to be something so entirely personal and idiosyncratic that no established publisher will want it.'

She opened her mouth to object so I rushed on.

'On the other hand, it may be a real find. The joy of the written word is that you just never know. Certainly the doctor led an interesting life. All I can promise you now is that I'll give it the best chance possible at a fair read by someone in a position to get it published. *If* it's something that may appeal to a larger audience.'

'Thank you,' she said. This was accompanied by a small, trembly smile. I only then realized she'd been expecting another flat-out rejection. 'That's just super of you. I do know you're busy and I do so much appreciate this.'

'You're welcome. But, as it is, no one is going to make the attempt to figure this out. And without a transcriber we will never know what these pages contain.'

'What does he charge? Doc Burke left me some money along with the manuscript. Ten thousand dollars.' She did a quick calculation in her head. 'That's about nine thousand pounds,' she added helpfully.

'Don't worry about money,' I said, brushing cookie crumbs off my blouse. 'Edgar owes me a favor.'

'Can he be . . . I mean is he trustworthy?'

'Absolutely,' I said. 'With Edgar, "What happens in Vegas stays in Vegas."'

'Hmm?'

Clearly she didn't get the cultural reference to the Las Vegas tourist slogan. I wondered what the British equivalent might be. Some place with gambling casinos. 'What Happens in Sheffield stays in Sheffield' didn't have quite the same ring.

'Tell you what. I have a retreat coming up in the spring – a writers' retreat in the mountains west of here – and I was planning on using the time for wrapping up my book. Giving it one more metaphorical pass through the typewriter, you know. I'll ask Edgar if he can get the pages transcribed and emailed to me by then. After that you and I can talk again.'

'The spring?' A lifetime away in teen years.

'That's probably going to be the best I can do,' I said. 'I know it looks like writers don't do much of anything with their time, but we answer to a lot of people and we always have a deadline for answering to them.'

'OK,' she said. 'Sounds good. Thank you so much. And thank Edgar for me.'

'Now I have a question for you,' I said. 'A favor to ask. Would you forward me a copy of the email you've been sending out to agents? I am assuming you sent them a summary of what the manuscript contains. At least, something of what the doctor told you it contains. That will give me a start in knowing what we're talking about.'

She dug out her phone and finding what she wanted, forwarded a copy of the message to me.

'Great,' I said. 'I'll read it later.'

I was struck by a thought.

'By any chance did you send your query to Rem Larsson?'

'I think I must've done. Is he in New York? I sent it to all the New York agents that didn't seem to be working out of their parents' dining rooms.'

'He's based in Washington, DC.'

'I sent it to a handful of those too. Yeah, I'm pretty sure I sent it to him. Why do you ask?'

'No particular reason.' If she had contacted Rem Larsson, the email would've been intercepted by one of his assistants who, unbeknownst to most aspiring writers, control the Game of Thrones that is publishing today. A way around these young dragons, I thought, might be to litter the email with references to hot young trendsetters in the book world. Whoever they were. Personally, twenty years into the business, I hadn't a clue who the new Dave Eggers might be.

'There's something else,' she said.

Isn't there always.

'Yes, Nell?' I smiled pleasantly. At least I hoped I looked pleasant. 'Something you forgot to mention?'

'Not exactly. I sort of wanted to find out who you are. What kind of person you are. Get a sense for *you*, you know. Before I told you this. Because it's really strange and I don't know what to do about it.'

'Go on. I'm listening. More coffee?'

I was not only listening, I was regretting saying 'yes' before I had all the facts, but I told myself I could change my mind, I could renege on my promise, depending on what she said next.

'It's just that . . . he's missing.'

'Who is missing?'

'The doctor.'

'I don't follow.'

'His body is missing.'

'Doc Burke? Your uncle?'

'Yes.'

'In what way is he missing?'

She honest-to-God looked over each shoulder in case someone could overhear what she said next.

'His body was released for burial. To his wife. That's what I was told when I called the place mentioned in the obituary.'

'I didn't know he had a wife.'

'I know. Most people don't know about it. They didn't live together.'

'They were still married?'

'Yeah. As far as I know they were, but again, they didn't live together. They were separated.'

This was news to me but not shocking news. A man his age, a man who travelled constantly, a man with a marriage in his distant past – nothing surprising there.

'But you say she came to collect his remains?' I asked. A picture was forming – had already formed – of a man with very few close ties, so it made sense that the person contacted by the authorities would be his wife, at least his wife on paper. No one would necessarily know they were separated.

'Yes.'

'What is her name?'

'Fatima. Fatima Alvarez Burke – I guess it's Burke; I don't really know if she took his name when they married. I was a child when I met her.'

'What did they tell you? I assume you are saying you called the funeral home.'

'Yes,' she said. 'Martin's Funeral Home. They told me the body had been released to his wife. Actually, what they said was the remains, the cremated remains. *Ugh*. The director of the funeral home – that's who I spoke to – was a bit snippy about it. I tried not to ask a lot of questions but by the third question he was – how do you say it here? Giving me the bum's rush. He didn't much like being called out on his way of doing business. Anyway, I thought that was odd. The cremation, I mean.'

'Why? Did Doc Burke have particular religious leanings that would forbid it?' I knew even the Roman Catholics, for a long time holdouts in that regard, had finally caved to the inevitable. The world was simply running out of space for full burials.

'Not religious beliefs,' she said. 'But he had tremendous belief in science. That we could all be, you know, resurrected, if there was enough of us left to grow our cells in a dish. Something like that.'

'We could be replicated, you mean. Like Dolly the sheep.'

'Yeah.'

I had read something about this new wonder of science. It was the twenty-first-century version of eternal life.

'So, did he leave a directive in his will to that effect? Stating his preference for burial?'

'Yes. After I got the heave-ho from the funeral director at Martin's I called the executor and asked specifically.'

'What did he say? The executor? About the wife's having claimed the ashes?'

'He was as dumbfounded as I was. He seemed to accept, however, that Doc Burke's wife had every right to claim him, even though they were separated. Every legal right. I didn't agree but he told me it was not going to be a winner in court if that's what I was thinking.'

'Were you?'

'I wasn't thinking anything really. I was just so surprised. So *shocked*. I did realize it was too late and what would be the point in legal action? I just assumed a relative would . . . you know. That a blood relative would be responsible for taking care of him. Someone from his immediate family, not a wife he may have hated, for all I know.'

'What about the funeral home? Martin's? I mean did the executor, this Mr Drake, think there was something fishy about what had gone on?'

'He looked into it and relayed to me that the wife, Fatima, had shown up with a marriage certificate. She mentioned that her husband had a weak heart and had been under a doctor's care. He routinely took one of those cholesterol reducing drugs.'

'Was this true? About the drugs?'

'I don't know.'

But – how did his wife not know or ask about the will? I wondered.

'They're a reputable old family firm, the undertakers – in business for fifty years,' Nell went on. 'I only know that from their website, but still.'

But still, I thought. During the pandemic more than one scandal had swirled around funeral homes, which had found themselves suddenly overwhelmed. A lot of record-keeping had probably got short shrift, even among reputable firms, so they could try to cope with the unprecedented demand for their services. Perhaps even now, the new normal was less rigorous than the old had been.

'Anyway, Mr Drake told me that a woman had appeared with a marriage license and had made all the arrangements. For the cremation, I mean. Paid for it upfront and all. That was in the funeral home records.'

'Had Fatima been in touch with the executor? With Drake?'

'No. Do you find that odd? I find that odd.'

'I suppose she didn't know about the will or the executor or any of it. It all depends on how long she and Doc Burke were separated.' I was struck by a sobering thought. 'Was there no memorial service?'

Nell shook her head sadly. 'No. Doc Burke's wife, this Fatima, told the man at Martin's there was to be no public ceremony. That's the part that really bothers me.' A flush of high color came to her rose-of-England cheeks. I was afraid she might start to cry. I nudged the plate of cookies closer to her.

'Like she was organizing a dinner party and deciding who

could attend,' I said, in perfect sympathy. 'In this case, only her, I guess. I am familiar with the type.'

What I didn't add – why stir the pot of anger that was clearly ready to boil over in Nell's heart – was that there being no public ceremony to mark the doctor's passing was no less than sinister, to my mind. I couldn't even say why that word came to mind immediately, but it did. *Sinister*. I mean, who does that? What 'loving' wife cuts a man off from those who care about him? Especially in the case of a man who had been so widely and universally loved.

Even if she'd hated him at the end for some reason of her own, and God knows love can curdle into hate, it took tremendous nerve to treat him with such disrespect.

What kind of woman, knowing there's a niece and perhaps other family members left to mourn him but living miles away, doesn't get in touch to say he's going to be cremated on such and such a date? Maybe have one of those online notice boards where people can comment?

Especially with a person as young as Nell, it seemed remarkably, unspeakably cruel to have almost literally 'dusted' Doc Burke from her hands and from everyone's life.

And in my experience when people do something inexplicably cruel in the aftermath of a death there are two reasons. One reason is that they are by nature cruel and operate whenever possible on a spite platform.

Another is that there is money involved. Count on it.

My time in the Desperados, the grief support group I had joined after Marcus's death, had taught me that much.

'Did he have any other family?' I asked Nell.

She shook her head. 'He never had children, and everyone else had already passed on. His parents were long gone, of course.'

'And Eleanor.'

'Yes.'

'No other siblings?'

'No.'

I wanted to ask what her mother had passed away from, as the woman couldn't have been that old, but as the information wasn't offered I wasn't going to pry. This is what makes me in so many ways a terrible detective.

Martin's Funeral Home was not that far from here. I wondered if I should look into things, in person.

Right. Just push that deadline back some more.

'Where does his wife live? This Fatima Alvarez?'

'Somewhere in West Africa, I think. Sierra Leone?'

'Is that where they met?'

She shrugged. 'I have no idea.'

'And I guess the idea is that she carried the ashes back home with her, is that right?'

She threw up her hands. 'They couldn't say. Those people at the funeral home . . . Reading between the lines they couldn't care less. They *think* she may have mentioned something about a burial at sea. They got paid and she left. Just disappeared into the ether. End of. That's why this is so frustrating. She had no right. Did she? I mean I know legally she did, but morally?'

I could remember when the engine that powered me through my teen years was moral outrage. The world beats that out of us somehow, out of all of us. With only little spurts of it reignited here and there.

But with Nell it was so new and raw. Why wasn't the world a better place full of honorable people?

'You were at the party where he collapsed,' she said. 'Did anything strike you as odd?'

'Believe me, I've thought about all that, a lot. The only unusual thing was that the doctor wasn't feeling well and removed himself from the group. Everyone else was just laughing and talking, enjoying themselves. It was a beautiful house in a beautiful setting. The weather with the help of outdoor heaters cooperated.' I shrugged. 'Nothing at all seemed out of the ordinary.' And yet . . . And yet. I had had an odd feeling. And nothing Nell had just told me made that feeling in any way subside.

'I've been thinking,' she said. 'I don't know any of these people who must have been involved. I mean if anything was fishy, it had to involve someone there at the party. I've almost thought, well . . . I've been thinking what was needed here is like one of those scenes where all the suspects are brought back together? Do you know? Like in some old Agatha Christie movie. Do you like Agatha Christie?'

'As it happens, I do, but those are movies. You mean like with Poirot gathering all the suspects in the library?'

'Yes.'

'No.' In real life they would all end up dead, I thought, and no one would ever find the suspect. I was finding it rather touching Nell didn't seem to suspect me of any wrongdoing. She only had my word I had no prior connection to the doctor, just as in Agatha Christie's books. Carn and Mary may have known him through some charity fundraiser or other, and the same with Rem and Montana. The two spies may not have known him at all but they were, after all, spies – how far could they be trusted? The housekeeper and the butler hadn't known him – that was all I felt could be said for certain. Well, almost certain.

The rest of the party were there at Callie's invitation. The common thread was Callie and her ambitions for a shot at an ambassadorship. What her ambitions had to do with the doctor was difficult to say except he had a luster attached to his name that would reflect well on her.

Aloud I said, 'The whole situation is very odd, yes, but it is, and I cannot emphasize this enough, a matter for the police.'

'I've been to the police.'

Nell was nothing if not full of surprises.

'The Old Town police? In person?'

'Yes.'

'OK,' I said. 'And what did they say?'

'They said there's nothing they can do. It can't even be classified as a theft, can it? Her taking his ashes. But there's nothing to investigate as far as they're concerned since the woman vanished.'

'This was Narduzzi you were talking to?' It didn't really sound like him to blow her off like that, but then again he dealt with a lot of people who left their crazy out on the porch. And it was a pretty wild story. Even I had to admit that, and I dealt in wild stories.

'No. He had been called out on another case.'

'Did the funeral home at least photocopy the woman's credentials?'

A firm shake of the head. 'They went squirrelly on me when I asked about that. Why should they, when you come to think about it? It's routine for them, like someone's coming to pick up a takeaway. She could pay for the services and she paid in cash. That's all they cared about.'

'I see,' I said, thinking she was probably right. Which was interesting and created the potential for all sorts of mischief. So long as money changes hands no one is too awfully concerned. The remains of a person are just that: remains. Who is going to rise up and complain?

'That's all they cared about,' Nell repeated, with the indignation only the young can muster at this universal truth: It's money *and* love that make the world go round. Sometimes you get both together, but not often.

I tried to remember if this was standard procedure for funeral homes. Looking back, although those days were a blur, it was standard when I buried my own husband. No one questioned I was who I said I was. I didn't even recall being asked for photo ID – just a marriage license. Which I had to go back to the house to collect because I didn't have it with me.

I tried to recall the entire procedure and what I could call up was the phone call telling me that Marcus had been in an accident. It was the police calling and it was the middle of the night. He was supposed to have been out attending on a case at Mount Vernon Hospital and he'd been coming home, taking the parkway, when he met with an accident. Some passer-by had found him and called an ambulance, and the ambulance had taken him straight back where he had come from, later taking him without much further ado to the hospital morgue. And from there – and this was where my memory really was foggy – from there the funeral home had collected him. Had collected him at my instructions, I suppose. I really cannot recall.

It had been one of dozens if not hundreds of car accidents in the area every year. Nothing to distinguish Marcus's accident from the rest of the tragedies, the phone calls in the middle of the night, the crushed metal heaps of cars containing the shattered remains of a family's dreams and plans.

And deaths that sometimes revealed more than the family really wanted to know about the deceased.

Nothing special about it. Except that Marcus was my husband and at the time he died he was the center of my world. I thought he was my best friend and my forever lover.

If not for the accident, would I ever have found out?

I still wonder.

'—and so I don't really know what to do.' Nell's voice broke into my thoughts. 'It's up to me. And not just because of the money.'

I dragged my gaze back to meet hers.

'Yes, yes. Of course.' Her words had reminded me of something. 'Do you know anything about the rest of his estate? I mean, I assume his wife inherited everything. Unless he had got around to changing his will once they separated.'

'The executor didn't talk about anything beyond my own bequest,' she said. 'I wouldn't have expected him to, really. Knowing my uncle, I assumed that the bulk of his estate, whatever he had not already given away to charity or spent on travel, would go to one of his favorite charities. There may not have been a lot left apart from his house, if he even owned that. The executor just mailed me the manuscript and the check.'

We chatted a while longer. When she told me she was staying in a nearby hotel, I nearly invited her to stay with me.

But something stopped me. Probably nothing more than my innate need for privacy. Coupled with a sense that I knew so little about a girl her age and how to keep her entertained. I did offer to take her out for dinner if she was at a loose end in a strange town and she answered quickly that she was fine. She was jetlagged and just wanted to get some rest. She was off the next day to complete her journey to California.

I showed her to the door, feeling strangely protective and wishing her safe travels. It wasn't until I returned to the kitchen to put the dishes in the dishwasher that I again saw the manuscript sitting on the table, now managing to look like a huge, obligatory, and onerous task weighing far more than a few pounds.

Scrolling through my phone's address book for Edgar Montesquieu's number, I wondered exactly what I had got myself into.

ELEVEN

It seemed to me there was one large missing piece to the puzzle. If this were one of my books, it might be a red herring. Or just one of those inexplicable things that do happen. Things I never write about because readers just won't accept that life is weird and full of loose ends. They don't buy a book for loose ends – those they can get from their own lives. There is so much we have to take on as part of being human, however bizarre. Unexplained phenomenon, like UFOs.

Still, the situation required, to my mind, an immediate follow-up, if only to free my mind to return to more mundane and necessary tasks, like doing the laundry and writing a book.

And that was to learn more about the heretofore unexpected existence of the Doc Burke's wife, Fatima.

Who possibly lived, or had lived, in Sierra Leone.

And who for some reason had swept into town to collect her husband's ashes.

Why would she do this? Maybe I only had part of the story and to get it all, I would need to find her.

Google to the rescue, of course. Fatima Alvarez as a search term pulled up some Instagram and Facebook accounts belonging to younger women. I assumed the Fatima I sought and Doc Burke had been separated for some time and that she had not been a child bride, but there was actually nothing provable attached to either of those hypotheses. I had to go with what was logical to my mind and then maybe branch out into very young women with young children or very elderly women older than the doctor's sixty-five years.

I also tried searching on Fatima Alvarez Burke, of course, and drew a blank, with Google wondering if I mean Bark rather than Burke, which I did not.

LinkedIn suggested it was housing some likely candidates. Because I had not logged in to my account for ages, I first had to jump through many hoops to satisfy them I was not working for the Anonymous hackers' group. I had of course forgotten my password and thinking it was Roscoe for my dog I tried a few versions of that before they locked me out and after more tedium which I will spare you involving two-factor authentication and the name of my high school English teacher (Elizabeth Barrow, if you'd like to use my account), I was able to narrow down the possibilities inside LinkedIn to five candidates. One was a licensed real estate agent operating out of Ohio, one was a youngish editor for a small press, one was an insurance claims adjuster, one was a banker, and another was a registered nurse.

Doctor. Nurse. Not an altogether unlikely pairing, as I'm sure you'll agree. This woman, who on her professional account used the name, Fatima A. Burke, happened to live in Freetown, Sierra Leone.

Bingo. Had to be her.

I looked up the time difference and saw Freetown was four hours ahead of Northern Virginia. Nine at night for her, then. I used LinkedIn to message her, then went to see what was in the freezer for dinner. Because I had ruined my appetite with those cookies of Nell's I wasn't that hungry, but it gave me something to do while I waited to hear back.

First I wrote down the goddam password in case I was automatically logged out after a certain time. But I didn't hear back until the next morning.

At six a.m. my time I logged in to LinkedIn and saw a message waiting for me from Fatima.

In the meantime, I had googled her name coupled with 'wife of Doc Burke,' which turned up photos of a slightly plump middle-aged woman with long brown hair and brown eyes. She was no one I had ever seen before.

I had messaged her to say I had been present at the passing of her husband and I was hoping she would be willing to talk to me about him. I chose my words carefully and kept it brief because I had no idea to whom I was writing and how she would react. She might have been completely estranged from David and hate the very mention of his name. She might have been in deepest mourning for him. Marriage was complicated; even unto death it was complicated.

I thought there was a real chance she wouldn't get back to me at all. Why should she? I hoped she would see from my profile that I was not scary and liable to ask her to wire me money for surgery on my ailing grandmother, but she would see I was a crime writer and that can be a real turnoff for people who aren't familiar with the genre. I mean used as a calling card, my profession can offer a dicey introduction. Someone who writes about murder is not necessarily someone you want to strike up an acquaintance with over the Internet, unless you happen to be a crime writer yourself or looking to hire a hit man.

I had thought of taking that 'crime writer' information off my profile before contacting her and disguising myself as a reporter or something and then realized that would be more alarming. For better or worse, I had to stick with who I was. I did update my profile to mention I was a *New York Times* best-selling author because since I last visited LinkedIn that had become true.

My instinct about not claiming to be a reporter was right on the money.

'You're not a reporter, are you?' was her message in reply. 'Because if you are, I'm sorry but I have no comment.'

I answered back right away. 'Absolutely not. I can put you in touch with my book editor or my agent if you want to verify who I am.' I thought about mentioning Detective Narduzzi as a reference and then thought better of it. For one thing, I really didn't want him up in my stuff. Not until I knew what was going on here. If I thought about it at all, I wanted to present him with a *fait accompli* if in fact there was something fishy about the doctor's death.

'As mentioned,' I went on, 'I was at the party where Dr Burke passed. I am still in shock, as perhaps you are, too. Maybe I can help you in some way. I live not far from where he lived.' Obviously, picking up his ashes wasn't going to be one of those ways. 'Are you in Sierra Leone now?'

She replied: 'Yes. My shift starts at eleven and I don't have much time. What was it you wanted to know?'

Awkward. I couldn't come up with a nice way to ask her about the ashes of her ex-husband and what she thought she was doing with them. This was what I hated about texting and emailing and all these other modern forms of communication: I wanted to be able to see her reaction. To see and judge her reaction.

To be able to tell if she might be evasive on that topic, or on any other.

From outside I could hear the bells of St Mary's ringing the hour from their gothic tower. They were a few minutes off, as always; over the years I'd come to think of them as a warning that the hour of our reckoning approacheth. The sound was mechanical, of course, not generated by a human bellringer, although I would totally apply for the job of Quasimodo if it were open. I always wondered why they couldn't set the timer correctly.

'Would you be willing to talk to me on FaceTime?' I wrote Fatima. 'Much better than texting like this. And then you'll have a better sense of who you are speaking with.'

A two-way street, of course.

She was agreeable and we did all the trading of information and button pushing necessary to bring that about. In due course, my phone screen lit up, announcing the connection. Once she got her video camera stabilized, I could see she was a bit older than I'd thought at first, closer to retirement age. Probably close in age to her deceased husband. She had dark brown hair, threaded with white at the temples and French-braided into a frame around her face. A mild expression. Large, tired brown eyes nestled in a web of dark wrinkles. She looked like she had seen quite enough already and she hadn't even started work for the day. I knew from her profile she worked at a local hospital in Freetown. St Agnes's. She wore dark blue scrubs – not the starched white uniform of the past, which had to have been impractical at the very least.

'Hello,' she said tentatively. 'Augusta?'

'Yes,' I said. 'How are you?'

'You don't look much like your profile photo. But I can see now that it is you.'

I let out a hoot of laughter. There are few author photos in the world that resemble the living author, and mine had to be ten years out of date. I kept meaning to do something about that, soon. It's not as if I'd look much better if I waited.

'I'm sorry,' she said. 'That must've sounded rude.'

'Don't worry about it. In fact, I resemble my passport photo and I'm one of the few people who can say that.'

She smiled. 'You knew David,' she said. It wasn't accusatory, which was a good sign. She didn't suspect some romantic tie or anything like that.

'Actually, I did not. I had never met him before the night of the party.'

'Oh, I see. What was the occasion? I only saw a couple of news accounts online. They just said he'd been taken ill at a dinner party. If anyone tried to get in touch to tell me more, I wasn't aware. I half expected to hear from the media but I would soon put a stop to that. It didn't happen anyway.'

'Right,' I said, thinking there wouldn't be a lot of point in a reporter's tracking her down, even if they knew she existed. 'The woman who organized the party . . . well. Let's just say it was a typical DC do. Everyone was brought together for a purpose, even if the purpose wasn't evident on the surface. I gathered David was there because the woman who hosted the party – she and her husband – had been contributors to one of his causes. In fact, he told me that himself.'

'I see. It doesn't sound like anything David would have liked. In support of his causes, he might make the effort. And you?'

'Why was I there? The hostess is writing a book and was hoping for a leg up in getting it in front of the right people. Nearly everyone at the party, apart from the doctor, was connected with publishing in some way. Some were writing a book; one of them was a literary agent. A politician and his wife; I'm sure there's a book in the offing there. Those people can't ever shut up once they leave office. Let's see . . . there was a man, his name is Montana – just Montana – who helps people "polish their public presence."' That would make a great slogan for Montana's business, I thought. All that alliteration. 'Helps them hone their media presentations, comb their hair, lose their accents, buy a good suit if they don't have one. He's sort of a voice-and-lifestyle coach, all rolled into one.'

'Was David using his services?'

'Not that I'm aware.' It was rather an odd question. 'Why? Would he, do you think?'

She lifted one shoulder in a shrug. 'The David I knew had a

few rough edges. Maybe if he was going hat in hand to get money for his causes, maybe – you know. Maybe he felt he needed to be polished up a little bit.'

Interesting. 'I hadn't really thought of that. He's awfully famous, with or without polish. He just was. People seemed to like him for, not despite that.'

'Yes.'

'Do you happen to know Callie Moore? The woman who threw the party?'

'I can't say that I do.' She lowered her eyes and I got the impression she was glancing at her wristwatch.

'I hope you don't mind my asking, but when were you two married, you and David?'

'Fifteen years ago,' she said briefly.

In their early fifties, then. A late marriage.

'And you've been separated from him how long?'

'It's been ten years since we lived together.'

So, they lasted five years in harness. Not much of a run, I thought.

'But you're not divorced. I guess I read somewhere that he had been married or was married – his situation was always a bit vaguely glossed over in interviews and so on. But I didn't know anything beyond that. He never seemed to be *with* anyone if you know what I mean.'

She laughed briefly. 'I know exactly what you mean. He was a complete loner. Even when I was married to him. Living with him.'

I waited. We might be in dangerous territory now and I did not want to scare her off, because taking time off to go chasing her down in Sierra Leone was not in my busy schedule.

'I was married to a doctor,' I told her. 'A pediatrician.'

'Oh,' she said. 'So perhaps you know.'

I decided to take a chance because I did feel I knew what the problem may have been. I mean, marriages go wrong for a lot of reasons, but marriages to doctors may fall into a special category only the principal players can understand.

'With Marcus it was like being married to a saint,' I said. 'And while I'd often bask in the glow of my husband's halo, it wasn't always easy.'

She laughed. 'Perfectly said. Everything David did was so noble and respected, I couldn't complain. How could I complain without sounding like a selfish, whining woman? Several universities gave him honorary degrees; several countries gave him honorary citizenship. Sarajevo and Mandrekka were the most recent.'

Mandrekka again. No wonder Doc Burke had been invited to Callie's party. Dropping his name as a friend or supporter could be another string in her bow, helping her win that coveted ambassador posting.

Fatima seemed to have kept up with some of the doctor's recent news. Natural curiosity, or something more?

'Is that what ended your marriage?' I asked. 'His elevated status?'

'I'm really not that petty. I just wanted him home more often. That and a few other things.'

'It was a car accident ended mine.'

Fatima left a thoughtful pause. 'You could say a car accident ended mine as well.'

Confused, I said, 'I mean my husband died in a car accident.'

'I see,' she said. 'I am sorry to hear that.'

I didn't say the usual: It was a long time ago, or I'm fine now, or any of the things people are expected to say. The listener, one hundred percent guaranteed, does not want to hear much more about your bald grief; I figured that out for myself very quickly. And I certainly didn't want to get into the things I learned about Marcus after his death. In this case, especially, what would be the point?

'Thank you,' I said simply.

'Yes, indeed.' She seemed to have drifted off somewhere into an old memory. 'Yes, you could say it was a car accident ended our marriage, too. My marriage to David. Not to diminish your loss in anyway, or blame David, but he told me he was involved in a car accident long before we met and was never the same after. He quit drinking cold turkey. People would press a drink on him – I don't know why they do that – so he'd pretend the water he was drinking was vodka or something else. Anyway, I think he saw our marriage as a sort of second chance at happiness. When I wasn't able to live up to that – wasn't able to save him, restore him to the man he'd been – I felt I'd failed him. I know that's wrong but for years I couldn't help feeling that way.'

I was thinking how taking on full responsibility for another person's life was always doomed to failure. Did the doctor even realize the burden he'd placed on Fatima? Depression, if that's what this was, may have given him a sort of tunnel vision.

'I'm sorry, but . . . do you mean there was brain damage? Mental trauma? Something like that?'

'I'm going to go with mental trauma and leave it at that. You haven't really said . . . Was there something in particular you wanted to ask me? Because I really do need to leave soon.'

I was losing her. I scrambled to organize the question I most wanted to ask in the most palatable way I could think of. Modulating my voice, I said, 'I understand you came to the US to claim your husband's body.'

If she'd been holding the phone, I think she would've dropped it.

'Do *what*?' she demanded. 'Claim his—?'

'Claim his, um, remains,' I said, stuttering over the words. I hadn't expected this astonished reaction. 'I was told by his niece that—'

'Nell?'

'Yes.' It seemed like a good time to shut up and let her tell me what was going on. I was pretty much out of questions that would make any sense at this point. But she just shook her head. 'I have no idea what's going on. I haven't left the country in ages, and even then it was a trip to New York to see relatives. I went nowhere near DC.'

I believed her reaction was genuine, and that what she was saying was true. It opened up a barrel of questions at my end, however.

'Why did Nell tell you?' she demanded. 'Why didn't she get in touch with me?'

'I don't know, really. I can't speak for her. I only know Nell arranged to meet me because the doctor – David – had left her a manuscript with instructions and a small bequest in his will.'

She was nodding. 'And all the rest to charity. Probably a foreign mission. That's how we met you know. I worked for

Catholic Relief at the same time he was in Sierra Leone as a volunteer doctor.'

'I don't know anything about the rest of the will,' I said. 'Nell only knew about her end of things, you see. I gathered the bequest was pretty much intended to cover her expenses in dealing with the manuscript. She took it on as a labor of love. I don't think there was any great benefit to her. In fact, I know there wasn't.'

'I haven't seen Nell for years,' she said slowly. She had calmed down enough to take in the news and try to process what was going on. 'I suppose I wasn't the first person she thought of. We barely knew each other. She was a girl of – oh, six or seven the last time I saw her. A little star, even then. But once I became David's wife in name only – well. It was a formality to get divorced and David and I just never got around to it. There were no children, no question of alimony, nothing like that. God knows he spent every dime he ever had on his mission to save the world. To save himself.'

'OK.'

'What are you saying? That someone claiming to be *me* collected his remains?'

'Yes, that's about the sum of it.'

'For heaven's sake. I can only say it wasn't me. You can check with passport control. I wasn't in the country.'

I was certain passport control wouldn't hand out any information to me, but I could run it past the police. Specifically, I could run it by Narduzzi. I didn't think any random police officer would accept the story at face value and not take it as the ravings of a deranged crime writer jabbering about purloined remains.

I may have been overestimating Narduzzi but, still. A cold call to anyone else at the station would get me nowhere.

Nell's story of her conversation with the funeral home was starting to gel but now the big question was – who in hell had turned up to claim the remains of Doc Burke?

Echoing my thoughts, Fatima said, 'Who was it then? Don't they ask for ID over there? Can someone just wander in off the street claiming to be a relative?'

'I have no idea,' I told her. 'Those are my very questions. Whoever it was showed a marriage license, but if it wasn't you . . .'

'What should I do? Do you think I should do something?'

'I suppose you could file a complaint,' I said vaguely. 'Do you know a person named Drake? That's the last name. Mr Drake is all I know. He's the one who got in touch with Nell.'

She shook her head. 'No idea.'

'Do you know anything about the manuscript the doctor was working on?' I had so many questions spinning in my mind I was almost throwing them out randomly, afraid she might stop talking to me simply because I was the bearer of weird news. 'Possibly a memoir?' And remembering the word, 'murder' – 'Possibly a work of fiction?'

At that she laughed.

'David was not given to flights of fancy. He was too serious for that. Too busy saving the world. Whatever he was working on would've been non-fiction and the topics would have been disease and world poverty and child hunger, something along those lines. He was far too literal-minded to write any other type of story. Look, I really must go.'

'Sure, sure,' I said. 'Look, maybe you want to get in touch with Nell, although I'm not sure she'll have much to add. She seems like a nice kid.' I gave her Nell's email address.

'Thanks,' she said.

'Did you know Nell's mother?'

'Not really, no. It's been years, and she lived in California. Then David and I split, and . . . you know. Drifted apart, she and I did. And we were not close to begin with – my time with David was so brief and Nell was so young. You do know she's dead – Nell's mother?'

'Yes.'

'She was a lovely woman – it was a real shame she died so young. But from what little I know she raised Nell to have a high regard for herself, for her own worth. That makes her sound insufferable, but I mean . . . there's a lot to be said for letting girls know how valuable they are. What I see here—' She shook her head. 'It would amaze you. When people are focused on survival, on food, self-esteem seems like a luxury. Look, I really have to go.'

I nodded quickly. 'If you hear anything . . .' But, what in the world was she going to hear? And from whom? If this was a con game, the last person the con artist would contact would be the person they had impersonated.

My internal warning bells were telling me I did need to hand this over to Narduzzi.

For once I decided to listen.

TWELVE

Detective Narduzzi was a busy man. If there was a murder, his underfunded office was what the citizens had to solve it, in a good-size town with a growing murder rate. When I'd first met him, he'd been accompanied by Sergeant Bernolak. I don't know that I ever got her first name or if she was even still with the force. She had always struck me as a fish out of water.

You would think the murder rate would reflect poorly on Narduzzi and his abilities but in fact the Old Town area and its budget had never fully recovered from the woes brought about by the pandemic. People get up to all manner of crime, most of it involving property, when they feel the world has gone to hell.

I'd been lucky: I worked from home so I seldom had to put myself at risk as we waited for the vaccine, and my income didn't suffer. In fact, it went up in a major way as people bought books to distract themselves. The only drawbacks were that I couldn't attend publishing conferences and see friends – any crime conferences and book signings where I'd normally appear were cancelled.

I almost hesitated to embroil Narduzzi in this but obviously something was very wrong and it was, after all, his job.

Besides, he had access to information I did not have. Whether he would share it with me was another question, but . . .

I had his phone number from when we first worked together. I didn't feel he would put it quite that way for he had gone his way and I had gone mine during the investigation, but in fact, I had been the one to solve the case, wrapping it in a package, tying it with a bow, and handing him the solution.

I was certain I would get his voicemail and possibly never hear back but he answered right away.

'I wondered when I'd hear from you,' he said.

'I've been busy,' I said. 'I have a PI license now. The test was easy.'

He laughed. 'I see you're still working on your self-esteem. Let me know when you're done.'

I wouldn't have to work so hard if you would give credit where credit is due, I thought. But I kept that to myself. It didn't seem the best way to go about worming information out of him.

He surprised me by saying, 'You're calling about the death of Doc Burke, aren't you?'

Why bother pretending? 'I am, as a matter of fact,' I said, one professional to another. 'Did you have any reservations about what happened to him? Because if you recall, I was on the scene. No one seems to be treating it as anything more than a normal heart attack – if we can use the word normal in this context.'

'It wasn't in my bailiwick,' he said.

'I did wonder. Well, whoever is running the show in Fairfax didn't seem to feel it was anything out of the ordinary.'

'That would be Henderson,' he said. I waited for him to elaborate but Henderson was all I was going to get, apparently. There was a wealth of information packed into those few words though. Henderson was a nitwit, a rival, looking forward to retirement years before daydreaming on the job would be appropriate, perhaps being investigated by Internal Affairs. Any of the above might apply. It was hard to say precisely but I gathered Narduzzi was not a fan.

'I did hear that you were at the soirée,' he said. 'And I did wonder.' Wonder what? I wondered. 'But there are rules about this sort of thing. Protocols. Since you called me clearly not knowing Detective Henderson is the one you should contact, I don't see why we can't chat a while on the topic. It's just that I'm not going to be able to give you a lot of information. Not that I can discuss a case with any random member of the public who doesn't have a distinct interest.'

'I'm not random, and I have a distinct interest.'

'I'm not surprised. Well, as I say, there are rules about this sort of thing.'

'Hmm. So are you saying I should call Detective Henderson instead of you?'

'In a perfectly ordered world, yes. A world in which everyone followed the rules. Absolutely, one hundred percent I would tell you that you must speak to the officer in charge. That I could not possibly comment.'

'So there is a case?' I asked.

'I didn't say that. Is that coffee shop still there near your house?'

'The Beanery? Yes.'

'Does it still havc that upstairs room?'

'Last I looked. Funny you should mention it. I was just headed that way.'

'It's about time for my coffee break.'

I was settled into a far corner booth on the second floor of the Beanery, laptop open, when Narduzzi emerged at the top of the stairs. Most tourists did not realize the space existed so it tended to be uninhabited, particularly at this time of day.

It was your typical American coffee shop circa early twenty-first century, striving to be cool with unpainted brick walls and exposed everything. It mostly succeeded in achieving that vibe and had been cleverly marketed to appeal to the thriving tourist trade seeking unthreatening hipsterism and a good cup of coffee, things the Beanery did very well.

Narduzzi was carrying a coffee and something in a brown paper bag. I assumed it was my drug of choice.

'Chocolate chip cookies,' I said, peering at the contents. 'How did you know?'

'Lucky guess,' he said. 'There's also a blueberry muffin if you'd rather have that.'

'That's far too healthy for this time of day. All those antioxidants.' I gave a pretend shudder.

He pulled out a chair across from me and sat down.

'How have you been?' he asked. 'I haven't seen you since the night of your book signing. Sorry I had to leave early. Duty called.'

The night, which in retrospect could only be called fateful, I had met Callie Moore. Although since she had engineered the whole thing, I supposed fateful wasn't really the word.

I waved away his apology. 'I figured it was something like that.'

'How did it go?' he asked.

Busy arranging my cookie on a paper napkin, I held out my left hand and toggled it back and forth. 'So, so,' I said. 'I may no longer be Old Town's favorite child.'

'I did order it online later.'

'Most people do that. The bookstores hate it but it's a David and Goliath game.'

I didn't want to ask how he enjoyed the book because it can be such a loaded question. He surprised me by saying, 'I enjoyed it. I don't know anything about police procedure in France, but it seemed accurate. That sort of leisurely Gallic way of solving a crime with lots of food and a few cigarettes involved and the occasional love affair in the afternoon.'

I laughed. 'That's what the readers respond to. The food as much as the crime, I mean. The love affairs, not so much. At least, I never get emails about that, telling me I did something wrong. I do get emails about the food. That sort of reader feedback is all I have to go on. I sort of steer the ship of my next book using their feedback. To tell you the truth, I have very little idea how they go about catching and processing murderers in the countryside of France. The gendarmes and police officers are not given to letting me into their confidence and my French is sketchy, anyway. I do the best I can, using my imagination.'

'I'll just bet you do.'

I felt his eyes on me and looked up from breaking off a bit of the cookie. I cleared my throat, suddenly uncomfortable.

'Writing books must be exhausting,' he said. 'Even though you seem fine to me.'

'It's a process. You're never quite *done*.'

'I feel that way most days.'

I nodded. 'So,' I said, in the pause before popping the bit of cookie in my mouth. 'I gather that you have questions about the evening with Dr Burke?'

'Not officially of course.'

'Goes without saying.'

'Does it?'

I made a 'cross my heart and hope to die' gesture. 'Yes. Absolutely. Is something up?'

'I got a phone call from a young lady named Nell Campbell. Ring any bells?'

'Yes, I spoke with her yesterday as a matter of fact. She told me you had recommended me.'

'I suggested she might talk with you, yes. I thought . . . I don't know what I thought, exactly. But she seemed like a nice kid who had just lost pretty much the only living relative who had meant anything to her – she was kind of broken up. And there was nothing I could do for her, then or now. Because the case is not a case, you see. I cannot say that strongly enough: There is no case. And even if there were, it is not technically mine. But I thought, when she started talking about memoirs, that you would be just the person.'

'Thanks a bunch.' If he caught the sarcasm it didn't register on his handsome face. The only thing I saw there was concern.

Part of me was wondering if he didn't have any other cases to work on. His *own* cases. And the other part of me knew Narduzzi was not the sort of detective to waste investigative time on pointless expeditions. He heard from a lot of victims every day – bereaved parents, wives, girlfriends, husbands, boyfriends – who were following up on cases new and old.

If Nell Campbell had got to him somehow, I knew he was going on instinct. And from what I knew of the man, his instincts were solid. That I wanted to know more of the man and his instincts was a thought I had tucked away in the attic of my mind. He was married.

'So,' I asked, 'what are you thinking?'

'So,' he said, 'what can you tell me?'

'OK,' I began, to break the impasse. 'There's something fishy going on and I don't know what it is.'

'Go on.'

'First of all, I just learned this or I would've told you before. I promise.'

'We'll worry about re-establishing trust later on. What do you know?'

Re-establishing?

'There was some funny business at the funeral home that took in the doctor's remains. Someone turned up and gave instructions to have Dr Burke cremated and the same person – I guess – showed up to collect the ashes.'

I certainly had his full attention. If this had been an interview with TV's Detective Joe Kenda, this would have been where he said, 'Well, *my, my, my*.'

'Nell didn't tell me that it was funny business.'

'She didn't know when she spoke with you and you sent her over to me with his memoirs. When she later contacted the police about the ashes, they brushed her off. She was hurt by what happened – as you say, her uncle's death left her pretty much alone in the world – but she didn't immediately think "funny business." She only wondered why the Doc's widow hadn't been in touch.'

'But you did. You thought "funny business."'

I struggled with whether to claim credit for that. In a way, it was just a fluke I thought to call the doctor's wife in Sierra Leone. I had been thinking she had collected the doctor's remains and had been astonished to learn she had not.

'I just had a feeling,' I said, trying to look mysterious and all-knowing but not too smug – a tricky balance.

'That was very good detective work,' he said. 'You say "someone" turned up at the funeral home. Pretending to be a relative of the doctor's.'

'That's right. Pretending to be his wife. His sort-of estranged wife but his wife, nonetheless. She spoke fondly of him, if exasperatedly. Fatima Burke.'

'Interesting,' he said.

'Isn't it just? It's Fatima Alvarez Burke, if you want the full name. Nee Alvarez, of course. I've already spoken with her.'

'Wow! You're saving the police a lot of time.'

He was smiling. But I did not miss the sarcasm.

'Do you want to hear this or not? I can always call Fairfax PD.' That was an empty threat, but I was counting on him not to realize it. 'Detective Henderson, wasn't it?'

It was like waving a red flag in front of a bull. This was interesting. I wondered what Henderson had done to Narduzzi, who did not strike me as a man given over to petty jealousies. Did he steal the sample noses from his Identikit? Hide his bulletproof vest?

Relenting, I said, 'She lives in Sierra Leone. She's about the same age as Doc Burke, who was sixty-five. Maybe younger. A nice woman from all I could tell.'

'What, you Zoomed her?'

'FaceTimed. I'll give you her contact information if you like.'

'That would be great.'

More sarcasm, but milder this time. 'I guess she's been there many years, possibly all her working life; I didn't have time to ask where she was from originally. She's a nurse working for a Christian charity. That's how she met Doc Burke, working for Catholic Relief. Still is, I guess. He was in the country as a volunteer.'

'On one of his many do-good expeditions.' Narduzzi nodded. 'Interesting man.'

'I can tell you I never met anyone less likely to be on the receiving end of a deadly attack. Even on short acquaintance I got the impression of a retiring man, not one to seek the spotlight. Trying to save the world but not butting into anyone's business as he went about it. Are the police sure it's murder?'

'I never said it was murder.'

I could almost hear that conversational door slamming shut. A wiser and less persistent woman would have changed the subject.

'Clearly it was murder,' I said. 'I mean, come on, isn't it obvious?' I leaned forward in my best cut-the-crap manner. 'Maybe he was an unintended victim. There was a mix-up of some kind. In any event, he died, but now we have no body to test. Which had to be the whole point of someone absconding with his remains from the funeral home. I mean, why else?'

'Why else indeed. What can you tell me about this impersonator?'

I shook my head. 'Nothing. She had a marriage license and that's apparently all you need. That and money to pay the expenses. From my own experience, that's true. I mean really, who would question why you were there? They would take you at face value as being the wife with every reason to make the claim. It's not like you're buying a car, in which case they'd be a lot more careful.'

'Did whoever it was show ID, or just the marriage license?'

'I don't know about the ID,' I said. 'But anyone who could fake a marriage license could just as easily fake an ID.'

'Are we really saying that someone showed up in disguise to claim the remains?'

'I'm not sure there would really be a reason for disguise. It's not as if the funeral home director was going to Google her image. I mean, would anyone expect him to? So anyone looking reasonably like they might be a spouse of Doc Burke could pass themselves off as Fatima. They might wear a dark wig, sunglasses, makeup. It wouldn't take much.'

'Said the woman who is such a master of disguise herself.'

'I thought we were past all that.' He was referring to a small, harmless caper of mine during 'The Case of the Missing Neighbors.' 'I was in pursuit of the truth. I've changed a lot since then.'

This was true. Having suffered unintended consequences in solving the mystery of my neighbors' disappearance, I'd vowed to become a better person and neighbor. That had lasted up until the next Home Owners' Association meeting during which landscaping fees had been discussed. Landscaping was always a thorny issue, no pun intended.

Moving right along, I said, 'I've drawn up a list of candidates. Would you like to see it?'

'Sure.'

I opened my laptop and turned the screen to face him.

'These are the women who were at the party who could conceivably pass themselves off as Doc Burke's wife. They're vaguely in the age range of forty-five or more, although that doesn't matter, does it? The funeral home guy wouldn't know what age of woman to expect to turn up. They are, in no particular order: Callie Moore, Felicity Overstone, Mary Hilton, and Zelda. She's the housekeeper. I don't have her last name, I'm sure you can find it.'

I hesitated, then said, 'It might even have been a man disguised as a woman.'

'Like, the funeral home was all dark so no one would notice? Maybe they had a power outage?'

'I'll admit, it's a long shot.'

'It's the sort of thing that only happens in crime novels,' he said. Was that a grin on his face? Yes, that was definitely a grin. A dimpled grin, rather sexy, which somehow added insult to injury.

I felt it might not be the best time to mention my sixth book, wherein I had used a similar ploy. A darkened French church; a figure in a dark coat – a man pretending to be a woman; a knife flashing from out of nowhere in the candlelight; the victim, an innocent woman cleaning the altar—

'So it follows, one of these people may have a lot of explaining to do,' he said.

'Although, nothing says it is one of them.'

'No. But if not them, who?'

'Right,' I said. 'Who would do such a thing, and why?'

'My first question is, how?'

'How was he poisoned or whatever, you mean?'

'Yes, let's talk about that. You were there on the spot. What did you notice? Walk me through it.'

'OK.' I cast my mind back to that night, that dinner, the drinks before dinner, the drinks during and after dinner. Put that way – drink after drink – it's a wonder any of us could remember our own names. Was that a deliberate ploy on Callie's part? If she had something to do with what happened to the doctor, wouldn't a party full of smashed witnesses be a great defense? Who would believe a word they said?

So I walked Narduzzi through everything I could remember, ending with, 'You see, nothing sinister, no sense of foreboding. I was actually enjoying myself – I don't get to many parties. If anything, I saw this as a chance to refill the well.'

'You mean get new ideas for your next book?'

'Or flesh out the book I'm working on.' I glanced at my watch; it was almost noon. 'Should be working on.'

'I won't keep you much longer,' he said.

'Are you kidding? I'll do anything to help. But the fact is, once we all had our dessert, the Baked Alaska, Doc Burke sort of drifted away. At first he said he didn't want dessert but then accepted a very small portion.'

'Did you see him eat it?'

'No.'

'OK, what happened next?'

'He said he was tired. Maybe he said he thought he'd sit down; I don't recall. I didn't think much of it; we were all pretty much in the bag by that point. We just carried on chatting and let him rest.'

'Wasn't that a bit, well, rude?'

'Of him, you mean? Not really. It was so clearly what he

wanted, to be left alone. In fact, I expected to turn around and see that he had left. He was not a party guy and I think he may have tried to slip out given . . . well, given time. Next I saw of him, I thought he was asleep.'

'Could the poison or whatever it was have been in the dessert you shared?'

I had already given this a great deal of thought. 'I don't see any way that's possible.'

'Were there – I don't know, sprinkles or whipped cream or something that came with it? Something decorating the plates?'

'No. And it would be difficult to poison just part of a cake. Unless a portion of it was marked off or tagged somehow as being for the doctor. Which means the butler had something to do with it. Or the butler and the chef-slash-housekeeper together. That's just way too tricky to pull off, I would have said. We all watched the butler serve out the portions and there was nothing added to the individual servings. No decorations, nothing like what you're suggesting. No chocolate sauce or whatever. Setting aside the question of motive we have to set aside the fact the doctor had just a suggestion of the dessert.'

'It wasn't possible the food from dinner was tainted?'

I shook my head slowly. 'I've thought and thought through that. I don't think so. I don't see how. I didn't consume all of the meal because I'm vegetarian and I focused on the meat-free offerings.'

'Did anyone know you were a vegetarian? Did you tell the hostess – Callie Moore?' The question confused me, what possible difference could it make, but I said 'I didn't say anything beforehand. I simply said something to the butler as he was serving.'

'Was anyone else a vegetarian, doing the same thing – refusing certain portions?'

'You know, I couldn't say for certain.'

'The doctor, for example?'

I shook my head, but I finally saw the point of his questions. He was trying to look for the one food that only the doctor may have consumed. But if so, that line of questioning was a dead end. 'I think he took a portion of everything that was offered,' I said. 'But now you ask me, could I swear to it? Like under oath? I couldn't be that sure. This is so frustrating. The thing is, when you're in the middle of what seems like a harmless enough party, you don't expect you'll ever be asked. I was focused on listening to the conversation.'

'I understand. Was the doctor sitting next to you?'

'Sort of caddy-corner across the table from me.'

'And who sat next to him?'

'On his left was Mary Hilton. On his right was Felicity Overstone.'

No need to ask him why he wanted to know. The only two people with access to his plate and his drink, apart from the butler, were the two women.

'Did you see the doctor take any medication during the evening?'

I had to stop and think about this. 'I don't think I did. If he shook a pill out of a bottle or something I think I'd have noticed.'

'Did you know he had a heart condition?'

'I did. The butler tried to give him more wine and he said something about having a dicky heart.'

'He carried heart medication with him, for emergencies, and he took a daily pill. We know that from talking to someone on his staff. Which was why there was no question, at least at first, of what had happened to him.'

'Thank God. I mean, I've been feeling a bit guilty about that. Because I was the one who diagnosed a heart attack in the first place. Sort of just piercing together what he said at dinner and the way he looked, there by the pool. When I told Zelda to call for an ambulance, I said it was for a heart attack. To tell that to the emergency services so they'd know what to expect.'

'All the signs were that he had succumbed to a heart attack but couldn't reach his medication.'

'His medication wasn't on him? When they took him to the hospital?'

'He had nitroglycerin with him but he didn't appear to have had time to reach for it.'

'Holy cow,' I said 'I can't *believe* this. Basically, everyone took my word for it that it was a heart attack. It was listed in his obituary as a heart attack, so I thought someone who knew what they were talking about had examined him. If it was something else, we will never know. Thanks to me. Oh my *God*.' I put the fingers of one hand firmly against my mouth, utterly appalled. If I'd kept my mouth shut, would they have done an autopsy and found out there was something wrong with him? That someone had done something wrong to him?

I took a deep breath, and said, 'Why would anyone listen to me? I'm not a medical professional.'

'Listen, don't beat yourself up too much about this. The fact that he carried medication for his heart confirmed the professional diagnosis. It is what it is now. And we can only go forward and see if there is something to investigate – which apparently there is.'

'There's something more?'

'Yes, but it doesn't amount to much. One of the EMT specialists that night noticed there was a melted glass in the outdoor firepit.'

'Not a broken glass, but a melted one?'

'Glass usually melts in heat rather than shatters, per our experts.'

'He didn't save the glass for analysis?'

Narduzzi shook his head: 'Remember, no one thought it was murder. He just made a note of what he saw in the immediate vicinity of the body. Did you happen to notice a melted glass? Did one go missing that night?'

I shook my head. If only I'd paid more attention, if only I'd not taken it on myself to diagnose a heart attack.

'You bring up an interesting question though,' he said.

I was dabbing away the tears at my eyes, tears sprung from out of nowhere. *Damn.* When would I learn to mind my own business? Stop being such an in-charge know-it-all? I was so busy berating myself my mind took a moment to catch up with what he had said.

'What's the interesting question? Apart from how did I get to be so dumb?'

'Who put the notice in the paper? The obituary?'

'Oh,' I said. '*Oh.*' I thought for a moment. 'It wasn't his niece. It couldn't have been.'

Narduzzi was looking at me, waiting for me to think it through, probably. Some days it was a long wait.

'It had to be the woman who showed up at the funeral home. Had to be.'

'They don't run those notices for free, and I would bet they don't take cash. She – or whoever – had to have used a credit or debit card.'

'Which would be wonderfully easy to trace. Unless it was one of those pay-as-you-go things. One of those cards that's not necessarily attached to the person who purchased it for cash.'

'I did think of that. But we will be following up that lead.'

'We?'

'Me. For now, until I've got more to go on, this is just me. And it must stay that way – do you understand?'

I nodded solemnly.

'This is sort of an off-the-books investigation.'

'Henderson.' He was worried about Henderson. Wow.

'Enough said.'

'Back to the poisoning,' I said. 'Let's call it what it was. Let's call it what we *assume* it was. Everything is a poison given in the wrong dose to the wrong person. Otherwise I couldn't do my job.'

'I don't follow.'

'Most of my book murders are poisonings. I don't know anything about guns so I just have someone give the victim too much of some otherwise useful substance.'

'Right. No knives?'

'Too messy.'

'OK.'

'The real question is how he consumed whatever it was. And the problem with most poisons is they taste bad or smell bad.'

'I may have an answer to that,' he said. 'Doc Burke caught the virus during the pandemic, and he suffered from long COVID as a consequence. This I got from his medical records, which I have had a look at. Don't ask me how.'

'My lips are sealed. So it wasn't just from talking to his staff that you know about his heart.'

He looked at me rather sternly and said, 'You're lucky I'm telling you as much as I'm telling you.'

'Got it.'

'Anyway. He came down with the virus at the height of the pandemic, a somewhat mild case – he wasn't hospitalized; he just tested positive and he had to isolate for a while. But when he recovered, his sense of taste and smell were impaired. It was probably a permanent thing with him. That happened with some people. In some cases, they recovered fully. In others, they never recovered.'

'Ah,' I said, nodding. 'That explains his only accepting a small slice of cake – he was merely being polite. He was full from dinner and had no inclination to stuff himself with cake like the rest of us. So that means anyone could have fed him any horrible thing and he wouldn't have known the difference. *Jesus*.'

'That is strictly confidential information. OK?'

'Yes, yes, of course. *Yes*. Because whoever knew that about him would know how easy it would be to taint his food or drink.' I sat quite still, taking in the ramifications. 'Jesus,' I said again. 'So if there were anything funny about his drink he wouldn't necessarily know it – in fact he probably wouldn't know.'

'Who did the cocktail mixing?'

'The butler, as far as I know.' I nearly added, 'He worked as a bartender once,' but remembered just in time I'd come by that information through less-than-orthodox means. 'The maid who was also the chef took our drink orders at some point. I didn't see our hostess Callie do anything but flit about. Here and there she would issue an order to the butler to fix a new drink for someone.'

'Is it possible someone made a mistake?'

'Huh? *Accidentally* put poison in his drink you mean?'

'No, of course not. If it's what we think it was, the deed was deliberate. What I meant was, could the wrong person have been killed by accident? Could the killer have screwed up?'

'Oh. Yes. That makes much more sense than anyone's killing the doctor.' I still found it difficult to see how anyone could hate or fear this humanitarian. 'I mean, he chose to use his skill to make money from the rich but he also used it to take care of the poorest of the poor. He gave everything away, really. Time and money. Who would kill such a man?'

I fell silent, remembering that famous people sometimes lead lives at odds with their public personas. Often their peccadilloes only come to light in divorce court or once they are dead. In this case, while perhaps it was too soon for any salacious gossip to have emerged, the mentions of the doctor's passing had been nothing but eulogizing.

In official notices such as that (now suspect) obituary in the *Washington Post*, the private nature of the remembrance service and burial was stated, with no details given to the public. That was what was odd about it. Very odd, for such a public figure. If I thought about it, I guess I'd assumed the doctor, being such a private and humble man, had left instructions that there be no fanfare at his passing.

'Jealousy and envy can take some very twisted forms,' Narduzzi was saying. 'Maybe someone Doc Burke went to medical school with felt he had surpassed them in fame, and they couldn't stand the thought. They saw one fawning article about David Burke too many and they just snapped.'

'Wow,' I said. 'I guess that can be par for the course in a lot of professions.' I paused, thinking. 'I would still say pretty much everyone else at that party was more likely to have attracted enemies than Doc Burke. Me included. Callie maybe especially.'

'Why do you say that?'

'She just got up people's noses. Anyone that ambitious is just plain annoying.'

'I meant, about you.'

'Oh. Well, writers annoy people all the time. Mostly reporters do. But anyone with an opinion and a Twitter feed.'

'I see. There's another thing.' I could see he was hesitant to tell me, so it must have been important.

'Yes,' I said neutrally, trying to hide my excitement.

'The doctor was quite deaf. He wore hearing aids in both ears. They were turned off. This was discovered at the hospital.'

'I remember seeing him fiddling about with what I assumed was a hearing aid. I thought he was turning up the volume to hear us better.'

'Looks more like the conversation bored him and he was tuning it out.'

'So if someone were to sneak up behind him, say, and tamper with his drink . . . He might not hear it. There was a little table beside where he sat. Whoever it was could have snuck up and put something in his drink and he'd never know.'

'Would the other people at the party notice?'

I shook my head. 'It was dark where he sat, and the others were too drunk. All except the doctor himself: He didn't drink alcohol at all that night, I'm quite sure. Whatever was in his glass was water or mineral water, something like that. And with the lingering effects of COVID . . .'

'Right. He'd never notice if the taste was off. So . . . he didn't leave a family, apart from his niece and this wife in Sierra Leone?'

'From whom he'd been separated for years. I'd say that's a dead end.'

'No children? Stepchildren? Adopted children?'

'Fatima said there were no children but she may have meant he had no biological children. That would be a good follow-up question. Shall I call her?'

He smiled. 'Let me handle that. If you don't mind?'

I waved one hand in the air magnanimously. 'You go right ahead.'

'Thanks.'

I sighed. 'While my experience suggests Callie Moore is narcissistic, she's not necessarily a killer. Which is too bad; she is such a natural suspect. But it's looking more and more to me like the doctor was the target, not Callie, the more natural target.' At least, she was the target I would choose, I thought.

'The doctor may have had enemies we don't know about,' said Narduzzi. 'He had the cosmetic surgery business in the region locked up – every year he was voted the best by his patients in some magazine poll or other. Personally, I think it was a combination of his skill and his reputation as a big-hearted philanthropist, generous with his time and money to those who would have to go without otherwise. That can generate envy among the also-rans – they simply can't compete with a saint.'

I thought a moment. 'I suppose doctors know secrets, too.'

'What do you mean?'

'I'm not sure. Maybe someone under the effects of anesthesia blurted out some long-buried misdeed.'

'That would mean trawling through all of his records. And I doubt there would be a notation in there of what any patient said under anesthesia.'

'But remember he's a plastic surgeon. What if – oh, I don't know . . . some drug lord on the run from DEA was wanting to change his appearance. He'd blackmail Doc Burke into doing it and then kill him once the operation was a success.'

'You've been watching too many movies.'

'Yes, I have. Or perhaps one of his colleagues bungled an operation and the doctor knew about it and threated to go tell the medical board.'

'You mean a fellow surgeon hired a hitman to take him out that night,' he said. 'You're reaching now.'

'I'm not,' I said. That was the plot of my eighth book. Or maybe it was the ninth. 'But if we have to widen this out to search for hit men . . .'

'Yes, that would get complicated, fast,' he said. 'And remember, he's officially a heart attack victim. Until I know why he was killed, or even if he was, I can't get any further. There was no physical evidence to speak of. It's motive – this is all about motive. And it's so confounded difficult because he was so likable. Usually, people are murdered for a reason and the reason is obvious. Not this time. Everybody loved the guy.'

'Or claimed to,' I said.

'Exactly,' said Narduzzi. 'Whoever did this is a good actor. Very good at hiding his or her emotions and feelings.'

'Maybe someone in his office would know if there had been a problem in the past with a patient or a fellow doctor.'

He sighed. 'This is shaping up to be a monumental task.'

'So what's our next step?' I asked.

'Our?' He laughed. 'I'll let you know. It might be best if you stepped out of it, right about now. If we're talking about murder, all the more reason.'

I nodded obediently. As if *that* was going to happen.

For I had had an idea. Actually, it was Nell's idea, to give credit where it's due. I had dismissed her suggestion at the time but now it made perfect sense.

I had to learn more. I simply had to. With the weight of police suspicions behind me, propelling me forward, it was clearer to me now than ever.

'Augusta, I mean it.'

'Sure,' I said. 'OK. Yeah.'

I had to learn more.

PART III

THIRTEEN

The day of my conversation with Narduzzi, I found a missed call from the woman organizing the writers' retreat I was scheduled to lead.

The retreat organizer was Janika Higginbotham, a slightly eccentric and extremely wealthy woman who had left the Hollywood scene where she had made a killing as a screenwriter (*The Last Mayor, Las Vegas Nights, Opposites Kill*, and many more), had then bought with her husband a large spread in the mountains of the Shenandoah, and put out a shingle announcing that they were opening a writers' retreat in the existing lodge on the property. Technically, 'they' were, but everyone knew it was Janika's idea. She was originally from the Blue Ridge region of Virginia and opening such a retreat had been her lifelong dream, in the local-girl-makes-good tradition.

Of course, these days a shingle is a website, and having done my due diligence I saw that several recognizably famous names had taught at the retreat. I had to say if it was good enough for Mary Higgins Clark, who had held court there two decades before, it was certainly good enough for me. More recent teachers (or gurus as Janika liked to call them) included James Rugger, and I will admit I saw no downside to having my name linked with his in some database as a person having sound knowledge of the writing process. Online reviews for his retreat session, which had been called 'The Breakout Book: Fact, Fiction, and Fantasy,' were all five-star raves. One reviewer gushed, 'He's so handsome I could just die,' which did not seem to speak to his writing or teaching prowess but perhaps a few days stuck in the woods with James Rugger was not considered by all to be the disaster I had envisioned.

I stopped reading the reviews after the Danielle Steel raves and tried not to let any of it get me down. Comparisons are odious.

Janika had left a message for me about the time I was saying goodbye to Narduzzi; I called her back as soon as I got home.

She usually spoke in a honeyed drawl but she sounded frazzled.

'Hi, Augusta,' she said. 'I'm afraid I've got bad news. It's my husband. I had to take him to the hospital with kidney stones and his surgery had a few "glitches." Not the medical term they used, of course. What they said was "adverse outcomes." They promise it's nothing serious, just routine, but they have to go back in there and he is scheduled for the very day you were going to start your course.'

'Well, that's scary,' I said. 'I'm sorry to hear you're both going through that.'

'The way he carried on you'd think he was giving birth to triplets. But turns out he wasn't exaggerating.'

'I've heard kidney stones can be extremely painful.'

'Yeah. In a way, it doesn't affect anything at the lodge but I'd worry less if we postponed your session. I generally want to be on standby during retreats in case anything goes wrong or needs to be done for the attendees. I never thought when I started this how much some writers can drink but so far it's been containable. I don't stay at the inn but I'm generally nearby.'

'Of course, I understand,' I said. 'But are we talking about indefinitely postponing?'

'With this group, yes. I will call everyone and let them know about refunds and possible new dates and other events they might like to sign up for instead. All the usual. It's too bad the way it played out because the earlier month was empty on the calendar. So this makes two months in a row.'

'Empty?'

'Yes, Tina Brown had to bail on her narrative non-fiction course. What a shame.'

'Hmm,' I said. I was thinking about Nell's Agatha Christie idea. The gathering of the suspects. Could I take over Tina Brown's spot? Surely Janika's husband was stable then, just between surgeries. Was it a bit risky having them all in one spot? Maybe. But I barely knew most of these people and it was a good way to get to know them better.

'Hmm?'

'Well, it's just that I have a friend who was suggesting getting a group of people together for a writing retreat. There would be

– let me see – about a dozen of us, a few of them married couples, which as I recall is the capacity for these retreats you offer.'

'I can handle twenty people in a pinch as long as some of them are married or getting along well, yes.' I could tell from her voice she was interested. It's not as if she needed the cash, but I was sure she would want to keep that publicity ball rolling and not make the online calendar look as if everything was dying off. A session by yours truly marked 'Sold Out' would make February look like the happening month it generally was not in that remote region, apart from the ski resorts.

'I'd love to do something on "The Art of the Memoir,"' I said. 'I've got PowerPoint slides and everything.' And may God not strike me dead for a liar, as my grandmother would say. 'So it would be a ready-made opportunity to take over the slot Tina's left open. I can't compete with such a high-powered profile as hers but I can guarantee you a ready-made group. They're all well-behaved, too. I can vouch for them.' Well-behaved except for the last time I saw them all together in one location someone had been killed. I didn't see any reason Janika needed to know that.

The only way to get to the bottom of what I was sure was a crime – a murder, in fact – was to regather the suspects.

'I'll just make a few phone calls and send you their names and contact information if I may,' I told her. 'And then you can concentrate full-time on making sure your husband is safe and comfortable.'

'That's great,' she said. 'Let's talk dates.'

And so a weekend in February was agreed upon and the game was afoot. If I couldn't corral all the dinner attendees who had been at Carrie's house, I'd make up for the absences myself out of my own pocket. As it was, I planned to foot the entire food and wine bill, enticing my captive audience with a free getaway. I'd have to phrase it so it sounded both attractive and beneficial.

And there was the rub: I had to figure out a way to make sure they all knew it was to their benefit to be there. That to *not* be there might look suspicious. That would be especially compelling to anyone with a guilty conscience.

But that would mean letting them know the police might have

an interest in what had happened to Doc Burke. I wasn't sure how far I could go without compromising the investigation. Because as far as most of them knew, the man had died of natural causes and no one innocent of his death would have any further, compelling interest in his passing.

But if anyone at that party had had a hand in his death, which was almost certainly the case, I was sending an invitation to a killer.

I coordinated the invitations using the tried-and-true conference organizers' method of attracting the marquee names first to make sure the others would follow. Only in the case of complete resistance would I bring out the heavy ammunition in the form of casually mentioning the police interest in the case, hinting heavily that Narduzzi would be there wondering about anyone who was not.

In the end bringing Narduzzi into it was completely unnecessary. They were all thrilled when I described the property: majestic views, trails for cross-country skiing, downhill ski slopes nearby (and a promise of decent snow by then), a sauna, and a massive fireplace for chats by the fire. I may have mentioned 'unlimited drinks on the house.' I did hint to certain persons that in addition to the world-famous agent they had already met at Callie's, Rem Larsson, my own agent and editor might put in a surprise appearance, absolutely panting to acquire a memoir or two for their lists with the editor willing to bid top dollar. Yes, there was nothing to which I would not stoop; it was essential they all accept the invitation so I could try to suss out connections and motives. Even one of them missing would be like playing chess without all the pieces.

Of course, I wanted also to make sure Nell Campbell could be there. Not only had it been her idea to have an Agatha Christie-style gathering, but I needed another set of eyes, someone I trusted, someone from outside to bounce ideas around with. And of course she had a vested interest in the proceedings. She wasn't *essential* to the proceedings but luckily, she was available and enthusiastic. The words 'golly' and 'gosh' and 'super' were used many times in my intervening conversations with her. She said she could arrange to be in the DC area and would join me on the drive to the lodge. When asked about her schoolwork she said, 'I'm doing all online courses at the moment. It'll be fine. They make special accommodation. Because of my family situation.'

I only ran into some slight difficulty with Montana. Of all of them, he was the only one with the sense to recognize that while he had always *wanted* to write a book, he was only in the planning stages and had nothing ready to show an agent or editor. Moreover, he had nothing he was willing to share 'out loud' in a writers-retreat type of environment. So with Montana, I had to resort to outright falsehoods. If you have stayed with me thus far, you will know how much I hate doing business that way.

But this was important. This was murder. And the more I thought about what Narduzzi had told me about the doctor, the angrier I got. I knew not only was it murder, it was murder by someone who was familiar with Doc Burke to the extent he or she probably knew he was hard of hearing and had lost his sense of taste and smell because of the coronavirus. Someone willing to exploit his vulnerabilities.

It seemed to me a crime of opportunity, however, with someone lying in wait to find him separated from the crowd. Callie's party presented all the right conditions for the attack. But if this opportunity had failed, they'd find another way.

Whoever killed him had added insult to injury by essentially desecrating the doctor's remains by claiming them under false pretenses. By denying him a proper burial with mourners.

This knowledge fully motivated me to do and say what was needed to recreate, as best I could, the night of Doc Burke's demise.

As Nell said to me, 'Among these people is a killer, someone who murdered Doc Burke in cold blood, and I want to know who it is. Or I will die trying.'

'No need for that,' I told her. 'We'll get them.'

So I told Montana I had put out feelers in New York and there was great interest in bundling his work into not just a book but a video or TV series, something along the lines of a TED talk. I kept that part vague. I told him we could talk more about it at the retreat but that I had to rush off. I just needed to get his buy-in because if he didn't want the space, I would have to find someone else.

It was the mention of a TED talk that did it. I gathered he had approached the gatekeepers there and got nowhere on his own. He took the bait, delighted to have the chance to move out of what was essentially a local operation grooming thuggy politicians and into the big leagues.

I put my head down and got to work on my own novel, knowing that whatever happened at this writers' retreat, so-called, it would involve a lot of detective work and little actual writing time for me. Within a few days I had managed to map out large portions of the as-yet unwritten parts of the book, and within a few more days I was coloring inside the lines I had created.

By the time the date of the actual retreat rolled round, I was no longer afraid to answer my phone, fearing it might be my agent or editor asking me how was I doing. They knew better than to ask how many actual pages I had written but I had reached the point I could volunteer, 'Maybe two hundred pages.'

And if you're wondering, what I told them was true. Caroline and Claude would live to unravel yet another crime in the Dordogne. I even knew who the killer was – the killer in my book, I mean.

I had it solved. I just had to finish writing it.

And now I could try to solve a crime in real life.

FOURTEEN

Luck was with us. A predicted storm in Virginia that would have blocked our path instead headed to West Virginia, leaving our route mostly clear.

Nell stayed with me the night before we left – I had picked her up at the airport and we'd gone out for dinner. As a matter of fact, we went to the same restaurant where Callie had finagled me into this situation. Try as I might to dampen Nell's expectations, her positive spirit was contagious. We *would* unmask the killer – and *not* die trying.

I couldn't say I regretted having been manipulated by Callie because if I hadn't been at the party, would anyone have questioned what had happened to Doc Burke? To whom would Nell have turned once her suspicions were aroused? The police, apart from Narduzzi whose business it technically was not, had not been particularly helpful. 'No evidence, why bother' seemed to be the general mantra of Narduzzi's nemesis, Henderson.

I reminded myself and Nell we had to be careful. Super careful. Whoever had committed the murder had clearly made plans in advance to cover it up by disposing of the body. In a way it was clever – they had not had to dig holes or drop the body at sea, anything like that. For a small price they had let officialdom deal with his remains, destroying any evidence there may have been.

From my book research, I knew that even had someone performed an autopsy, running lab tests on the doctor's blood, it wasn't a given that anything would be found. More often than not, the medical examiners need to know what they're looking for before they can find it. Arsenic would be tested for and a few other standby favorites, but the doctor's medical history as well as his age would almost certainly preclude any extensive testing.

One avenue I wanted to explore during the weekend was this: How did anyone know beforehand Doc Burke had a heart condition – anyone who'd been planning him harm? It wasn't as if he had announced it, apart from what he'd said to the butler.

As Nell and I prepared for our trip, I found it was nice having another human being in the house. It wasn't anything I'd want to make permanent, but Nell was a considerate guest in cleaning up after herself: emptying the trash can in the bathroom and fitting it with a new liner; stripping the bed the next morning and leaving the sheets by the washing machine. I wondered if she was such a paragon at home but realized the boarding-school life probably did not produce many slobs. It would be part of the curriculum to learn how to take care of yourself and your surroundings.

We left with Roscoe around ten that morning, Nell again in shredded jeans and Doc Martin boots. I waited until rush hour traffic had poured into Washington DC via the various bridges. The place had been built on a swamp and was still surrounded by water, almost like a remote island.

No matter how you try to game it, though, you're going to hit traffic and however many roads they build and widen around the area, it's only getting worse. I inched the Jeep through various construction zones wondering why it always takes at least five people to stand around staring into a manhole until at last I could join Route 66. I followed it all the way to Highway 81, which would take us to New Market and Harrisonburg.

We stopped in New Market for a sandwich and grocery shopping before continuing past horse farms dusted with snow and small villages tucked among the silken white fields divided by dry stone fences. Here and there horses in blankets dotted the pastures. Some of the farms had been there forever but most had been newly acquired by the wealthy. The Jacqueline Kennedy mystique had not worn off entirely, although Democratic operations had largely moved to Massachusetts and Delaware. It was lovely even at this time of year with everything dormant, waiting for spring.

'It's beautiful out here,' breathed Nell.

'It is nowhere near as beautiful as the countryside I've seen in Great Britain, but we have some pockets of beauty, yes, we do.'

'It's so *big*,' she said.

'Yes,' I said. 'Not big enough some days. We're running out of unsullied space like this.'

The directions Janika had emailed me described winding roads that wormed their way ever closer to the Shenandoah, climbing the sides of mountains until they reached government-claim land. At last I saw a small hand-made sign for the Higginbotham Lodge Writers' Retreat. In smaller letters underneath, it read: For Peace and Productivity.

Well, amen to that. I turned the Jeep into the parking lot a little after two p.m.

In a separate email, Janika had sent me the code to the front door and the alarm system. She knew I would be arriving early to get the lay of the land, but of course I had not let her in on my mission. She had already assigned rooms for what she believed was a memoir-writing group and I'd printed out the list. I could only hope Janika would not send out a customer satisfaction survey once the weekend was over because the reviews were bound to be mixed, to say the least. In due course, I would fill her in on what was really going on, assuming there was anything to tell. I suspected she'd be thrilled with the whole idea. I knew she was a mystery fan from way back.

I'd tailored my pitch to fit all the invitees. As mentioned, the ones writing a book were the easiest – the congressman and his wife, and Felicity and Fred Overstone. The TED talk lure worked on Montana, but Larsson was a harder sell, since his idea of a perfect weekend away would not include being chased after by hopeful authors with manuscripts. In his case, I played on his obvious interests and fears, promising him the weekend would bring the situation to a head and hopefully allow him to move on with his life, free from fear of – whatever it was. I'd told him Callie would be bringing evidence for her memoirs – I had wrangled that promise out of her, pointing out she'd need to bring her materials with her for a memoir-writing weekend, especially if she wanted my help. I also think, good agent that he was, Rem saw the potential for a book in the set-up. He knew or suspected something was up and I don't think he could resist being on the scene of a crime being solved.

With Callie, I had to go bold, letting her think we were playing a game called Catch the Killer and I might need her help. One of those murder-mystery weekends. She'd been pleading conflicts and so on, possibly a stalling tactic to postpone either showing me the evidence behind her memoirs or admitting she had no proof, but when I threw out the 'game' angle she loved it. If she had a guilty conscience about anything, it wasn't in evidence. I think she had convinced herself the doctor's death was simply inconvenient, which made me start to think she might be innocent of his death, after all.

She had a favor to ask: Could she bring her husband, because he loved to ski? I said I didn't see why not.

In fact, Callie's inviting her husband played well into my plans. I had not forgotten Tommy was technically part of the murder scene and I had been wondering how to include him.

Since Callie had thrown open that door, I tentatively suggested she bring Antoine and Zelda. I left it to her whether she wanted to put them to work or give them a break. She hesitated and I realized that might be a step too far. When I offered to pay for their stay, however, she couldn't think of a way out of it.

'Sure,' she said. 'Why not? By the way what's the dress code for the weekend? Maybe Zelda can make herself useful ironing my things. I just hate it when clothes get wrinkled in the luggage don't you? Even though I tell her to roll not fold, it doesn't seem to make much difference.'

'How did you happen to, well, "acquire" Antoine and Zelda?' I took the opportunity to ask. 'Did you arrange to bring them to this country or were they here already?'

'Why do you ask?' she asked, in a way that confirmed my suspicions their legal status might not be all that the immigration services might desire.

'Believe me,' I told her, 'the immigration officials and I have no bonds of friendship or anything else. As far as I'm concerned, it's strictly "don't ask don't tell". Well, unless people are being exploited.'

'Exploited?'

Clearly the wrong word to use.

'I don't mean exploited *exploited*,' I said, wondering what that even meant. There were no degrees when it came to subjugating people. 'I meant, of course you treat them very well; I can see that for myself. Pay me no mind: It's just an angle I'm working on for my current book, and since I don't employ servants I don't know how these things work. But I am required to let the owner of the lodge know who is staying there. For security reasons, you understand.' Security reasons had become such a catch-all phrase we were all conditioned to snap to attention whenever it was invoked. 'Do they have a last name? I mean, they are married right? Same last name?'

'I'll have to ask and let you know. I just call them A to Z. It saves time. I pay them in cash so there's no, you know . . .'

'Paper trail?'

'You could put it that way. I would not. Besides, it was how they asked to be paid. It wasn't my idea at all. Usually, I like to have everything documented in triplicate and laid out on spreadsheets. And have an accountant look over the files.'

I decided to stop her. This rubbish could be visited another day. It would still, I was sure, be there.

The great thing about Callie, if the words 'great' and 'Callie' can be used together, was that she really didn't take offense. I was pretty much accusing her of human trafficking. Not only immigration but internal revenue might be fascinated by this little domestic arrangement, since if Callie was withholding tax on their paychecks and entering the amount into a spreadsheet, then I was a deep-sea diver.

'You met them in Mandrekka, their native country, am I right?'

'Well, sure, yeah, OK. I was there scouting the location. You know.'

So why did you lead me to believe you knew nothing about the country? That was a question for later. I was more interested in how and why she brought them here.

'Oh,' I said. 'So you brought them over here on a tourist visa?'

'They brought themselves. I merely told them if they came to visit our beautiful country, they should look me up. They were working in the embassy in Mandrekka, you see, so I felt that they would be, you know . . .'

'Useful,' I offered.

'And so they have been, yes.'

'And they are free to go home whenever they wish.'

'Naturally.'

'And when did they arrive in the States?'

'Oh, about a year ago. Maybe more. Time flies.'

Interesting, I thought. A typical tourist visa to the US was only good for six months. Antoine and Zelda had officially entered a pact with the devil. Theirs was a *Hotel California* arrangement, for sure.

I had many things to explore with Callie but for now I let this go. On the off chance – and I really hoped it was an off chance – Antoine and Zelda had had anything to do with the death of Dr Burke, I wanted them to be somewhere they could easily be found. I wasn't going to alarm them by stirring all this up and banging on about their immigration status.

But I was certainly going to ask them if they were staying in the country of their own free will and if not, do what I could to return them without penalty to their own country. The embassy in Mandrekka might no longer welcome them back but surely they had family who would.

I wondered idly if Narduzzi knew anyone in immigration.

When Nell and I arrived at the lodge we quickly began emptying the Jeep of groceries and luggage. She was using the same tote bag which had held Doc Burke's manuscript and I was carrying a Gladstone bag I'd picked up in England years before. I turned Roscoe loose with strict instructions to stay close by and not try to make friends with a fox or a skunk.

I had debated whether to bring him as backup, even knowing how much he'd love it, or leave him with the dog-sitter. Would he be in the way? He was fairly useless as a guard dog. In the end I figured, worst case, he could spend a few days chasing squirrels in the fresh air and alert us to any midnight strangers.

I punched the code into the pad by the door and on entering deactivated the alarm with a separate six-digit code. The main door opened into a hallway where an archway to the left revealed a large living area like a hotel lobby. Picture windows ranged across the front of the room. I could imagine deer or other wildlife peering in, hoping to find food or warmth.

On the other side of the hallway was a door into a dining room, which held a table large enough for about fourteen people. A door at the back led presumably to the kitchen.

Nell and I dropped our bags in the living area, taking in our home for the next two nights.

The focal point was the sort of gigantic stone fireplace one might find in a castle in the Scottish Highlands or a hunting lodge in Wyoming, minus the moose heads, deer antlers, and stuffed trout adornments. Its mantle lined with thick white candles, it commanded nearly the entire left wall.

The setting was ideal for the exchange of writing wisdom and witty bon mots over a brandy or two. I could have stayed forever, pretending to write or actually writing, having called off what I was sure Detective Narduzzi would call a fishing expedition.

A dangerous fishing expedition.

That man was such a worrier.

The cathedral ceiling soared twenty feet above us, and a wide set of stairs at right led up to a balcony ranged along a narrow hallway, off which were doors presumably to the bedrooms.

Furniture-wise, everything that could be carved out of wood had been carved out of wood, including the lamps and shades made of thin bark; large chairs and sofas upholstered in soft plushy fabrics invited afternoon naps. Janika had thoughtfully provided a large spray of winter blooms and branches on a table ranged behind the seating area. She had promised not to disturb us on retreat, which she seemed to regard as a sacred time, but to be there if I needed anything.

I had packed my snowshoes, the only winter sport in which I was unlikely to actually kill myself. I had reached that conclusion after several heart pounding encounters with ski lifts, trying to impress Marcus when we were first dating. He was an expert skier, having grown up near the Catskill Mountains. If you haven't grown up around that kind of thing you just don't know what you're doing, and you can put everyone at risk as they try not to ski right over your inert body. Being from Maine you would think I would be a little more acquainted with skiing, but it's an expensive sport and anyway my parents preferred indoor sports like yelling and slamming doors.

'Let's go scope it out,' I said to Nell. Pointing to the printout of a schematic I'd received from Janika, I added, 'There's my room, and there's yours next to it.'

We trudged upstairs with our bags. I was glad I wasn't barefoot because the whole thing was unpolished wood, inviting splinters. It was clear the aim was to immerse the writer as much as possible in a natural setting, but for most writers a natural setting is a coffee shop or maybe a bar or, in earlier centuries, an opium den. But the exposure to all-natural everything was probably meant to jump-start creativity and who was to say it wouldn't work? Just because Janika had (after much internal debate) installed Wi-Fi didn't mean this lodge couldn't have come straight out of a survivalist's handbook. The Ted Kaczynski model for gracious living, with tips on how to store your ammunition. My stepson would have loved it, as his place in Vancouver was very much like this, on a much smaller scale, and with pigs.

Nell and I opened door after door, peeking inside. The smallest double room with private bath had been provided for the congressman and his wife. I had of course had to tell Janika the full names of the attendees, even knowing she might put two and two together if she had read news coverage of the night the doctor died, so this assignment might or might not reflect her opinion of Carn Hilton's politics. I trusted her otherwise to be discreet should the whole idea turn to crap before my very eyes. Once the invitees came to realize the actual purpose of the weekend, I fully expected a couple of them to drive off.

The Overstones, Felicity and Fred, had been given a large room at the left end of the hallway overlooking rolling hills in the back, now covered in snow – a lovely view. I could see the tracks of a herd of deer in the otherwise undisturbed snow. Callie and her husband had been given the room with private bath next to them.

I had requested a room in the dead center of the action – in the center of the hallway – and my room connected via a bathroom to Nell's. Montana had the next room down the hall from Nell and next to him was Rem Larsson – they too had a shared bath connecting their rooms.

Jumbled together at the far-right end of the hall were three single rooms; two had been assigned to Antoine and Zelda – an ad hoc servants' quarters. They would share the bath in the hallway.

I entered each room looking around for I don't know what. Given the anticipated presence of the Overstones, I suppose I had in mind electronic bugs hidden in the wooden paneling or inside the cute little toothbrush holders Janika had provided. The fact that the Overstones had not yet arrived to bug the place did not dissuade me from this idea; I was certain they had their ways and their resources. But if there was a bug in any of the rooms it was far too sophisticated for me to spot it. I also saw no hidden cameras, nothing that raised any alarms.

I opened every free-standing closet and peered inside every cabinet. Nothing.

Nell, taking my cue, did the same.

After half an hour of this, she shook her head. 'Nothing. I guess we should watch what we say, though. Just in case.'

'Good idea,' I said, miming, 'Let's go outside to talk,' walking my index and middle fingers across the palm of my left hand. At least that's what I thought I was miming.

'What?' she said.

I pulled a notepad and pen out of my back pocket and scribbled a message to her. I showed her the writing, then tore the page out and crumpled it up. I stuffed it in my back pocket to be burned once we got the fire going downstairs. Which we needed to do right about now; it was getting cold even with the central heat.

'Aren't you going to chew it up and swallow it?' she asked. 'Maybe dissolve it in acid?'

'Very funny,' I said. 'Come on. The others will be arriving soon and we have things to do.'

'I'm afraid to ask.'

'Nothing illegal, but we have to get our stories straight.'

I was going to add, 'nothing dangerous,' but was that true? That positively was not true and I was basically dragging a kid into a very adult murder. She seemed smart and savvy and sophisticated beyond her years, but what scared me most of all, beyond failing to find the truth over this weekend, was putting her in danger.

This was undoubtedly why I had let motherhood pass me by. With a mother like me, my kids might not have lived long enough to make it to college.

FIFTEEN

They began arriving at around four thirty. The snow seemed to come with them; each new arrival complained loudly about the roads. Apparently, the snow crews had believed the forecast just like us civilians and were not ready with salt, as well as being short on snow ploughs, so the first dusting of snow turned instantly to ice. I had been prepared for it with my trusty Jeep, but that hadn't been foresight on my part. Foresight would have had me postponing the event for a different weekend.

Callie and Tommy arrived first. She had packed – or more likely Zelda had packed for her – three suitcases and a tote containing a large laptop for a two-night stay. Her necessities filled every available inch of the Bentley. Tommy was making do with one small valise.

'It's a writer's retreat,' I reminded Callie, as I took in the supplies she'd brought. '"Peace and Productivity."'

'Absolutely!' she replied. 'I am halfway through chapter ten. You have no idea how great your timing was in organizing this event now. It will really jump-start my imagination. And with a mystery weekend to boot!'

'Chapter ten?' Now I'd got her here, I was rather hoping she'd forget the mystery weekend angle. 'Wow. How many words?'

'About 2500.'

'You must be using the James Patterson technique. Short punchy chapters, so all the page-turning will keep the reader active and awake.'

'Learn from the best!'

'Totally.' At my nod, Nell picked up Callie's tote and one of the suitcases, and I pointed Callie and Tommy upstairs to their room. The frigid air had blown in with their arrival, and I got to work stoking up the fire with more wood. Callie seemed to take it as given the place came with a bellhop.

Nell and I had discussed how to explain her existence, apart from being a general dogsbody. Introducing her as the niece of

Doc Burke was a sure way to put the wind up everyone, especially his killer. So I introduced her as my niece, who was writing a Harry Potterish book about her days in boarding school. She decided immediately that wasn't a bad idea and she might start work on it right away, 'for authenticity's sake.'

'No,' I told her. 'That will have to wait until you are back in school. This weekend, I need you available to be my eyes and ears where appropriate. If anyone asks, just tell them you're procrastinating. Perfect cover for a writer. Totally authentic.'

This seemed to confuse her but she agreed to go along with it.

'I actually have a mission in mind for you, if you're up for a bit of skullduggery. I'll explain later.'

'Super,' she said.

Next to arrive were Zelda and Antoine, driving a car nearly as antique as the Bentley but in not nearly as good a shape. It was in fact an old Honda with bumper stickers I suspected had been left behind by the former owner. 'My driving scares me too,' read one of them.

Nell showed them to their separate rooms in the 'servants' quarters.' When later I asked Nell how that had gone over, she said, 'They're fine with it. They just put most of their stuff in the center room and plan to use the small bed in one of the other rooms to sleep together.'

The congressman and his wife showed up in a BMW and were followed by Montana and Rem Larsson. They were sharing a car, a classic Mercedes. I learned later it belonged to Montana.

The two spies brought up the rear – the Overstones, Felicity and Fred. They didn't arrive until six. I had a sense of them hanging back, perhaps hiding in some side road as they watched the others come before them, following some manual directive for trailing suspects, not wanting to be rear-ended or forced off the road. I imagined a movie played in their minds most of the time if they were anything like other CIA and FBI employees I had met.

Part of me wished Narduzzi was around, if only because he had a gun and probably bear mace and I did not have so much as a hatpin or knitting needle. And perhaps he had a bit more training in apprehending a suspect. *And* legal standing to ask the tough questions, whereas I only had a healthy dose of curiosity and strong motivation to bring Doc Burke's killer to justice.

On the other hand, I was sure I could flush out the killer on my own, and have Narduzzi send backup in an actual emergency. The situation would be much too difficult to explain to local law enforcement.

As the suspects arrived, they were told dinner would be at seven. It would be a simple repast of 'homemade' acorn squash soup with bread and butter and chocolate cake for dessert. All courtesy of the Harris Teeter store Nell and I had shopped at on the way.

And all the wine they could drink, on the house.

Tomorrow's breakfast would be bagels, scrambled eggs, and bacon for the non-vegetarians. Lunch would be sandwiches they would make themselves from cold cuts and bread and condiments. Tomorrow's dinner would be lasagna and salad from the Harris Teeter deli. I didn't mention the menu to anyone beforehand in case it made them want to change their minds. But we weren't here to enjoy a gourmet meal as we had been at Callie's house. We were here ostensibly for a literary salon, to talk about things written and unwritten. And of course, officially, for me to get some answers.

I had chosen the menu to minimize my time in the kitchen. Nell would act as server. Anyone willing would assist with dishwashing and cleanup.

Callie had offered the services of Antoine and Zelda for the occasion, which I suppose was nice of her, but I wanted those two to be free to mingle, to just be themselves. To forget, despite their cramped quarters, their lowly status. Honestly, if I'd known how cell-like their rooms would turn out to be I would have organized a swap. As it was, they might find it a bit odd to be thrown in with the guests in such a democratic way, not at all what they were used to, I was sure. But that was exactly what I wanted: to put the cat amongst the pigeons.

I had announced free time before dinner for them to get settled in and explore the grounds if they liked, although it was a bit too cold for that. Most of them chose to hang about the fireplace until dinner was served, helping themselves to the drinks cart Janika had provided at my request. I wanted them to be as thoroughly sauced as they had been the night of Callie's party, if only because being in the same mental state might loosen up some hidden or forgotten memories.

Dinner was a surprisingly cozy affair, although no one could fail to notice the guest list was comprised of everyone who had been at Callie's gathering the night Doc Burke had died.

A couple of them tried to cajole me into revealing what was up – were we here for a mystery weekend? *Goody!* (This was mostly Callie, but the others caught the spirit of it as well. Felicity in particular seemed to think a sleuthing challenge would be great sport, but then she would. I was certain her training had included staged scenarios requiring derring-do, codes, and dead letter drops.)

Carn and Mary visibly relaxed at the idea this was all just a fun game, and Rem and Montana got into the spirit by offering to be the murderer and the victim, respectively. As another bottle of wine went around the table (I had counted five so far), I rang my glass with a spoon to get their attention.

'Welcome to the Higginbotham Lodge Writers' Retreat. Of course, the main reason we're here is to write, or if you prefer, simply to reflect on our lives, on what we may want to write about one day.' I nodded at Callie, who gave everyone at the table a broad, happy smile. 'I hope you will enjoy yourselves, away from the hustle and bustle of your daily lives. But it so happens – as several of you have mentioned – we were all present on the sad occasion when Doc Burke passed away. And I think, as none of us were able to mourn his passing properly, it would be appropriate for us to take this occasion to raise our glasses now and toast his memory.'

They all murmured some version of 'Hear, hear,' or 'Rest in peace.'

'He was a saint,' offered Nell.

'Did you know him?' asked Felicity.

'Just from reading the news,' lied Nell smoothly. I beamed with something like maternal pride. I would make a proper sleuth of this girl yet.

'Now, let's gather by the fire where it's warm,' I said. 'If you'll take your own plates and silverware out to the kitchen, please. Nell has offered to do the washing up.'

I had kept an eye on the paned windows throughout the meal,

watching snow collect in the corners. It was a winter Wonderland out there, and I suspected we would soon be shut in. We could always ski or snowshoe out but driving might be dangerous for a while. I planned to check my weather app after dinner to get a handle on that situation.

I let them think we were through commemorating the doctor, watching their faces at the table for signs of relief and a 'Thank God I got away with it' expression. But I saw nothing. They all seemed to be enjoying themselves, not a care in the world. There was a moment of throwing on a mask of sober reflection to mark the man's passing but quickly removing the mask to have a good time the rest of the night. I saw Felicity and Fred exchange glances suggesting banked passions. I saw nothing of the sort passing between Carn and Mary Hilton, which rather confirmed my suspicion they were in a marriage of political convenience, a common state of affairs (so to speak) in Washington.

Callie and Tommy I couldn't read, but the word 'convenience' seemed to be in play there as well. This attractive married couple who should have delighted in each other's company were behaving as if they had struck a bargain of being on good behavior, at least for the weekend, and were determined to stick to it. I gained the impression handsome Tommy did as he pleased, if taking care not to get caught, as perhaps did Callie. Also that I was in the presence of two very strong-minded people who for whatever reason had stayed together out of habit and conjoined finances. I wouldn't myself fancy going up against Callie in a divorce court. Tommy would likely be left owning only his boxer shorts.

Eventually they all drifted into the sitting area around the fireplace while Nell and I loaded the dishwasher. Antoine and Zelda offered to help, but I refused.

'This is meant to be a break for you, too,' I told them. Their reaction was odd, and they kept insisting on wanting to help. Were they so used to taking orders they hardly knew what to do if left to their own devices?

Montana and Rem Larsson were particularly pally. I hadn't really seen that coming, but why not? Two good-looking, successful men of about the same age. I wondered how Rem was coping; he'd been nearly distraught the last time I'd seen him.

If I had a chance to get him alone, I would ask. But for right now, pulling him away from Montana looked like it would be a challenge. I had plans for keeping my promise to Rem about Callie's memoirs but I wasn't ready to share those plans, anyway.

They all settled in around the fire, which threw off a welcome blaze of warmth. Roscoe had staked out a spot just close enough to the flames to avoid singeing his fur.

The picture windows revealed a definite trend toward blizzard-like conditions now. The sense of claustrophobia was fed by the hypnotic fall of snow. We might find ourselves confined indoors for the weekend; that road to the house didn't lend itself to anything but four-wheel drive and even that would be slow going.

I checked my phone for the area, and saw I was right. Oh, well. I certainly had no plans for fun outdoor activities now. I had spied a snow shovel on the kitchen porch near the pantry. It looked as if we might be getting some healthy outdoor exercise taking turns shoveling snow.

SIXTEEN

It was Callie who opened the conversation once everyone was nestled round the large coffee table. I'd splashed out on a good brandy, and everyone had taken a generous pour. They looked comfy sitting there. I was sorry/not sorry to have to disturb them.

Callie had released Antoine and Zelda from the gathering, probably finding it uncomfortable to hobnob with the help. I didn't after all try to dissuade her; there would be plenty of opportunity for me to talk with them later. No doubt they welcomed a respite from her company.

'How do you want to start?' she asked the room. 'Maybe we could all summarize what we're working on.'

I broke in. 'As some of you have guessed, in addition to a chance to talk about all things literary, and to get my comments on your sample pages if you have brought them, I wanted to talk about Dr Burke. Doc Burke, as the world came to know him.'

Carn Hilton raised his glass. 'Here, here,' he said. 'Great man.'

'He will be sorely missed,' agreed his wife.

More comments of the thoughts-and-prayers variety were murmured round the circle, even though we had already toasted Doc Burke at dinner. Fred and Felicity Overstone were particularly vocal in their praise.

'In his later years, when he should have been enjoying his retirement, he went to countries even the CIA avoided,' said Felicity. 'He was fearless. And fun? So dashing. When he was a younger man he had all the girls. Out clubbing every night. Those were the days.'

Clubbing? Dashing?

'I thought you barely knew him,' said Fred.

'I knew *about* him from Berlin,' she said, in a flippant way that did not seem to dispel his concern. 'It was before you and I met. I was practically a kid. He was in school there for medical training.'

'Wait a minute,' I said. 'All the girls? That was never my impression of him. Are you saying he was a . . .'

I sought the right words. 'Playboy' was the only one that came to mind. Not in a million years did the man I met at Callie's party fit that description. Distinguished, quiet, polite, yes. Cautious and hard to draw out, if affable enough. But party guy? No. He didn't even drink.

'I know. Sometimes events change people suddenly. Your hair may not go gray overnight, but your brain circuitry gets, I don't know, short circuited. After the accident he was never the same. It's a form of PTSD, I would say.'

'Accident?' I looked over at Nell, who shrugged. Fatima had hinted at this, but Nell may not have been told.

'Yeah, it happened after I left the country.' Felicity sat back, in her element telling war stories. Definitely a memoir brewing there. 'I wasn't ever sure what had happened or when or where. But I left behind some colleagues I kept in touch with and they said, to a person they said, it completely changed him.'

I looked around at all the faces glowing in the firelight to see if this came as a surprise to anyone. Apparently, it did. Only Rem Larsson said, rather sharply: 'I heard rumors like that but that's all they were. Rumors.'

'Yes,' said Montana. 'Let the man rest in peace. He's earned it.'

Putting somewhat of a damper on my intention to get to the bottom of things. It was hard to tear down a saint. Although of course, that wasn't what I was trying to do.

'Accident,' I repeated, aiming my words at Felicity, who seemed to know more about Doc Burke than I'd realized and furthermore to be in the mood to reminisce. Leaning across the table, I topped up her brandy.

'OK, I don't really know, so this is hearsay, right? Plus, this was about – thirty-plus years ago? But he was driving a car over there and had a terrible accident.'

'Had he been drinking?'

'Yes.' No one liked that answer, she could see. She hastily added, 'Not a lot. Enough, apparently.'

'Was he alone?' I said hesitantly. I was afraid to ask because I feared the answer.

'No. I'm not apologizing for him, anything but that – I hate drunk drivers. To put it in context, in those days we all drank like fishes, it was part of the culture, and no one thought anything about it. Especially in the CIA – the drunker you could get your source, the better, you know?' I nodded. All evening I had been taking a page from the CIA spy handbook. 'These days I take an Uber even if I'm stone cold sober because the traffic is so bad but this was Berlin. The Germans are much better drivers than Americans but they drive very fast, the speed limits are crazy, and foreigners over there think they know how to handle it. They don't. Believe me they don't.'

I was nodding my head rapidly, in that way we do when we want someone to just get on with it. 'The accident. You said he wasn't alone.'

'His fiancée was with him. Coming back from a party, so probably on a weekend night. Although the partying in those days, as I've indicated, was pretty much non-stop.'

'What was he doing there anyway? His practice was in DC.'

'This was before. He did some of his training in Berlin. His mother was from there.'

'He spoke German? I didn't realize.'

'Sure. We all spoke loads of languages. Besides, I don't think they taught medical courses in English in Germany.'

'And his fiancée? Was she German?'

'I don't really know. The place was crawling with Americans, with people of all nationalities. Everyone spying on one another, you know. It was crazy. At that time Berlin was really one of the "happening" places in the world.' She drew ironic air quotes at the word. 'And it was a hub of clandestine carry-ons: We were keeping an eye on everything, the German connections to Libya, Syria, Iraq. The Germans never stopped being our rivals, no matter what it looked like on the surface. A unified Germany was nothing but a threat to us economically. So we kept an eye out. We went to the nightclubs, where we kept tabs on the diplomats. We've never really stopped watching them, even now. But what was different was this: When we needed a little extra help – you know, something to use as leverage, let's say – in every decade there are things people can be blackmailed over and if they were one of ours . . . you know. Compromising positions.'

She turned to Rem. 'This is all going into the memoirs, as much as isn't classified.'

'The doctor wasn't involved in anything like that, was he? Sex, drugs, arms dealing?'

'Nothing we ever spotted. There's probably a file on him somewhere, we kept tabs on everyone, but it would be very thin. He was what he appeared to be: a student, but a student not that interested in books, more out for fun. For all the wine, women, and song he could pack into one lifetime, you know the type. He had a pal in medical school named Greenfeld, as I recall, and together they cut a wide swath.

'Then he met the woman he wanted to marry, and everything was bliss. He seemed to be settling down and then . . . the accident. As I said, it changed him – radically. He kept his head down so he could finish his training early and head home. He clearly did a lot of thinking about the meaning of his life and began planning to make as much money as he could in private practice. But the money was to go to make reparations for what he'd done, so he could live with himself. I think there are worse things, worse ways to straighten yourself out. Most people in that position just drink more and give up.'

It seemed to fit with everything I knew about Doc Burke – from Fatima, from my brief time with him. He had met Fatima after years of beating himself up over causing the death of his fiancée – years of trying to make up for it by being not just a good man but the best possible man. He tried to make a new start with Fatima, who came across as a nurturing soul by nature, but the attempt had ultimately failed. He simply had too much baggage.

What was it she had said? 'You could say it was a car accident ended our marriage, too.' Of course, I should've pressed her for details, but I was so afraid she'd realize there was no reason to be talking with me at all. We had so much else to discuss: the whole weirdness of someone using her name, collecting her husband's ashes. We somehow never got back to the core of what she was telling me about her husband's car accident because it seemed beside the point.

It did sound as if he'd had a complete personality change. It is said people cannot change but I know it's not true. A shock like this will change them, for better or worse.

'Now you know what I know,' Felicity said. She was starting to slur her words. Setting down her glass, she nearly missed the coffee table. 'I don't even remember the woman's name, if I ever knew it. But the whole thing screwed him up in a big way. It's not that he was a hopeless drunk and the accident scared him straight. But he'd been living it up, round the clock. And in his mind . . .'

'And in his mind he killed her.'

'They didn't test him? They must have done,' said Montana.

'Sure. He wasn't over their limit – which is, by the way, very strict. Stricter now but always has been.'

Carn Hilton, who had been closely watching this exchange, spoke up. 'You mean to say he killed someone who was in the car with him and the Germans were fine with that? I can't believe it. They are very strict, the Germans.'

Felicity shrugged. 'For whatever reason he got lucky in the legal sense. There was some proceeding or other, but nothing came of it. Maybe his mother helped with a good lawyer.

'But you know as well as I do, congressman, that sometimes luck has nothing to do with it. For whatever reason – which I would not go into even if I knew, OK? – he was not prosecuted or punished.'

'And since no one else would punish him, he decided to punish himself,' I said, nodding. 'For the rest of his life.'

SEVENTEEN

The conversation moved on after that. I kept trying to return them to the subject of what had transpired poolside at Callie and Tommy's house, but now they were skittish. Understandably they were. It was something they wanted to forget. Innocent or guilty of his death, they were here in a picturesque, rustic mountain lodge to have the good time they'd been promised. Well, they were here to write which is often diametrically opposed to having a good time but my test questions as we sat around the fire, thrown out to gauge reactions – questions along the lines of where everyone was standing; did they say anything to the doctor, and when; did he cry out for help; did they notice anything amiss – drew a blank. The blank of the innocent, if I can call it that. They truly seemed as baffled as I was.

But that was all in the past and here we were, effectively on a mini vacation in the virgin snow among the evergreens. I had given the sauna a test drive before dinner following a brief excursion on my snowshoes, and I had been able to report that all was working well in that department if anyone wanted to give it a spin. For now, everyone just wanted to stay warm by the fire.

Part of my mind was toying with the idea, of course, that the doctor's self-imposed punishment might not have been sacrifice or revenge enough for someone. Not horrible enough. Not *dead* enough. Had Doc Burke not in fact compounded the injury by becoming a revered, internationally known icon? By going from mere Dr Burke to Doc Burke? He hadn't approached Princess Di status as a humanitarian, but he'd come close.

Only Rem Larsson called me on it. Why was I asking all these questions? There was no question Doc Burke's death was anything but what it appeared. Was there?

I had to cross that Rubicon sooner or later. So long as they all thought or hoped it was a natural death, and so long as the murderer thought he or she got away with it, they simply were not going to play along with my 'mystery quiz.' They thought I was just rehashing a painful night for the heck of it.

After stealing a glance at Nell, who was sipping an age-appropriate sparkling water, I looked straight at Larsson and said, 'I believe there was something unusual that happened to the doctor that night.'

'Something that hastened his death?' I knew he'd had his suspicions, but with no reason to suspect anyone or anything he had put his doubts aside. Now here was I, reigniting those doubts.

'Do you have any evidence for your belief?' This was Carn, on high alert for anything that might drag him into a scandal, just when he thought this particular episode was over and done with. Mary had the same watchful look on her face, precisely as if someone had pulled a string in her back. Since they both looked like they might jump up, pack their bags, and drive away, I said, 'Nothing for *you* to worry about. Nor anyone else here, so far as I know.'

'Then why bring it up?'

I answered that very good question in my own way. 'I have been approached by someone with information that suggests the doctor was not universally loved,' I said. 'I mean everyone, especially anyone in the news, attracts people hoping they will fail. Believe it or not, lovable as I am, I have people like that in my life.' I added a self-deprecating smile to show I was kidding. Not even my frenemies in the publishing world much cared what I did.

'But I have no reason to believe anyone in this room had a grudge against him,' I added, untruthfully, of course. I suspected all of them. 'So what I'd like to do is simply discuss it, try to process it for my own benefit if no one else's. It was a shocking event and I find I'm not sleeping well as a result, turning it over in my mind, wondering if I could have helped him.'

'You were the first to reach him,' said Montana. 'That's all I remember.'

'Yes,' I said. 'And if this were a novel, that would make me a suspect. You have to take my word for it I had no reason to do anything but help the man.'

'Nor I,' said Carn Hilton. That was interesting since he and Mary had hung back as far as they could without landing in the pool, distancing themselves from the whole scene. They probably contemplated fleeing on that occasion too but realized the impression that would make. (Congressmen like Carn, even those on their way out, must be hyper-aware these days of the blogger armed with a video camera.) To leave without thanking their hostess for a lovely evening, even when the night had ended in murder, was not covered in the etiquette books.

I decided to chance my arm. 'Callie, if memory serves, you were speaking with Rem about the time I noticed something was wrong with the doctor. Is that right?'

She looked up from examining her nails. 'I may have been.'

'She was,' said Rem Larsson.

'Felicity and Fred? I must admit, I wasn't paying close attention to anyone in particular.'

'We had split up, hadn't we, Fred? I had to powder my nose. I also took the opportunity to place a call to someone. It was something work-related – nothing to do with the party.' She turned to her husband. 'I'm not sure who Fred spoke with while I was gone.'

'I don't think I spoke with anyone at all,' said her husband. 'I just sort of hung back and watched everyone. It was getting pretty cold out there and I was thinking we should leave anyway. Too bad I didn't act on the thought.'

'Too bad we all didn't,' said Montana.

'And then when I discovered there was something wrong with the doctor, what did you all do?'

They exchanged glances.

'Well, I wasn't even there,' said Tommy. 'I mean not *there* there. I came out of the house when I heard the hubbub – the shouting and sirens so on.'

'Yes,' I said. 'You had been at a meeting?'

'The meeting was cancelled so I came home. I wasn't really in the mood for a party so I just went into my office, did some work.'

'On your computer?'

'Yes, on my computer, if you were thinking of getting the police to seize my computer and examine it. Although when you think about it, it would only prove that I was at the house catching up on email, which is not anything I'm denying.'

He said all this with more than a touch of snark than I appreciated. But then again, I was basically accusing him of murder, so I gave him a bit of leeway.

'If you don't mind my asking, who was the meeting with?'

'I do mind. My business affairs are highly confidential. People don't pay me as a lobbyist to blab their business everywhere.'

Fair dinkum. I had one more question for him. 'Did you have any dinner when you got home? I mean did you maybe take a plate of leftovers into your office? If that's not violating the confidence of the cattle lobbyists or the Fruit and Vegetable Association.' I could do snark if that's how he wanted to play it.

'No, I'd had dinner and—' he broke off. 'Why do you ask?'

'You had dinner in town, did you?'

You could tell he did not want to answer and was weighing the fact that I had no business asking against the chance of looking really dodgy in front of his wife as well as the entire group. Finally, he said, 'I went to The Exchange if you must know. The bartender knows me there; he can tell you.'

Well, that was interesting. You may recall I mentioned earlier that The Exchange is where the spies hang out, swap coded messages, shoot each other with guns disguised as lipstick cases, or whatever it is spies do. You would think by gathering in the same place they were making it way too easy for the people paid to keep an eye on them but, hey. I'd have to ask James Rugger one day, although I doubted he knew. Like me, he just made stuff up for a living.

'But take my advice,' said Tommy. 'This is not an occasion for amateurs to ask questions. There's no point to it – the man died of natural causes, but for all you know it could be riling up the wrong people unnecessarily.'

'My husband's right,' said Callie. He looked at her, surprised. I imagined it wasn't often he heard those words from her lips. 'The media has gone away, lost interest – it was a seven-day wonder. I mean I feel terrible for the man but . . . I thought this was supposed to be a fun weekend. You promised.'

I knew children who could reproduce that exact expression, the little red pout, the trembling lip, when their trip to Disneyland had been cancelled.

'There, there,' said Tommy, patting her hand.

I waited for her to stomp her feet and cry. How did he stand it? I wondered.

'Anyway,' I continued. 'When it became evident there was a problem with the doctor, what did you all do?'

Montana said, 'I started giving him CPR, as you know, but anyone could tell it was a lost cause. Then the butler took over – wasn't it the butler?'

'It was Felicity.'

'That's right,' he said. 'I'd forgotten. It was such a jumble after that.'

Which reminded me, 'Felicity, do you always carry a gun?'

'I never carry a gun – what do you mean? I do know karate.'

Of course she was lying. I saw her pull out the little gun clear as day, but I had no recourse except to say, 'Liar, liar, pants on fire.' Instead I let it go, as it didn't seem important. No one had been shot that night, after all. Only poisoned.

'I hope you didn't bring it with you,' is all I said. Even though I knew she must have a concealed carry permit, given her profession, I was not comfortable with the idea of anyone on the premises running around with a gun, however professionally handled.

Almost done now.

'Rem, I saw you taking a video on your phone. I'm just wondering when you were going to mention that? It would save a lot of my asking people about their movements, wouldn't it?'

'It would but it was of very poor quality. I'm afraid my hand was shaking and I'm not ashamed to admit it. The entire scene was chaos. I deleted the file.'

Wouldn't Narduzzi be interested to hear that? If Rem subscribed to a cloud service, the police likely could retrieve the video. I wasn't sure it would be necessary, as I was nearly positive it wouldn't prove anything. It could only go to show that he hung back from the action, like most of them did. I guess I'd been thinking all along in terms of a fast-acting poison used on the doctor, but at the time Rem Larsson was taking his video, the poison had already been administered. The real time of interest was at some point before the doctor collapsed. And no one seemed to be able to make a good accounting for themselves during that time.

That was pretty much a wrap as far as I was concerned. I had some things I needed to do, a call to make, and I felt it was best for me and Nell to split up now. By prearrangement, I'd leave her downstairs to see if anything happened – if they felt freer to talk with me gone – while I took some private time in my room. We would meet up later. I was playing it by ear as I had no idea what my next move might be. It did seem like time to put in a call to Narduzzi, just fill him in a bit.

Just, not yet. I didn't really have anything to report. And there would be plenty of time, I thought, to bring him into the picture. Maybe with a murderer all wrapped up and tied with a bow.

EIGHTEEN

I'd left my phone charging in my room, and saw I'd missed a call from the transcriber, Edward Montesquieu. He had called while we were having dinner.

It was close to ten p.m. In New York that would be the start of the evening; in Washington it tended to be when things shut down – everyone seemed to have an early commute, especially the ones who worked for the government. But from the tone of his message, it seemed it might be important enough to disturb him.

His news was brief but rather thrilling if you like treasure hunt-type stories, which I did. We exchanged the usual pleasantries, his rounded up with a warning about the weather, since he knew I was in the mountains.

'You're not going to be able to get out of there before Sunday afternoon, if then. They never seem to be really prepared for a big snowfall no matter how often it happens.'

'With any luck maybe we can beat it out of here,' I said.

'I doubt that very much. It's on the way. I'm looking at the radar map on my computer right now.'

Looking on the bright side, it gave me more time to worm information out of everyone. 'So did you find anything in the manuscript you'd like to tell me about?'

'There's nothing special about the book itself. It's interesting, in its way, but it's mostly a prolonged apology. The doctor was involved in a car accident. He was completely responsible for the accident, to hear him tell it, and he *was* driving, but you know what? The roads were icy and visibility was bad and the pair of them were arguing and there were a lot of factors, but he decided he was to blame. The authorities didn't see anything to prosecute, a simple accident. That much becomes very clear the more you read. He was really beating himself up. Page after page. I doubt it's publishable, to be honest. But I'm not the one to judge. He says things like, "I knew the roads were bad and I shouldn't have been drinking at all, I was distracted. It was a new car and I was showing off for my darling Helen."'

'Helen,' I repeated. 'Did he give Helen's last name?'

'No.'

Well, that was all right. If it mattered, surely there was a public record that would name her. I would get Narduzzi on that if needed to help connect the dots.

'I looked it up,' said Edward. 'I have access to all kinds of databases.'

I should have realized.

'The less said about how I have access, the better, though. Capeesh?'

'Got it.'

'Her last name was Rogers. Does that help?'

I shook my head even though he couldn't see me doing it.

'Nope.' I sighed. 'But thanks, good thinking, above the call of duty and all that.'

'Could you figure out what he meant by the murder he mentioned?' I asked. 'By the way, congratulations on being able to figure out his chicken scratch.'

'Nothing to it,' he said. 'Once you get used to it, it's like a replacement code. That "a" that always looks like an "e" is actually an "n". Anyway, the murder. That was only in reference to himself. He thought of himself as a murderer. I mean it's really kind of twisted: The man should have talked to someone, a professional. Sure, she'd still be alive if not for him but even by his own account, it wasn't as if he was reckless or blind drunk or anything like that. He was wearing a seatbelt; so was she. And if they were arguing, well, it takes two to remember now is not a good time to get distracted, discussing in loud voices who forgot to buy milk and toilet paper. It's one of hundreds of stupid, preventable accidents that happen just that way every day, I'm sure. In fact, I know.'

Edward was a paraplegic from a spinal cord injury when he was a teenager. He had been hurt in a car accident where he'd been driving distracted by a call on his mobile phone. 'No one to blame but myself,' he'd told me when I'd first met him. He'd been helping me research some obscure topic I needed to understand for one of my books, a topic even Google couldn't help me with. Something about guns and blanks and residue, as I recall. 'But for years I tried to blame everyone unlucky enough to wander into my orbit.'

'At least your transcription helps close that line of inquiry,' I said. 'I'd rather been hoping he'd seen Callie stab someone to death.'

'If anything, he may have been the one who wanted to do the stabbing. I did gather she wasn't always a ray of sunshine, although he discreetly describes her, gentleman that he was, as "flexible and adventurous."'

Interesting. So he had known Callie from before, and from the sound of it, not just as a donor.

I said hesitantly, 'I hope this whole thing didn't bring up memories for you. Of course, I had no idea what he'd be talking about when I asked you to do the transcribing.'

'Of course, you didn't know, and it's OK, regardless. Other people's accidents and griefs belong to other people. Mine is unique to me. Besides, his handwriting was the sort of challenge I enjoy.'

'I'll bet.' I never know quite what to say to Edward, but he was so good at putting people at their ease I'd completely forget his challenges. I'd start talking about my latest hiking trip or cross-country ski adventure and realize mid-sentence I was probably being incredibly tactless. He'd guess what the problem was and encourage me to go on. He always wanted me to tell him every detail, and text him the photos. 'But he did mention Callie,' I said. 'Calypso. Right?'

'Yeah. Apparently, they were lovers. I should mention, the list of the doctor's lovers was long. Which surprised me a bit. That is not at all what I thought I knew of the man.'

'I'm just learning there were two Doc Burkes. One was pre-accident and the other was post-accident. One was a player, a woman in every port, and another – I don't know. People keep calling him a saint, but I guess a better word would be a penitent. He had nothing alcoholic to drink the night of the party. I thought nothing of it at the time, but it sounds as if the accident scared him sober. So, he and Callie were lovers? That's all he wrote?'

'I'm sure Callie would think that was plenty.'

'I'm sure you are right.' Would she care all that much, or not at all? She might not want Tommy to know – she'd lose the upper hand – but it was a very long time ago. Before they were married? I could find out but what difference would it make?

'So, dead end?' he asked.

'I'm not sure,' I said. 'Let me read you a list of names. And you tell me if he mentions any of them in the manuscript.'

'Shoot.'

'Overstone, Felicity or Fred. Overstone probably wasn't her married name then, but Felicity is a bit unusual. Tommy Moore. Carnegie or Mary Hilton – no idea what her maiden name was. Remington Larsson. Montana – don't know if that's his first or last name, I can find out all of this if need be. Antoine or Zelda – no last name there, either. Again, let me know if any of those names show up.'

'No,' he said. 'There's nothing like that. Nothing like any of those.'

'Of course, there's nothing to say they couldn't have changed their names.'

'Did you realize there was something tucked in the bindings?'

'Hmm?' I was called back from speculating over who might have had some secret, long-ago connection to Doc Burke. Also, whether Tommy would care about Callie's long-ago fling.

'There's a letter, folded and tucked into the bindings.'

'Did not know that,' I said.

'It's addressed to Nell. Is it OK for me to read it to you?'

I had to admire Edward's ethics but, no time for principles now.

'It's a murder investigation,' I said. 'I'll tell her about it later. Right now she's busy observing the suspects.'

'OK,' he said. 'It is undated, handwritten like the rest.' He read aloud:

> *'Congratulations, my dear niece. When I heard the news, I was astonished although astonished is the wrong word. I always knew you were amazing – different, special, tremendous, bound to do good things in the world. I don't have the words, really, but your engagement is wonderful news.*

You are my dearest girl and to think of you marrying a Crown Prince is only right and suitable. For you are, my dear, a Princess born in more ways than one. With love, your uncle David.'

Nell a princess? What the actual—

He went on, 'Then there is a PS: *I think my manuscript will be worth a lot to a publisher.*'

David Burke had been a writer to the last, bless his soul. Come what may, he was sure his outpourings were worth a ton of money.

What I was wondering was why Nell had never mentioned she was getting married. She wore jewelry but nothing that looked like an engagement ring. We had sat through that long drive together to get to the lodge, sometimes stuck in traffic, more often driving through bucolic scenery and admiring the horses and little villages, up and down hairpin turns and winding roads with nothing to do but chat about our lives. I had told her about Marcus, about my travels to France, about my books. She seemed fascinated by the publishing industry, and I told her it was a business like any other but I couldn't think of a business I'd rather be in.

She had told me how her schooling had changed during the pandemic, explaining why she seemed to be so footloose and fancy free. 'Have computer will travel,' she said. 'The lectures, the reading assignments, the papers – they're still letting me do most of it online. I have to go back occasionally for in-person tutes. But a lot of the teachers prefer we zoom in.'

Not a word about a husband-to-be, presumably waiting for her back home in the UK, playing horse polo or losing a fortune at the blackjack tables to pass the time.

But above all, what was this about her being a princess?

For the doctor had not been using the term as an affectionate term. I had Edward email me the thing so I could read it for myself.

The Doc had literally meant, Nell was going to marry a prince.

'You have some explaining to do,' I said to Nell a while later. I had texted her to leave the party, as I had news for her from 'E'. 'Battle stations,' I wrote.

Then I stood guard outside Callie's room while Nell went in to 'borrow' Callie's tote bag.

The only thing we found in there remotely of a compromising nature was a sketch of a nude man who may or may not have been a member of the royal family. It's not as if any of them would have a tattoo of the family coat of arms on their backsides. There was no diary kept by her dear Aunt Davinia, no letters, no photos.

We took mobile phone photos of the sketch and of the pages of Callie's work in progress before returning the tote to Callie's room. I'd only skimmed the pages which seemed to describe Callie's childhood, during which (she wrote) she had been hailed by her teachers and family as a prodigy. If Rem Larsson had feared some sort of dark revelation, she didn't seem to have got there yet.

My advice to him was going to be to play along, see what she produced, and promise to represent her as the best way to vet what she was up to. Once she showed me what she'd written, I would praise it to the skies and convince her she didn't need a ghostwriter, but that I was willing to review her pages. In that way, I could keep Rem in the loop and get myself off the hook as her ghost-writer. I could also confirm her claims of having dynamite material about other people for her memoirs was mere fantasy.

Now Nell and I were seated safely in two cozy chairs in my room by the window, the homespun curtains framing the constant downdrift of snow.

'That's if you wouldn't mind,' I said, 'I would appreciate an explanation.'

I had told her what I'd learned about the Doc's memoirs. Then I told her Edward had discovered Doc Burke's letter to 'Princess' Nell.

'Just out of curiosity, when were you planning to tell me?'

'I didn't really have a plan.'

Yep. 'Congratulations, by the way,' I said.

'No need,' she mumbled, turning to stare out the window.

'Oh,' I said, immediately contrite – my tone had been on the sharpish side. I kept forgetting how young she was. 'You mean it's been called off. Well, that sucks but, "too many fish in the sea," you know?'

'That's not it,' she said.

'OK. I'm listening.'

'My name is not really Nell Campbell.'

'OK.' What was this? 'And your relationship to Doc Burke is . . . what, then?'

'OK, here's the thing. I'm travelling under someone else's passport.'

'I don't follow. Is this a new fad like *Dungeons and Dragons*? I guess you know it's illegal to travel under a fake passport.'

'Who said it was fake?'

'Stolen, then. Is that better?'

'She *gave* me the passport.' Nell actually sighed as if she couldn't believe I hadn't guessed that. She pulled the document from her hip pocket. 'I'm doing a favor for a friend.'

I was really out of questions at this point so I just let her go on as I stared at the photo of a young woman named Eleanor Campbell.

'Nell asked me to deliver the manuscript. Doc Burke is her uncle. Was her uncle.'

'So you're impersonating Nell. That sounds rather dangerous if you don't mind my saying so.' I was also thinking it was a bit dangerous for me to be sitting here having a cozy chat with a young girl who might be completely unbalanced.

'The impersonation was a risky thing to do, I guess, but I didn't realize it at the time – I was just helping a friend. It seemed like a lark, you know?'

I was casting my mind back to the halcyon days when a scheme like this would have just seemed like a lark. Honestly, it wasn't a stretch. I would have been all over it. The question is, would I have got away with it? I'd like to think I would have. The further question was, would the occasion have arisen? The truth is my upbringing was chaotic, but more sheltered, less mean streets. Impersonating others and flying under a fake passport had not played a big role. I'd been too busy writing for the school newspaper and trying out for the pep squad and hoping to attract the attention of Derek Merk. Luckily for me, the pep squad had astonishingly low standards even if the newspaper did not. Derek's standards also were high. He never strayed from the side of his chosen one, the prom queen.

I tuned back in to 'Nell's' story.

'I heard recently my friend had been attacked in London despite all her security detail, with her bag stolen, and it was only then I realized how this could all go south. The attack was probably random, just thugs, but it did make me realize.'

'That's good. Awareness is good.'

'Yeah. Maybe not my best move, to impersonate someone so high-level.'

Shaking my head, I realized this hare-brained scheme, ripped from the pages of some novel they'd read (maybe even one of mine), probably did seem like a fun thing to do. Illegal and now dangerous but fun.

'So, what is your name? If you don't mind my asking.'

'Pippa Harp.'

'And your friend is Nell Campbell.'

'Sort of.'

Exasperated, I said, 'What do you mean? Cut the . . . cut it *out*. This is no time for "sort of" answers.'

'She travels under a family name for security reasons. Her real name is Princess Eleanor of Herzoslovakia-Bering. She moves under several passports but it's with the full knowledge of Interpol, who keep an eye out for her. I think it's all rather fun, don't you? Having options like that. I came in one of her private jets. You skip the security screening and metal detectors altogether. No one asked questions. With makeup, she and I look pretty much alike.'

'Jesus Christ,' I gasped. While not up on all the world's young royalty and their comings and goings, their pairings and separatings and reunions, no one could escape knowing something of the antics of the beautiful young woman known to the world as Princess Eleanor. Princess Eleanor of H-B, for short. She would have been as famous as a fashion model with or without her title but as it was, she was frequently photographed going to and from ski resorts and beaches where the young and beautiful gather to cavort in expensive clothing brandishing expensive equipment.

'You can see why I couldn't say anything. She's engaged to marry the Crown Prince of Mandrekka.'

Of course she was! Mandrekka. Right. *Of course*. Why did I not see this coming?

'How in the world do you come to know Princess Eleanor?' I asked.

She – the girl I must now train myself to think of as Pippa – shrugged. 'Boarding school, and a sort-of summer school in Switzerland before we started sixth form. Like a finishing school, only we weren't there to be finished. We both just needed a place to stay that summer. It's where we became close friends.'

'Old school ties,' I said, nodding, as if I benefited from those all the time, trying to imagine what the sort-of finishing consisted of. How to Order from a French Menu? Seating Charts 101? Mastering the Slalom?

'Sure.'

I was reminded there was a whole universe of people traveling by private jet in social circles far grander than mine, people with castles and trust funds and inherited top hats and tiaras nestled in velvet-lined boxes and all the rest of it. I wasn't particularly jealous of them – what, after all, did they do all day except shop and be photographed going to openings and receptions? I was simply baffled by their lives.

'And her uncle?' I asked, then remembered something. 'Her half-uncle, I mean. Wait, don't tell me, let me guess. She heard he had died suddenly, under what might be mysterious circumstances. Meanwhile this manuscript came to her attention via the lawyers. She couldn't just jump on a plane, however chartered the plane—'

'Private.'

'Oh, excuse me. However *private* the plane and come investigate his death. So she sent you anonymously in her stead so the media wouldn't get wind of it.'

'Right.'

'And she was alarmed that his ashes had apparently been stolen.'

'Right.'

'But one question, after "why you?" And that is, "Why me? Why not some other writer?"'

'Because we'd read all your books, of course, and we knew you were the one for the job. Also, Callie Moore mentioned you in an online interview she did with a Mandrekka reporter. She said you were helping her write her memoirs. It all seemed a perfect fit. *You* seemed a perfect fit.'

Aha. I'd been right. Briefly, I tried to recall which books of mine had featured people travelling under fake passports – there had been more than one.

'As to "why me," I looked enough like her to pass. I mean, it's not as if anyone was going to do a DNA test. But above that, we are besties. It's what best friends do for each other.'

It was as if she were speaking from a parallel universe. The age gap, the American/British gap, the gap of privilege. Ordinarily, mentioning my books favorably would be the way to my heart and probably a token legacy in my will, but I was seriously peeved and determined to be firm with this young miscreant before me.

'You did a great job pretending to be broken-hearted by Doc's passing, by the way.'

'I was not *act*ing,' she said, 'if that's what you are insinuating.' The color rose in her cheeks. 'I knew Doc Burke quite well. He would come to the school to see Nell and he would always include me in what they were doing – taking me out for dinners and shopping and ice creams and all of that. He wanted to make sure I was part of it. The school was simply ghastly and quite unbearable in every way, you see.'

'Quite.'

She sat forward, looking directly at me, pleading for understanding.

'He knew I was alone up there, you see. My parents are divorced, and each of them has remarried some *person* and started new families and has no time for me.' This was not said in a particularly 'woe is me' kind of way. Apart from the emphasis on the word 'person' which seemed to be a stand-in word for 'monster,' it was a statement of fact. I wondered for the first time if parents comprehended what they were doing to the child excluded from their bright new lives. 'He was a very kind-hearted man and I did love him for including me in those outings so I didn't have to hang about the school on weekends and holidays, no parents or siblings to take me in. It was his idea I go to summer school with Nell. I think the people we truly love are the people who have been kind to us, don't you? – unless there's something very wrong with us in the first place.'

That was nothing but the truth, I thought, abashed to have accused her so unjustly, despite the wild impersonation and despite my annoyance that now the case had been confused by this international, passport-swapping charade.

Or had it been confused? Was this the entire point of killing the doctor? His memoirs, a sort of *Confessions of St Augustine* crossed with the adventures of a real-life Don Juan?

Were they the reason his niece – his real niece, the Princess Eleanor – had been attacked, her bag stolen on the streets of London? Is that a coincidence, London (and other large cities where the Princess could often be seen on Twitter cavorting in fountains) being a more dangerous place than it used to be?

And might the princess's friend here before me, one Pippa Harp, be a target? Does the attacker not realize the manuscript is no longer in the princess's possession, no longer in Pippa's possession, no longer even in *my* possession, but in the possession of a hapless transcriber making thirty-five dollars an hour to transcribe the chicken-scratch handwriting of Doc Burke?

Had I unwittingly invited someone to the lodge this weekend who might want to harm *anyone* who stood in the way of their retrieving Doc Burke's manuscript?

The first order of business would be making sure Edward was safe on the off chance whoever had attacked the princess, presumably wanting the manuscript, had followed Nell here.

Reluctantly (I hated admitting I couldn't do everything myself or be in two places at once) I placed a call to Detective Narduzzi, knowing I'd probably get his voicemail this time of night. I left a rather scrambled and lengthy message – so lengthy in fact I had to leave three separate messages to get the entire story out.

Next I called Edward to warn him not to leave the house, and not to open the door to anyone who did not identify himself clearly as a police officer. Preferably one by the name of Steve Narduzzi.

I looked at Nell-now-Pippa, wondering what on earth to do with her. So long as I didn't understand what was going on, I couldn't keep blundering through this investigation without taking basic precautions.

I pointed to the double bed.

'You're sleeping in here tonight. For your safety and mine.

First, let's make sure that connecting door to the bathroom is locked from inside.'

If she was in danger, in any way, it was my responsibility to get to the bottom of this without jeopardizing her further.

After all, I had to answer not only to myself, but to her pal, the Princess of H-G.

If we all got out of this alive, maybe I'd even get an invitation to a royal wedding.

NINETEEN

The next morning, I made my announcement. I had barely slept but I made my way downstairs around six a.m. to put out fruit and butter croissants and jam for their breakfast, and to get the coffee pot started.

It was the aroma of French roast coffee that seemed to do it. By seven they had all trickled downstairs. Callie was dressed in her best apres-ski clothing in a Ralph Laurenesque design that managed to be a nod to both Scandinavia and the Indigenous Indian population of the US.

I waited until they were all together and had their first cups of coffee before them.

'I'm afraid Nell is too ill to join us,' I told them. 'I won't beat about the bush: I believe she's been poisoned.'

You could hear the proverbial penny drop as they all exchanged glances. It was Montana who spoke first.

'You're joking,' he said.

'So it's a mystery weekend, after all?' asked Mary hopefully. 'She's not really sick?'

A look of relief passed through the group, an indefinable dropping of the shoulders and relaxing of the eyes, and I was tempted to call back my words. I wasn't sure I could see this through.

But I had rehearsed for most of the night what I was going to say and how I thought I could draw them out. Letting them role-play a pretend mystery wasn't going to cut it.

I *had* toyed with the idea of letting them think a pretend poisoning was part of the writers' retreat events, a test of their ability to observe. But what if they didn't want to play 'Mystery Weekend,' and preferred to run around playing in the snow or the sauna?

They had to think there was a real danger to themselves and others.

After all, wasn't there?

Not willing to risk lives, I had told Detective Narduzzi to get out to the retreat lodge on the double himself, if possible, but in any case to notify the local authorities, and – again, if possible – make sure none of these people were allowed to leave. When they realized what was going on, I figured some of them would try, regardless of the road conditions, and I wouldn't have any grounds or legal standing to stop them.

Nor would the police if it came to that.

The fact it would make them look guilty if they left might not prevent them making the attempt.

I decided to up the ante for good measure. I didn't have to fake the tremor in my voice. It was a risky maneuver with no guarantee of success.

'Look,' I said. 'I'll be honest with you. Nell is very ill and I'm not sure she's going to make it.' This had the desired effect. Both Hiltons pressed their fists hard against their mouths in alarm, no doubt thinking of his already checkered career ending with a murdered girl in a remote lodge. Not too different from his usual scandals, really, except his victims usually survived.

Montana looked ready to wrestle anyone to the ground who tried to leave. I was finding Montana, with all his military training, to be a most useful stand-in for the police.

Larsson was harder to read. He wasn't particularly thinking of himself and his career, so far as I could tell, but he looked distinctly uncomfortable to be part of the sort of scandal that wouldn't result in a million-dollar book deal.

Antoine and Zelda looked strangely unfazed, as if this was for them all in a day's work.

So did the Overstones. For them, I was sure in a way it was. But there was an excess of tension to their postures, as there was to Montana's, as if their adrenaline gates had opened.

'Tommy?' said Callie. He returned her worried look with a shrug, not looking particularly perturbed. Another day with Callie, another fiasco, might have been the man's motto.

'I've already called for an ambulance and put the EMTs in the picture,' I said, 'but I think it's poison so any thoughts of leaving . . . Well, I really wouldn't. They indicated they'd like to speak with you.'

'They?' Callie wanted to know. 'The ambulance attendants?'

'No, the police,' I said. I had the satisfaction of watching her turn pale beneath her expertly applied blush. 'Besides,' and here I swept an arm across the nearly whited out window. The snow acted as a curtain, darkening the room. 'Look at the snow coming down. I wouldn't chance it, myself, for lots of reasons.'

'This is ridiculous,' offered Callie. Her ambassadorship must have started to look like a tiny ship last seen on an ever-receding horizon.

'It's more a horror film,' I said. 'But while we're waiting for them to get here, it might be helpful if you all explained your movements last night. Did any of you go outside, for example? Or see anyone else go outside?'

'Why would we go outside?' asked Felicity, not unreasonably. 'You said yourself there's a storm out there and it started yesterday. In the middle of the night, what are we supposed to do? Go night skiing with a torch?'

The touchy tone was interesting. I thought secret agents knew how to keep their cool.

'None of you went outdoors to get to the sauna?'

'We were going to,' said Callie. 'But it was so cold out and we decided against it. Right, Tommy?'

'Why are you asking?' This was Felicity again. 'What does the sauna have to do with anything?'

'It just so happens there is a sort of potting shed out by the sauna.'

'So?'

'It's a place where the gardener keeps his tools, the fertilizer and the leaf blower and the lawnmower and so on. He also has some very interesting poisons. An old tin of rat poison, probably decades old. That stuff is unmistakable. It has the skull and crossbones on it and everything. As a warning, of course, because it's deadly.'

I had their attention now. The actor in me was finding it all rather thrilling.

'You know what's really interesting?' I asked. 'There are footsteps out there. In the snow. I followed them right to the potting shed. But I was careful not to disturb them. Even though, by the time the authorities get here, they may be obliterated.'

Did I imagine it or did someone breathe a giant sigh of relief?

I thought it might've been Carn, but he and Mary were so much in sync even unto their breathing, it might've been her.

'I was able to get some really great photos on my phone, though,' I said, looking directly at them, one by one. 'These new cameras are wonderful, aren't they? You don't need to be an expert anymore to get a good shot. The flash, the three-lens camera that really captures things in high relief if you have the settings right. Which I did. I love my camera phone so much. I got it as a Christmas present last year.'

There was not a sound. They absorbed my lies and gush about photos of the footprints without a peep.

'What kind of footprints?' Felicity finally asked.

'They look like hiking boots to me. But I will leave that for the experts to decide; I really couldn't say. I can only say for certain whoever it was, they weren't wearing high heels. Ha ha!'

If I was hoping someone would make a lunge for my phone, which happened to be in my back pocket, I was disappointed. They didn't look thrilled by the news, they all looked to some degree nervous and uncomfortable, but no one looked like they were ready to knock me to the ground, grab my phone, and run.

This was disappointing. I had hoped for so much more panic.

'Where is she?' demanded Mary.

'Nell? She's in her room, of course; I'll be checking on her in a minute. I told her to keep her door locked – the doors to both the bathroom and her room – and to not let anyone but me inside. No worries, she's perfectly safe. Now. She's young and we can only hope that given the right treatment in time . . .'

'How would anyone know there's an old tin of rat poison out there?' asked Montana. 'How would they know to look there? It would have to be someone who had visited the lodge before. Or maybe the owner . . .'

'The person was seen,' I said, playing my last card. 'But none of you admit being outside. Interesting.'

Crickets. These guys were good. They didn't scare easily.

I was just getting ready to herd them into the living room – that warm room, big and high-ceilinged yet welcoming, with its outsize fireplace. I was reminded of the lovely outdoor firepit the night of the murder of Doc Burke. The night all of this started.

Hopefully this would be the day it ended.

I thought I sensed movement near the door into the dining room. A scuffing sound, a slight displacement of air. Tommy, turning his head in that direction, seemed to sense it also. I listened closely but heard nothing else.

Aloud I said, stalling, 'We just have to wait until we get help out here.'

Definitely I heard something on the stairs. One of the steps creaking ever so slightly. Just then the wind shifted in the growth surrounding the house. Perhaps only a tree branch moving, then.

'Besides,' I went on, improvising as I prayed for help to arrive, 'I think the weapon used against Nell was ketamine. Veterinarians and doctors and even the police use it to quiet suspects. It's an anesthetic. Combined with alcohol it can really knock a victim flat, as it did Nell. I used it in one of my books that featured a fatal poisoning of a victim – a high enough dosage can kill. And Nell is not a large person.'

'Neither was the doctor,' said Mary.

'He didn't drink alcohol,' put in Antoine. 'I tried to serve him that night and he refused everything but water.'

'A good point,' I said. Not having a clue what poison really killed the doctor, and with no way to determine it without a body, was totally getting in my way. Ketamine was my chosen shot in the dark. I'd done research on it and I was counting on them, with the possible exception of Felicity, to know as little about it as the usual layperson.

'Nell wasn't drinking last night, not that I saw.' This was Montana's contribution. It was a small slipup on my part. I chose to blow right past it.

'She has a small build. The question is, who among us would have had access to the drug? Granted it's a street drug and anyone could have acquired it easily, but this crowd isn't really the type to hang around Adams Morgan hoping to buy illegal drugs. For one thing, there's no need. It is readily available in some circles, medical and otherwise.

'I kept coming back to this: Who had drugged Doc Burke, killing him? It had to be someone with access to drugs, like a nurse or another doctor. Maybe a police officer? A veterinarian? Perhaps a pet owner who had access to a vet's drug cabinets?'

'This is purest speculation,' said Zelda, piping up at last. 'I know what ketamine is. But how do you know what killed the doctor and sickened the girl? It could have been anything.'

'I did a little search of your rooms while you were getting your breakfasts,' I said.

Another bluff, of course, but I closely watched their faces and among looks of befuddlement I saw that one person had the look of a deer caught in the headlights. A little fear, a lot of concern. Was the penny dropping for someone?

Interesting.

'And what did you find?' Zelda asked.

'I'll wait to tell that to the police,' I said.

I was really pushing it now. I expected someone to ask who I thought I was, searching their rooms. But no one did.

'Ketamine takes effect in thirty minutes and lasts an hour – depending on the amount used, the person's body weight and so on,' I said. 'I noticed last night that Nell, when she came to say goodnight to me, seemed confused – her movements were clumsy and her speech was slurred. Moreover, she claimed to have seen a ghost outside the living-room window. She was hallucinating from the drug, you see. I put her to bed in her room to sleep it off, thinking she'd got into the drinks cabinet. This morning, when she still wasn't well, I called for help.'

'Is there a snowmobile in that garden shed by any chance?' asked Montana. 'We don't have to sit around here waiting. I could take her into the nearest town.'

'No, worse luck. We're here for the duration. Now I'm going to go and see how Nell is doing. Why don't you all get settled by the fire? Take your coffee with you. It will take the authorities a while to get here, and we've got nowhere to go. I noticed there were some board games on one of the shelves if you feel the need of a pastime. Cluedo, anyone?'

I went up the stairs slowly, listening for I knew not what. The more I thought about it the more I was certain I had heard someone lurking outside the dining room door. But there was no one there when I passed through the hallway.

Halfway up, one of the stairs behind me creaked. I turned and saw Tommy had followed me.

'It's OK,' I told him. 'I'll be right down.'

'I want to use the bathroom,' he said.

'There's one downstairs off the kitchen,' I said. 'I don't want anyone up here with Nell.'

He hesitated, turning as if to go, but he was called back by my next words.

'Get away from that door,' I shouted.

From my vantage point halfway up, I could see a woman standing near Nell's room. A woman wearing a bulky parka with a fur-trimmed hood and ski pants.

'Who the hell are you?' I demanded.

'Barbara,' said Tommy.

'Tommy,' she said.

'What the actual?' I said to Tommy. 'Do you know her?'

'She's my assistant.'

I could just make out her features in the shadowy hallway. Perhaps in her fifties, pretty, lots of eye make-up on small bear eyes a bit too close together.

'I was just . . .' the woman began, trying to think of a way to explain her presence.

'When did you get here?' asked Tommy. 'How did you get here? The roads must've been impassable all night.'

'I . . . I spent the night.'

'Here?' he demanded. 'Where?'

I understood immediately. It explained why Roscoe hadn't raised the alarm. She'd been here practically from the start.

'There was one spare room. Next to the two rooms where Antoine and Zelda were meant to be. They moved in together so they could sleep in the same bed, leaving the middle room empty except for their bags. So there was plenty of privacy for you. You wouldn't be heard moving around in any case but that made it extra safe for you.'

'I don't understand . . .' began Tommy. 'You said you had plans with friends.'

The look she gave him was so forlorn I almost felt sorry for her. *What friends*? But my mind was scrambling to think of reasons she would effectively break into the lodge and skulk about in secret. Looking for someone or something? Was she somehow connected to Doc Burke's death? She hadn't been there that night.

I had a lot of questions but overriding all those was the question, 'Why?'

'Why don't we all go downstairs where we can be comfortable and discuss this?' It was an attempt at normalcy that seem to work. So much so that I added, 'You must be starving by now if you've been here all night.'

'I brought some power bars,' said Barbara, patting the pockets of her parka. 'But I'd love some coffee.'

TWENTY

Downstairs the group swiveled their heads as one to see us arrive with the newcomer.

And with Nell.

'I thought Nell was supposed to be sick,' said Callie. 'She looks fine to me. And what is Barbie doing here?'

'Don't call me that,' Barbara snapped. I didn't know their usual boundaries – Tommy's assistant versus Tommy's wife – but I felt sure Barbara had just crossed one.

'The girl looks fine to me,' echoed Felicity. 'You lied to us!'

I watched the blood drain from several faces. Some were probably imagining the headlines if any of this got out.

I noticed Felicity had retrieved her gun from somewhere. She wasn't pointing it at anyone but held it at the ready.

'Put that gun away,' I told her. 'There's no need.'

'CIA,' she said briefly, as if that explained everything.

Oddly, she was staring not at Barbara, but at Nell, who may have been alarmed but had a good poker face.

'What are you doing here, anyway?' I asked Felicity. 'The real reason.'

It was Fred who spoke. 'We're keeping an eye on Nell.'

And doing a lousy job of it, I thought, if you don't realize you're protecting an imposter.

I would have to leave that for Narduzzi to sort out, I thought, praying he'd hurry up and get here.

'Of course, I lied to you,' I said. 'When I'm on the track of a killer, lying is the least I can do. And better a liar than a killer like you.'

I was pointing now at an angry, startled Barbara. 'You didn't really think, any of you, that I'd leave Nell in her room, with a killer on the loose? You were listening at the door when I told everyone Nell had been poisoned. Were you thinking you'd finish the job someone else started?'

Barbara shook her head. 'You've got it all wrong.'

'Don't try to deny it,' I said. 'Bad luck for you, Nell was safe and sound in my room.'

'She was never in any danger. I just wanted . . .' she began. She wrung her hands for a moment, then with a glance at Tommy seemed to collect herself. 'No comment.'

'Wanted what? Were you searching all the rooms? Why? Hoping to find what?'

Mulishly, she shook her head.

'Why are you really here?' I insisted. 'If we're to believe you meant no harm, what were you doing here unannounced? Were you keeping tabs on someone? Hoping to surprise someone? Breaking and entering charges will be the least of your problems if you don't start telling the truth.'

Involuntarily, her eyes flitted again to Tommy and as quickly flitted away.

'The door was unlocked. I walked in. I've nothing more to say.'

'We'll see about that.' I had pushed her into a corner where I thought I'd let her stew while I cleared up a few loose ends. 'Callie, why were Carn and Mary invited to your party?'

She crossed her arms, leaning back into the sofa. 'Networking. I thought the congressman would like to meet my agent.'

This was the limit for Rem, who started to say, 'I'm not your agent,' but I cut him off. The only way to keep Callie under some control and find out what she had was to let her think we were helping her publish her memoirs. But I'd not had time to mention this plan to him.

'There was no other reason? Come on, Callie, we're trying to solve a murder here.'

She shrugged. 'Fine. I wanted his help with my ambassadorship. I'd asked my state senator and he'd said I wasn't qualified. *Me*. Can you imagine? When you think of the unqualified people who have been made ambassadors for this country.'

'Yes, indeed. We have a continuing proud tradition in that regard.'

'There you go,' said Callie, fussing about with her woolen collar as she listened to only the first part of my comment. 'So I wanted Carn to put some pressure on him to get my name before the foreign relations committee. I also wanted Carn to write a letter of endorsement for me.'

'Because you'd given tons of money to his re-election campaigns. Even though you're married to a lobbyist. Got it.'

'Don't look so shocked,' she said. 'It's how this town works. One hand washes the other. No big deal. I'm starting to wonder if you're the right ghostwriter for me, after all.'

Oh, Callie, I thought. Wonder away. My heart leapt for joy until I remembered my plan to keep tabs on her with Rem.

'My next question, of course, is why Barbara was involved in this plot against Doc Burke. If she was.'

'You're not pinning that on me,' she said.

'You were Tommy's alibi that night, weren't you? If asked you were to tell investigators Tommy was with you the night of the murder.' Pure guesswork on my part, but it had the desired effect. Her eyes, pleading, never left Tommy's face. 'You were willing to lie for him.'

'Lay off her,' said Tommy.

'I will if you tell me where you really were.'

'I was with a friend. At a meeting. The friend had a bad cold so I left early to return home.'

'Where you chose not to let your presence be known until there was so much racket you had to come see what was going on in your back garden. And you continued the lie about where you'd been earlier – "at a meeting."

'But, Barbara, when you learned there was a sudden death at Tommy's house, you agreed to lie for him.' Her expression confirmed my hypothesis. 'If asked where he was, you were to say he was with you the whole time.'

'Why would I do that?' she asked. 'There was no need.'

I turned to Tommy Moore. 'Why would she do that, Tommy?'

'Because she's . . . she's in love with me.'

Barbara, freed from the bondage of her charade of indifference to her boss, gave him a glistening smile.

This didn't appear to be news to Callie. Still, I thought it was Tommy's 'friend' who worried her, not Barbara, and Tommy was probably not completely off the hook in that regard. She scooted away from him, as far as she could get. Barbara looked longingly at the void left by her departure.

I wondered if Barbara had started to accept that Tommy would never leave Callie, at least not for her. Maybe she was here to catch him unawares in this romantic setting, find out what was really going on with him and Callie, see if she stood any chance at all.

I believed that was part of it – it explained her stalkerish behavior – but I also believed there was more. She had been creeping about upstairs like someone looking for something.

Had he asked her to be here? To snoop about?

'If there were questions about the doctor's death,' I continued, 'Callie and her husband, the congressman and his wife, and the politically well-connected literary agent could count – rightly or wrongly – on the police treating them with kid gloves because of their positions and political clout.'

'I say,' said Carn, 'that's not true.'

'That's often true when politicians are involved,' I insisted. 'With a congressman, especially, you can't say what they might do to protect their career.'

'Do I need my lawyer here?' Carn demanded.

'The more the merrier,' I said. 'The suspect easiest to overlook is the husband of Callie Moore. Thomas Moore. Tommy. He is at the house when the murder takes place. But no one realizes this until he comes out of his study wondering what all the hullabaloo is about. Perhaps he's been in his study with headphones on but even through the headphones he can hear something is up. Is he the one who caused something to be up? Why was he home?'

'I told you, my meeting was cut short. This is not a big clue for you to dissect.'

'Yes, your meeting. I don't suppose you can tell us who this meeting was with? No? That's fine. If the police ask what you were up to I'd suggest giving them her name.'

He said nothing. But his expression spoke volumes. And Callie's look suggested she would not be short on words for him either.

He turned to her, palms up. 'It was a friend, that's all,' he insisted.

'You're wondering how I know, aren't you?' I said. 'I know because – and it's the oldest cliché in the world – but when you emerged into the mayhem of the murder scene, you had lipstick on your collar. It was not a shade Callie happened to be wearing

– she had on bright red lipstick, which I gather is rather a signature look for her. She was wearing it when I first met her. The lipstick on your collar was a peach color.'

'A friend,' he repeated weakly.

'But these are mere diversions from the true story of murder.' Callie was doing something on her cell phone. 'Would you mind not doing that now?'

'The media will be all over this,' she said. 'They'll want an interview. I'll need hair and make-up.'

Shades of Norma Desmond, I thought. Ready for her close-up.

'Well, while you make your hairdresser appointment, you won't mind if we try to unravel the death of Doc Burke?'

'You go right ahead.'

'Great,' I said. 'The first I knew there was something problematic about his death, which confirmed my uneasy feelings about it, was when Nell told me his ashes had been collected by a woman claiming to be Doc Burke's wife. I remembered a recent news story: a funeral home had charged two widows, one bearing a fake marriage license, for burial and cremation.

'If this was indeed a case of murder, there was nobody to test. Meaning: no *body* to test. Was someone wrapping up a loose end? Maybe someone who was very, very good at wrapping up loose ends, because it was their job?

'Anyway, someone trying to hide evidence of poisoning shows up with a fake marriage certificate and has Doc Burke cremated immediately, then retrieves the ashes. She mentions a burial at sea. It doesn't matter – it is no longer the business of the funeral home what she does.

'The real wife of Dr Burke doesn't learn of his passing for a while because they've been separated for years. Besides, she's been working round the clock in Sierra Leone and didn't get the news right away. She is a nurse missionary, which is how they met. They didn't have children together. No one thought to tell her. There was only the doctor's sister and her daughter, his sister long deceased, and when his niece called to make funeral arrangements for him, she was told his wife had already collected the ashes and there was not going to be a service.

'His niece is stunned – hurt, but not terribly suspicious – when she learns the doctor's ashes have probably already been scattered at sea.'

'Could this really happen?' asked Montana skeptically.

'I'm telling you, it *has* happened. A woman shows up to claim the doctor's body, producing a marriage certificate to prove her relationship. A bogus certificate, of course. It is in the name of his estranged wife, Fatima Alvarez Burke. Who promptly disappears back into the ether after ordering the remains to be cremated and coming back to collect them.'

'Who fits the bill of someone who could pull this off? In this group there is at least one person with a secret-agent-type background. Fred Overstone is an expert with computers, and perhaps at forging documents for foreign operatives? How difficult would it be for him to fake a marriage license? He is CIA as well as his wife. He may at times claim to work for an insurance company but I think that's an extremely useful as well as boring cover, don't you?'

'It's quite fascinating work,' he said. 'Actuarial charts. You have no idea.'

'Please, say no more. The fact is, to be fair, absolutely anyone these days with a decent computer and photoshop and a modicum of skill could have forged a marriage license.'

Fred clearly took offense at this. 'Not just anyone.'

Felicity was aiming 'shut up' looks at her husband. She still held the gun loosely in her hand.

'But let's leave that for now. A notice is placed in the newspaper to say services would be private and, boy, were they. None of his friends made inquiries, thinking they would be intruding on the family, not knowing there was no family left to speak of.'

'So, who placed the ad?' asked Montana.

'Montana, that's a very good question. I called the *Washington Post*, the department that handles obituaries and memorials, and was told simply that his wife placed the notice. They wouldn't tell me any more than that, but I assume there was a cash card to go with the fake ID to pay for the announcement.

'In fact, the doctor's real and only wife lives in Sierra Leone and had no idea he'd died. She probably would not fly out to claim his ashes but just in case she took it into her head to do so, the killer covered that base.'

'Wait,' said Larsson. 'So, *were* his ashes scattered at sea?'

'I have no idea but I doubt it. If they were, it would not be to satisfy some urge to show respect to the man, of course, but to destroy the evidence of the crime committed against him. Chances are there would be no autopsy on a man of his age and medical history but his killer was not going to take the chance, thinking: What if some stray relative shows up and makes a fuss and demands an autopsy? It wouldn't be the first time in history.'

'I don't see what this has to do with me,' said Barbara. 'I should leave. I've got work—'

'Callie was writing her memoirs. God only knew what was in them, but you'd do anything to protect Tommy.' That was a shot in the dark but at the mention of memoirs, or protecting Tommy, she got very still. That, I thought, was interesting. I went on. 'The doctor had a heart condition and was in an age group where they don't necessarily test for foreign substances. It looked like a natural death – a heart attack. The murderer could so easily get away with it. If only Nell hadn't uncovered these shenanigans at the funeral home.'

'You haven't said *why*,' pointed out Felicity. 'What is the why of this?'

'No, you haven't,' said Fred.

'Do I need my lawyer here?' Carn demanded again.

Callie looked up from her phone. '*Sixty Minutes* says they might be interested.'

Had she lost her mind completely? 'Put that phone down,' I told her. 'You can get back to them once you have the full story.'

Reluctantly, she put it down. 'This had better be good,' she said.

'But these are mere diversions from the true story of murder. The real story. As Felicity says, the why of this.'

'Diversions,' Carn repeated. 'Go on.'

'I think Barbara was protecting someone,' I said, with more confidence than I felt. 'I thought at first it was someone *she* thought had killed the doctor to protect Callie: Tommy.'

'Why should he suffer, being ridiculed alongside her in the media?' Barbara said, looking around the group. 'You know what those people are like. *Animals*. Like wolves. They'd drag him down with her.'

'Protect me from what?' demanded Callie. 'I've got nothing to hide.'

'How about a charge of bigamy?' Barbara said. 'Callie *Jonas*? Or do you prefer Calypso?'

For once Callie was speechless. And I stopped to wonder how Barbara would know anything about Callie's younger days.

'Let me guess,' I said slowly. 'At the time you were with Doc Burke, Callie, you were a married woman. The doctor carried a lot of guilt, and he wrote something about being with other men's wives.'

'Why did you never tell me?' Tommy said. He didn't look angry; he looked wounded. 'When we met you said you'd never been married.'

'I meant to tell you. I fell in love with you and I sort of . . . forgot to do anything about it. I didn't want anything to, you know, delay things. Get in the way. You wanted to elope right away to Las Vegas, so . . .'

It was vintage Callie, but this seemed like something these two needed to unravel on their own. I couldn't see how it played into the death of Dr Burke.

'It was in another country,' she went on, with unconscious reference to Christopher Marlowe. 'I didn't think anyone would find out after all these years. *Or* care if they did.'

'But you did get divorced? Our marriage was legal?'

'Uhm. Well, I . . .'

'You didn't. You were still married when you married me. How could you? All these years?'

'I just, you know, sort of forgot.'

Strangely, I believed her. Callie would forget whatever was inconvenient to remember. I could picture a younger Callie being swept off her feet by a younger, dashing Tommy and – like a child – not wanting anything to get in the way of her happiness.

But was Tommy just pretending? Did Tommy know the threat the doctor posed to his wife's reputation and his marriage?

Did he care? Barbara seemed to think he did.

I turned to Barbara.

'You knew, didn't you? About Callie's first marriage. About Doc Burke's accident. How did you know?'

She wouldn't answer at first. Finally, she said, 'Once in a while *some*body has to play judge and jury.'

'Play God, you mean.'

'Have it your way. You'd do the same in my shoes. Anyone would. Helen Rogers was my sister.'

'Your sister?'

'Yes. Barbara Rogers was my maiden name. I was briefly married to a man named Keller. But now I just answer to Barbara or *Barbie*, anyway. Like a servant, you know? The perfect servant doesn't need a last name. But mine was Rogers.'

'You can't have been very old when your sister died,' I said.

'I was eighteen, and I worshipped her. I wanted to be her. Besides, I owed her everything. And when she died . . . let's just say things at home went from bad to worse.'

'So you had a double motive. You wanted the world to know what the doctor everyone worshiped had done to you. And you wanted to embarrass Callie by exposing her bigamy so Tommy would leave her at last.'

'You're wrong. You've got it so wrong. For one thing, nothing would embarrass that silly cow.'

'How dare you?' Callie said, diverted from her phone screen. 'After all I've done for you.'

'Done for me? Done for *me*? You did nothing but use me as free labor. Type this, transcribe this, shop for this, organize my parties, get me tickets for that.'

'I was exposing you to the finer things, you hillbilly *Okie*.'

I thought Barbara might lunge at her and we'd have to intervene to pull them apart. Since hillbilly is technically a conflicting slur for someone from Oklahoma, the word nerd in me wanted to point this out. Fortunately, we were all saved from this geeky intervention when Barbara took a deep breath and said, 'I was protecting Tommy. It was Tommy who asked me to . . . help.'

'Asked you to help with what?' This was Callie but it was Tommy who spoke.

'Go on, Barbara. It doesn't matter anymore.' Barbara looked at him, instinctively obedient, taking orders as she always had done.

A lawyer would have told her to shut it right about now, I thought.

'To get hold of the doctor's memoirs,' she said.

'I don't understand,' I said. 'How did you or Tommy know what was in his memoirs? That they even existed?'

Again, Barbara looked to Tommy for permission before speaking.

'Tommy got this . . . this demand for money.'

'Blackmail, you mean?'

'Yes,' said Tommy. 'It was blackmail. Whoever it was told me to leave cash at a dead drop location and I did. I paid them once, but they came back wanting more. I knew I'd never be free of whoever it was until I got hold of the memoirs.'

'How did you know they had them?'

'They sent a photocopy of the pages having to do with Callie.'

'Handwritten?'

'Typed.'

So someone besides me had transcribed the pages or had them transcribed. I was thinking a dead drop location sounded like something from a spy movie. And while a lot of people watched spy movies, the only professional spies in the room were Felicity and Fred. I willed myself not to stare at them.

I said, 'Like Robert Hanssen, the FBI agent who passed secrets to Russia by hiding classified papers under a footbridge in Northern Virginia.'

'Exactly. In fact, they told me to use a spot in the park not far from there. If I didn't do it by a certain date and hour they'd go to the press and put an end to Callie's dreams of an ambassadorship.'

'Go on.'

'That's it.'

'That's far from it. You say they wanted more money.'

'Yes.'

'Meaning they'd kept a copy?'

'Yes. They told me they'd leave the originals but finally I realized I was being played. They might have hundreds of copies. I had to hit them back, harder.'

'Why not just go to the police?'

'I was going to. But I knew once they were involved, it would be totally out of my control. Then Barbara here said she'd handle it.'

'This demand for money, did it come to your house or to your office?'

'The office.'

'Why didn't they try Callie for money? Isn't it logical she'd want to cover this up, even more so than you?'

All eyes in the room swiveled over to Callie.

'I'd already paid them.'

OK. 'Paid them not to tell your husband he was not legally your husband.'

'Right.'

'And they gave you the doctor's memoirs – or at least a copy – in return for the cash.'

'Right.'

'Just out of curiosity, how much money?'

She mumbled something.

'How much?'

'A hundred thousand.'

Jiminy Cricket. I looked at Tommy and saw the blood drain from his face. I wondered how much he'd paid, but it didn't seem to matter for the moment. I didn't want to lose Callie while I had her attention.

'And did they give you the memoirs?' I asked.

'Yes. I thought that was the end of it. How was I to know the greedy bastards would go to Tommy for more?'

'Bastards, plural. Meaning more than one?'

'I don't know, do I? Maybe it was one person. But whoever it was had a lot of nerve.'

'I'd agree with you there. So, you got a full copy of Doc Burke's memoirs, not just the pages pertaining to your marital status?'

'Yes.'

Something wasn't adding up.

'You only got the relevant pages?' I asked Tommy, who nodded.

Which meant . . . which meant Tommy never saw the parts of the doctor's narrative where he had done his big mea culpa over the car accident. Unless . . .

'What did you do with the doctor's memoirs, Callie?'

'What do you think? I burned them. In thc outdoor firepit.'

'You didn't read the whole thing?'

'Nah. Someone put sticky notes on the pages having to do with me. I didn't care about the rest. *Bor*-ing.'

This was so completely in keeping with her character I believed it.

'When did you burn them?'

'I don't know. A few days later. First I put them in my office safe and then I thought I'd better get rid of them.'

'The office safe. In your home office.'

'Yep.'

'A combination safe?'

'Yep.'

'Who knew the combination?'

'No one. It's written on a piece of paper I kept under my desk blotter.'

I looked at the people she called A to Z, Antoine and Zelda.

'Don't look at us,' said Zelda. 'I knew the combination was "hidden" like that – a silly place to hide it and a combination too easy to guess – her birthday – but I never would open the safe. Neither would my husband.'

I was thinking Tommy might have found the combination, even if he didn't already know it.

And there was Barbara, who had frequent access to the house and home office, doing her various dogsbody chores. I looked at her.

'Don't look at me,' Barbara said. 'I never opened the safe.'

'But you were often at the house. Helping Callie with her party planning, bringing files to Tommy, making yourself indispensable.'

'I never opened the safe,' she repeated.

I believed this virtuous denial, although I didn't imagine for one minute she didn't take advantage of her access to snoop around the house, keep an eye on any signs of progress with Callie's own memoirs, paw through documents and family albums. My brain was churning with the possibilities.

'You didn't *need* to open the safe,' I said finally. 'I mean, why would the blackmailer send Doc Burke's entire document to Callie, but then turn around and send only a few pages to her husband?'

Rem and Montana looked at each other. 'To save postage?' Rem said, smiling to show he was joking.

'I don't think so. They would send the whole thing to Tommy's office, helpfully marked with sticky notes as they did for Callie.' I looked at Barbara. 'You. You sorted Tommy's mail every day. Didn't you?'

Barbara opened her mouth to speak, but her answer was drowned out by the sound of an approaching helicopter.

The road must have become impassable by car. It had to be a search-and-rescue team.

Help was on the way.

'You read the whole thing, didn't you? And saw the parts not just about Callie, but about your sister. And you showed the pages having to do with Callie to Tommy, thinking if he paid the demanded blackmail money, the whole thing would just go away.

'But Tommy asked for your help, knowing you'd do anything he asked. Including murder the author of the memoirs once it became clear the blackmailer wasn't going to go away.'

'No,' she said. 'It wasn't like that.'

'No,' I agreed. 'I don't think it was. The man you regarded as the murderer of your sister had been handed to you. And you realized you could help Tommy *and* avenge your sister – in one strike.'

'So, who was the blackmailer?' Barbara demanded.

'In part, you were.'

'That makes no sense. You're crazy. Tommy told me to find out who it was. That's why I was here. To look around while people were out of their rooms and see if there was anyone here who wasn't what they appeared. You stopped me before I got very far.'

'You were, after the fact, part of the blackmail scheme. Although you didn't profit from it – money wasn't what you were after. You hoped that the scales would at last fall from Tommy's eyes once he knew the truth about Callie. That's partly why you only showed him the relevant pages once you had the doctor's memoirs in your possession. Unlike Callie, you had read the whole thing. And realized your sister's killer, as you thought of him, had been delivered into your hands. In his own words, he'd condemned himself.

'You must have been torn, perhaps hoping if Callie got the

ambassadorship, she might go to Mandrekka alone and you'd have Tommy all to yourself. Especially once, as I said, the scales had fallen from his eyes.

'But you misjudged Tommy's reaction. He loved Callie, despite everything. Despite his occasional exasperation with her. He wanted to protect her.'

I almost said, 'despite the infidelities,' but I didn't want to send Callie off on a tantrum just then.

'He wanted this ambassadorship for her because *she* wanted it so much. He also saw the potential embarrassment to himself if this unlawful marriage was made public – that Callie had fooled him over so many years. You wanted to save him from that embarrassment.'

'I told you, I just sort of forgot,' said Callie.

'You thought you knew Tommy, Barbara. But you did not. Callie knew him, but you couldn't see the man he was. Love makes fools of us all, doesn't it?'

'You're wrong,' she said.

'It not only made a fool of you, Barbara, it made you a murderer. You killed a harmless man because you thought his memoirs would tarnish your beloved Tommy.'

'Harmless?' she said. '*Harmless*? He killed my sister.'

'And spent the rest of his life trying to make reparation for her death. But combined with your need to avenge your sister, the dual motives proved irresistible, pushing you right over the edge.'

'But . . .' This was Mary. 'But who was the blackmailer? Who blackmailed Callie to begin with?'

'Someone who hated Callie, for a start. Someone who needed money to be free of her. Someone who got hold of Doc Burke's manuscript and saw how valuable its contents were, how much Callie, hopeful ambassadress, would pay to keep the contents secret.

'The one who best fits the bill is Zelda. But of course, Antoine was in on it.'

'Nonsense! You can't prove this,' said Zelda.

She may have been right, although their connection to the embassy in Mandrekka, where the doctor had been awarded an honorary citizenship, indicated otherwise. The dates of this honor being bestowed and their employment at the embassy would line up, if so. If the doctor stayed in rooms at the embassy, as he most likely did, he'd likely have had his memoirs in his luggage, so he could update them with this latest honor.

Most people working in an embassy are skilled at sussing out people's secrets. American embassy employees are often accused of being spies. Because so often, they are.

I was more interested in avenging the doctor. He'd had so much more to give to the world, and the chance to give more had been stolen from him.

Outside the sound of a helicopter had been joined by the unmistakable roar of a snowmobile. I ran to look out the front window. The person at the wheel came to a halt by the front door and pulled off his goggles and helmet.

DCI Narduzzi to the rescue.

EPILOGUE

A few months later, the appointment of Callie Moore to the ambassadorship of Mandrekka was announced. I should have known: It would take a lot more than a little local scandal to stop her.

She and Tommy, staying together in the honored custom of political marriages, would be leaving DC before the end of the year. I assumed their lawyers took care of that pesky business of Callie's first marriage and they were now properly wed.

How did this happen, you may be wondering? You may well wonder, but then, you probably live someplace normal, like Iowa. Callie became credited with – grabbed credit for – saving the life of Doc Burke's niece. That his niece was never in real danger was beside the point, but the garbled account repeated in the mainstream media had the desired effect of raising Callie from relative obscurity if not disgrace to being the first name thought of, behind closed doors in the halls of power, for the US ambassadorship to Mandrekka.

I refuse to be bitter about this travesty. I do, however, often fear for my country.

About the time of this appalling announcement, I was on the phone with my agent Holly. I had jokingly mentioned in an email I'd recently met someone who was writing a memoir of his time working for the IRS. Holly loved the idea (IRS memoirs apparently are hot right now), knows just the right publishers (she predicts a bidding war), and begged me to have the author get in touch.

'But that's not why I wanted to talk with you,' she said. 'Tell me the whole story of Doc Burke. There's a book in this somewhere. Let's start with: How was it done? The poisoning?'

I replied, 'It was a conjuring trick. A magician's trick. The eyes of the audience must be kept focused on the right hand, concealing what the left hand is doing. The goal is to divert attention from what is really happening while the actual magic is taking place somewhere else. In this case, Baked Alaska was the diversion, it being a showcase of a dessert. We know now that Callie insisted on it at Barbara's urging.

'Zelda said she had tried to talk Callie into something simpler but Callie insisted. She wanted to impress and be talked about as a grand hostess, a famous thrower of parties, and Barbara had convinced her this was the way. Callie got it into her head any ambassadorship required hostessy skills, which is true. She told Zelda one of the guests was from Alaska and she wanted to honor that guest. As it happens that was not true. A silly lie thrown in to persuade her this dessert was necessary.

'While all eyes are on the flames of the Baked Alaska, Barbara eased her way out from the trees surrounding the house, dressed in black, and slipped the poison in the doctor's drink on the table by his chosen seat.'

'No one saw her?'

'No one did. She'd parked down the road. It's a remote house on a big plot of land. She thought Tommy would be at a meeting so even though the crime took place on Tommy's property, she thought he wouldn't be implicated. She may have been hoping in her heart of hearts that Callie would be implicated. Callie in prison for murder would certainly free up Tommy's time for her, Barbara.'

'How did she get the poison?'

'Do a search online. You'll see. You can buy anything you want using a Tor browser. When the police went through her search history, they could see her searches for fast-acting poisons. It could have been anything, but nicotine is the hands-down favorite for most poisoners wishing to escape detection.'

'Which would be most of them.'

'Right. Besides, there's enough nicotine in a few stop-smoking patches to kill anyone, and you don't need the dark web to buy them. All you have to do is soak them in water. It's tasteless and odorless – although in this case, with the victim's senses impaired, those things didn't matter.

'Callie, meanwhile, created an even greater scene by adding alcohol to the Baked Alaska, making the flames go ever higher, making people step away and into the surrounding shadows. She was wearing her black elbow-length gloves and later I thought it was to help hide what she was doing in the darkness, like a magician. Everyone's focus was on not catching their clothing in the flames, on keeping the flames from the overhanging tree, also – not on what Callie or anyone else was up to.'

'But what happened to the glass the doctor drank from? That glass must have had the dregs of poison.'

'It went missing, or so it was thought. Antoine and Zelda, the butler and the housekeeper, thought it had been broken or thrown away, maybe into the river, maybe into the forested area around the house. But by the time anyone thought to wonder about it officially, too much time had passed, anyway. One of the EMT specialists that night noticed there was melted glass in the outdoor firepit. But all he did was make a note of it. You have to keep in mind, no one thought it was murder. He was just being diligent.

'Still, it was a clue, the only small clue there was that something odd had happened the night Doc Burke was murdered. The big clue being a stranger, impersonating his wife, later coming to claim his remains. That glass must have contained poison at one time in the evening or why would anyone have bothered to toss it in the firepit?'

'So, was it a spur-of-the-moment crime?'

'No, but Barbara did have to act fast and improvise. On any other given day, she'd have had to track the doctor down in his office or somewhere else far more open. But when she learned of the dinner party from Tommy, she felt luck was on her side. It was to her a sign. She knew the house, she knew the layout, and she knew the doctor would be there. So she made up her mind, do or die. Her hyper-efficient nature took over and, for the love of Tommy, she eliminated any potential threat to him. At the same time, avenging her sister's death.'

'How did you know he was poisoned there at Callie's?' Holly asked. 'Maybe he was poisoned before he ever got to the dinner.'

'It depends on the poison, of course. I too thought he may have been poisoned earlier, perhaps with something disguised in one of the capsules used to treat his heart condition. There's no telling when or where that could have happened.'

'And at the party, during cocktails?'

'I wondered about that, too. Had something been put in his

drink to upset his stomach or give him a headache so he might ask his hostess for an over-the-counter remedy? That seemed unnecessarily complicated, inserting that extra step.'

'How about during the meal?'

'There would have been too many witnesses to someone's tampering with his food. But once we were all outside, Barbara was free to act. Again, she was instrumental in getting Baked Alaska on the menu, and the safest – and most dramatic – way to set it aflame was to do it outdoors.

'There was a lot of drinking, a bit of chaos and laughter, and it was dark, the only light coming from the fire pit. Dark except for when the Baked Alaska was set on fire, and even then the light was localized, like a spotlight. In fact, the dessert was Callie's reason for the near darkness, to dramatize the moment when the alcohol was set alight by the butler. And it was in this near darkness the killer – Barbara – tampered with the drink.

'The doctor had chosen that rather remote chair and established it as his base, putting his glass down on the little side table while he mingled. Barbara tampered with it, in no danger of being spotted. Everyone's attention was focused on the fiery dessert and she could act with impunity, staying in the shadows.'

'She got lucky,' said Holly. 'If we can call it that.'

'If she'd failed that night for some reason, I've no doubt she would have tried again. When much later the doctor's death began to seem suspicious with all that carry-on at the funeral home, it was too late to look for evidence. His body, containing the only remaining evidence, had disappeared. That wasn't luck. That was Barbara, covering every base.'

'But why Doc Burke?' she asked. 'That was the overriding question.'

'Why poison this man who was not only harmless but had done so much good in the world? That's what made it so bizarre, so nearly impossible. I kept thinking I had it all wrong. He'd been killed instead of some other intended target. Some more deserving target.

'But I had to take the case as it was, with the evidence that was there. I had to think like a murderer; a murderer desperate to get rid of this harmless gentleman who was for some reason a threat or needed, in the killer's mind, to be punished. I kept coming back to that, too. Why Doc Burke? Was it something in his past? Something he'd witnessed?'

'You are talking like a detective,' said Holly.

'Sorry. It's becoming an occupational hazard.'

'The PI license hasn't gone to your head, has it?'

'Of course not. But this is the second time I've been drawn into a crime – a real crime, not one of my books – and actually managed to solve it.'

'It's taking you away from your writing,' said Holly sternly. I reminded myself Holly relied on her authors to help her pay the rent. Solving murders was all well and good but it didn't pay her bills or mine. 'And while that's great for book publicity,' she went on, 'it must be interfering with your next book. Should I talk to your editor about getting an extension?'

'No. I'll be fine, honest. Getting right back to it today. Honest.' I was aware that the two 'honests' probably cancelled each other out in terms of believability, especially since I had a lunch date with a friend that would get me back to my desk, a little the worse for a glass of wine, late in the afternoon.

'The *New York Times* is on this story, by the way, wanting to interview you.'

'No kidding. That's wonder—.'

'I told them you wouldn't be available until next week.'

'Next week?'

'You have to go back to work, Augusta. Something really must give here.'

Great. Now I not only had an agent, I had a nanny. You'd think she'd be proud of me, but no.

'Do you want to hear the rest or not?'

'Sure.' See, how complicit she was? How enabling? The woman was sending mixed messages. But I thought I might ask her to get me that extension after all. Just in case.

'So. There was no possibility this death was accidental – that one glass of port, for example, had been mistaken for another. That he put down his glass and picked up the wrong one. It turns out he didn't drink alcohol – and we now know there was a reason he was teetotal – so with water, he would have noticed most poisons right away. The fact his sense of smell was compromised led me astray, thinking it had to be someone with aceess to his medical records, but only for a while.'

'With Doc Burke being the only teetotaler, the killer knew, or believed . . .'

'The killer believed that would have to be taken into account. Barbara, part of the planning for the party, knew his preferences. Alcohol can hide smells and tastes far better than water or the flavored sparkling water he was drinking. It looked like he had been drinking sparkling rosé most of the night while the rest of us drank pinot noir and port and God knows what else. He stuck with his fake alcoholic drink. It was his wife Fatima who later told me he always did that to avoid the type of people who, seeing him drinking plain water, would try to force a "real" drink on him. This was equivalent to telling a junkie that one little shot of heroin wouldn't hurt. He avoided the whole thing with his glass of pretend-rosé wine.'

I paused, remembering his struggles to overcome, only to end up murdered. It still made me angry to think of the loss.

'There were so many suspects,' I finally said. 'I couldn't discount the idea Callie's husband may have had a lover – someone who might have been persuaded to kill the doctor to protect Tommy for whatever reason. He himself was at home and could have let this accomplice in at any time, and given her instructions on what to do. But overall, Barbara's motivation was overwhelming. Not only was she out for revenge, she was besotted with Tommy and would've done anything for him, anything to have him in her life. Anything he asked. Anything he even *suggested* might be helpful.

'And she so nearly got away with it! No one was investigating until we – Narduzzi and I – realized it was murder and not a natural death. And we didn't realize *that* until what I thought was Doc Burke's niece turned up with this wild story of her uncle's ashes vanishing after being given to someone pretending to be his wife. That might not shout "murder," but it certainly shouts foul play of some kind. The mystery became, what happened to the good doctor's ashes. And who "Fatima Alvarez Burke" really was.

'The man who runs Martin's Funeral Home told police the woman who collected the doctor's ashes, the woman we now know was Barbara, had said she was separated from her husband but was simply trying to do right by him. By the way, the police may be looking into practices at Martin's, but the fact is, they did nothing particularly illegal. During the pandemic, standards slipped and never were entirely restored.'

'Good to know.'

'Anyway, later I spoke with a friend of the doctor's from his younger days. Dr Greenfeld. Doc Burke mentioned him in the memoirs as a close friend. He is currently working in New York. We talked about how the Doc had started doing pro bono surgeries after he crashed the car with his fiancée in it, disfiguring her, killing her.

'As I spoke with him, a motive for the doctor began to emerge. By that I mean, the motive behind his radical personality change.

'Dr Greenfeld is a psychiatrist specializing in facial dysmorphia, a condition in which a person has a warped image of their appearance. The sort of people who have repeated facelifts and nose jobs and so on even though the surgeries are unnecessary. I could see easily how the two doctors had continued to cross paths over the years, the man specializing in facial reconstruction and the man specializing in persons who don't see how they really appear to the world outside their own mirrors. I emailed Dr Greenfeld to see if he would FaceTime me, as I knew from his website this was a service he offered his patients. I told him I'd be willing to pay for his time.

'He was reluctant to talk. He kept saying it was all water under the bridge, but then said the truth was Doc Burke was at one time just an ordinary if accomplished man, everyone's friend, the type of man who never met a stranger. He was also completely drunk half the time, but no one held that against him. People loved him. That was a theme of this case: the victim's overall wonderfulness.

'But what people liked were two different men. There were two *faces* of the same man, as it were: the rather foolish young man and the man he became after a horrible accident for which he was responsible. He went from being a "hail fellow well met" type to being a sober, straightlaced, practically humorless man who suddenly started doing pro bono surgeries for poor children in war- and poverty-ravaged countries. He went from a career treating fashionable wealthy women with nothing much wrong with them to trying to change the lives of these poor children.

'What was that about? Most people feel guilty for a brief time and then move on. He'd never shown this charitable side before. In fact, if his friend Dr Greenfeld was to be believed he was totally into medicine for the money – for fast cars and women, a fancy penthouse, luxury vacations. He was a very good surgeon, and later charged a fair price for an excellent job. But he pretty much followed the scriptures in giving away much of what he had to the poor and working for the poor – making sure the proceeds from his wealthy clients went to fund his good works. What in the world happened?'

'The accident, of course.'

'Yes. He'd been driving over the speed limit, distracted, himself too close to the legal alcohol limit. He crashed the car, sent it flying though a barrier and down a hillside, barely escaping with his own life and destroying the woman beside him. The young woman he had planned to marry. The woman with injuries too awful for him to fix, even had she survived.

'It changed him. How could it not? Most of us tell ourselves the stories we need to get through the day and the day after that. But this calamity was so, well calamitous, the damage to this woman so severe it changed him overnight. He went from fun-loving, hard-living playboy to driven doctor intent on saving as much of the world as he could. On healing the disasters of the world since he could not restore the world of the woman he had destroyed. It became his never-ending penance.

'Finally, on one of his missionary trips, he met Fatima Alvarez, and it seemed to him he was to be allowed a chance of happiness after so much pain and loneliness. They had much in common and she tried to help him, to be both friend and lover. But she had taken on too massive a job. She was one of those people who wanted to help, who wanted to *fix* people, and who refused to see that their love would never be enough to fill the bottomless void. They refused to see that until it was too late, in many cases, and their own lives were in ruin.

'He met Fatima in Sierra Leone where she worked for an orphanage. Their marriage was his late bid for happiness but it simply wasn't to be. She told me he was tormented and depressed, that he never slept more than four hours a night, and all he wanted to do was work. To make money to support his charity work. He was expiating that guilt 24/7. They never got around to divorcing but she knew she couldn't live with him anymore.

'She never wanted to remarry and neither did he. It may have been a true love match but Doc Burke had too many demons. The key information she passed along to me of course was that she had not shown up to recover his remains and had no idea what that was about.'

'Darn,' said Holly. 'Here I was thinking the whole thing was a political scandal.'

'I nearly went down that road myself. With a congressman, you can't say what they might do to protect their career.

'Now, Rem Larsson, the agent, is an interesting case of someone with an inside track to everything that's going on in DC. He would make a perfect CIA informant, very connected, and at the center of the scoops and scandals.'

'But, what was up with him and Callie? Why would he waste his time with her?'

'Yes. Callie. I wondered, too, why Callie seemed to have him running scared. He finally told me his mother still lived in Mandrekka and was an outspoken critic of the regime over there. You can see it was a delicate situation. He felt he didn't dare anger Callie in case by crazy chance she got the political posting she was angling for. Turns out, crazy chance was on her side.'

'Have you heard any more from Nell? I mean, Pippa? Pippa Harp, was it?'

This made me smile. 'Pippa wants to drop out of school and follow in my footsteps.'

'As a writer?'

'No, of course not! As a sleuth or private eye. I'm discouraging the drop-out-of-school idea – she wasn't being entirely truthful with me about how free she was to just zoom in to her tutorials and lectures. Adventure called, you know. She's back swotting away at her A levels but she might take a gap year under my wing. I'd love it if she did.'

She sighed. 'I was sure you were going to say the butler did it.'

'Antoine and Zelda are spies, not murderers. And good spies:

They certainly had me fooled. They accompanied Callie and Tommy to Mandrekka, by the way.'

'That must be awkward.'

'Yes, I'm sure the idea is to continue keeping an eye on her. They knew all about Tommy's affair, of course. Maybe they were holding it in reserve as leverage. But apparently Callie has decided to forgive Tommy, at least for now. She still needs him and his connections.'

'Makes me glad I live in New York,' Holly said. 'Anyway, pages by next week, all right? Meanwhile, leave this life of true crime behind. And stay away from Detective Narduzzi.'

Just as I was nodding, I saw another call coming in. It was Narduzzi.

'Sure thing,' I said. 'Look, nice chatting, but I have to take this call.'